Demon Season

The Demonborn Series
Book 1

Elizabeth James

Thrall of Darkness

Chapter 1

Demon Season

Taylor skidded into the classroom and got into his seat just before the teacher turned around to face the students. Good; Mr. Hill didn't notice that he had come in a few minutes late. Taylor tried to look nonchalant and hide the fact that he was out of breath, instead pretending that he had been here the whole time. Mr. Hill's eyes paused on him, but then they continued their sweep of the classroom as the teacher mentally took role. Taylor sighed in relief. Mr. Hill was known for yelling at students for being even a minute or two late to class, and this was not a good day to get yelled at. Today, after all, was the start of demon season and this was the first year Taylor was old enough to participate.

He fingered the black birthmark on his wrist nervously. Starting tonight, when he went to sleep, demons would visit him and if he was very lucky, one of those demons would bond with him for the rest of his life. For the next three days while the moon was the weakest, demons would visit all the students with the same birthmark on their wrists – the demonborn – and everyone would be competing for the demons' attention. If he didn't bond with a demon this year, though, he would have three more seasons to try. Demons only appeared to humans

1

between their eighteenth and twenty-second years, for reasons no one quite understood.

Mr. Hill ought to know that he and the other students were nervous and give them a break, but the ornery teacher lectured as usual about mathematical principles they were unlikely to ever use in real life. He ignored the occasional hand that went up as he once again started going too fast and left the class behind. The only thing Taylor learned in this class except was that his GPA was going to be a lot lower than he hoped when he entered the college. He would have switched out of the class, but for some reason it was required and it wasn't taught by anyone else. Everyone in the university was stuck with Mr. Hill and his frustrating math that seemed to have no relation to anything in the real world.

Taylor glanced over at his best friend Natalie, her hands flying as she frantically took notes with an expression of doomed determination. Even though she wrote down everything Mr. Hill said every day, she was still getting a bad grade in the class, like everyone else, because she couldn't make sense of his lectures and figure out what anything meant. She caught his eye and shook her head. Sometimes they passed each other notes, but today it looked like she was really focusing on Mr. Hill and might actually be making some progress. He didn't want to disrupt her if that was the case.

Which meant that he had to stew in his worries alone. He glanced at one of the older boys in the class who had put off the class until his senior year. A cat lay curled up at the boy's feet. The cat was a demon, of course, who had a strong enough bond with the boy to have taken on a physical form. It was what they all dreamed of: a demon powerful enough to take on a form in the real world, not just the dream world. But for a demon to take on a physical form, the demon had to be extremely powerful and the relationship between the demon and the human had to be exceptionally close. Demons fed off the emotions of the human, so the match between human and demon was very important. If the demon chose a human who didn't express the kind of emotion that fed the demon, then the pairing would be surface level at best and the demon would only exist in dreams.

That was how most pairs were, because it was rare to get a good match between human and demon. Most humans didn't produce enough emotional output to fully feed their demons to the extent necessary for a physical body. The main exception to that rule, of course, were the succubi. Taylor blushed and thought of the beautiful, half-naked women sometimes seen drifting behind their humans. Only their blood red eyes gave them away as demons, though to be honest their beauty did as well. He had never met a human half as beautiful as a succubus. They fed on human pleasure, and rarely had any trouble taking on a physical form. Occasionally there were male pleasure demons, too, called incubi, but they were far rarer. Only one incubus was currently alive, and he was paired with an older woman halfway around the world.

The bell rang suddenly, unexpectedly, and Taylor glanced over to see Natalie groan. Apparently it hadn't been a productive class after all. He headed to her desk as all the other girls in the room began squealing and gathering together, talking excitedly about something as they hurried out and were met by more noisy girls in the hallway. Natalie didn't join them, naturally. She was an outcast, like Taylor himself, and the few times she attempted to be nice to the other girls led to all sorts of hurt for her. Now she tried to observe them from a distance and avoid direct contact. Taylor felt bad for her, since she was such a wonderful person and a loyal friend, but he knew how it felt to be betrayed by others.

He himself had attempted to befriend some of the other students at the college and was met with cold glares. He didn't understand, since college was supposed to be a welcoming environment, but he backed away quickly. He suspected it had something to do with his unusual birthmark, but he never knew for sure. He was just glad he found Natalie when he did, because he had rapidly been sinking into depression with no friends in this strange place.

"What's up with them?" he asked, jerking his thumb back at the squealing girls.

"There's a rumor that the prince of demons is looking for a partner this year," she said.

"Aren't there royal demons nearly every year?"

"Princesses," Natalie said. "But there's only one prince, and he hasn't been seen in years. Plus, they say he's an incubus."

A delicious thrill ran up Taylor's spine. If he were a girl, he would have been squealing too. As it was, he had to try to look nonchalant once again, as if the thought of a prince incubus meant nothing to him when in fact his heart pulsed a quick tattoo and the thought of a handsome young demon pressing him into a bed and kissing him tenderly was the only thing his poor brain could focus on. But no one at the school knew he was gay, not even Natalie, and he was determined to keep it that way. Then he would really be an outcast.

"Well, I'm still hoping for a succubus," he said with as much conviction as he could muster, and to be fair the image of a beautiful woman dressed in one of the succubi's sheer outfits with those exotic eyes was enough to make his mouth dry, but he couldn't help his mind from straying to the potential prince and what that would be like.

"Any demon will do for me," Natalie said. "I'd kind of like a cat at my feet, like John has, or a hawk like Nadia. But I suppose a demon controlling my dreams would work too. I just don't want to get left out."

Taylor nodded. Natalie got left out of so much, and it wasn't fair. She deserved the incubus prince more than anyone else, and he hoped she got him. Surely a prince would be able to see how deserving she was, how intelligent and loyal and worthy. He still didn't know why the other girls had chosen her as their target, but he suspected it was because she played too fair and refused to gossip or hurt feelings or talk behind others' backs. Those seemed to be the only things the other girls did and refusing to participate alienated her to some degree.

"I guess I just want one too," Taylor said. "You're right, it doesn't matter who or what I get as long as I'm chosen. I don't want to be one of those students who has to wait year after year, and then find out I've been passed over completely and have to live with the regular humans. But I'm worried that I will be, with my birthmark and all."

"It's not that unusual," Natalie said, reaching out to take his hand and examine the birthmark on his wrist.

All demonborn children were born with birthmarks in the shape of a demon on their wrist. They were the only people that demons were able to bond with, and their willingness to bond and be fed on by the demons was the only way that demons survived. Everyone's birthmark was exactly the same, except for Taylor's. His was crooked and had a hole in the center so small it was almost unnoticeable, but clearly visible if you knew to look for it. His mother worried about it constantly, but Taylor always pushed it aside. It was likely the reason no one on campus really accepted him; he had an incomplete birthmark and therefore no real right to be on this campus full of demonborn students.

His mother's demon—his father—said that the birthmark was a joyous sign and indicated that his future would be blessed, but neither his mother nor his father could save him from the bullying at school when people found out he was different. He had never met his father in person, since he only existed in Taylor's mother's dreams, but Taylor's mother continued to report that he viewed the birthmark as a blessing. Taylor didn't know if his father actually said this or if his mother made it up to make him feel better.

He pulled his hand away from Natalie and rubbed the birthmark nervously.

"I guess we'll find out tonight, won't we? If any demons come, even just to examine me, we'll know it doesn't matter. But if they don't even bother with me, then we'll know I'm really cursed and don't belong here."

"If you don't belong here, then I don't belong here," Natalie said. "And I believe that we do. You just need more confidence."

"Unless I bond with a demon that feeds on insecurity," Taylor muttered, but Natalie heard him and burst out laughing.

"That's the spirit. Now come on, we're going to be late to our next class."

They rushed to the next class, a far better class than Mr. Hill's. The teacher, Ms. Winde, nodded at them as they came in a little late. She never yelled at students and never pointed out their tardiness, even though she always made a mental note of it and recorded it. If they had too many late arrivals, she would talk to them in private, but Taylor had only been late once before when Mr. Hill held them for too long. Natalie settled down in her chair and began taking notes, but Taylor couldn't relax. Thoughts of an incubus demon prince kept flitting about his mind.

What his mother would say if he came home with an incubus in tow? His father, being a demon, would have no qualms about any demon Taylor bonded with, but his mother would probably be shocked to her core. It was known that incubi and succubi had sex with their humans, and if Taylor was paired with an incubus... He shivered. Could he actually go through with it?

The thought of sex with a man was pleasant enough, but he had never had sex with anyone, not really, not since the time he tried not to remember. He was far too shy, and the only person he was close to was Natalie. He never thought of her in a sexual way. The thought was amusing, and he glanced over at Natalie. She was pretty enough, with mahogany skin and short spiked hair dyed a reddish black. Her face was beautiful, in his opinion, with an upturned nose and wide, dark eyes. But she was like a sister, and he couldn't even imagine having sexual feelings towards her.

He thought briefly of the time when he was six and met his first demon hunter, a woman who befriended his mother for some reason and then spent time alone with him. She had touched him, then, and done things to him that he shivered to remember. He didn't want to repeat any of that and he was sure it had something to do with his fears of sex, even though he didn't like to think of it. Ever since then, he was more afraid of women than attracted to them.

None of the girls in the classroom sparked his attention, but neither did any of the men. Maybe he was just broken, and he couldn't love anyone. Or maybe, he thought, maybe he was just holding out for someone special, someone like a demon prince. But he wouldn't be able to just jump into bed with anyone. Not after what had happened to him as a child. Even if he paired with a succubus, who were notorious for having sex with their humans at the first possible chance, he would need to be wooed first. He had no intention of giving up his heart or his first time easily, no matter how hot the person was. He wanted romance and love, not just sex. But if he partnered with a demon, would that demon understand what he needed or would the demon just take what it needed to feed? Demons weren't known for their ability to compromise.

He shivered. Partnering with a demon was beginning to sound dangerous. He knew that humans who weren't demonborn often thought of the demonborn as slaves to their demons, but he had never thought of it like that before. He always assumed that the human would be in control of the relationship because the human controlled the food source. But now he realized that once the bond was formed, the demons could do anything they wanted. After all, they could use magic and play tricks on their humans' minds to cause them to do whatever the demon wanted. It wasn't anything like slavery, but the demons were in control, weren't they? Taylor gulped. The idea of an incubus prince seemed less desirable all of a sudden.

Let the girls have their prince, he decided. He would, like Natalie, be happy with a cat or a hawk, or even a demon that didn't have a physical form at all. But even though it was beginning to sound more and more like a trap, he still wanted a demon. It was what he was born to do, what he had trained all his life to do, it was his destiny. But please, he added silently, let it be a good destiny.

Chapter 2

First Dream

Taylor undressed slowly in the dorm. His roommate was already asleep, clearly not suffering from nerves like he was. Jordan had made a quip about hoping to find a succubus in his dreams, climbed into his bunk, and started snoring before Taylor even had his shirt off. The cool night air caused a ripple of goosebumps on Taylor's arms and his nipples hardened as he pulled his shirt off completely. He toed off his shoes and socks, then pulled off his pants. He wondered if there were demons around them even now, watching yet invisible. He wasn't quite sure what the limits of a demon's power were, but just because they were limited to dreams didn't mean they couldn't affect the real world at times. He quickly pulled on a pair of sweats to sleep in, then climbed the ladder into his bunk.

Both he and his roommate had elevated their bunks and put their desks underneath so that they could fit a comfortable chair and television in their dorm room. Jordan could most frequently be found playing video games in the chair, which had become his chair for the most part. Jordan was a relatively good roommate, but he did get on Taylor's nerves at times and they weren't exactly friends. Jordan avoided seeing him outside of the dorm, and when he caught sight of Taylor's imperfect birthmark, he started treating Taylor as more of a curiosity than a person. Sometime Taylor caught Jordan watching him with a strange look in his eyes and he wasn't sure what it meant. But while it wasn't the best relationship, they did get along.

Taylor sighed and tucked the covers under his chin. He lifted his wrist and stared at the birthmark. It was black now, but if he bonded with a demon then it would turn red, like a demon's eyes. He heard that unbonded demons had black eyes that turned red when they bonded with humans, and in demon society it was a status symbol to have red eyes. He didn't know much about demon society, though, despite having grown up as a demonborn with a demon for a father. He, like most demonborn, didn't really know his demon parent because they didn't have a physical form. Physical forms were beneficial because they allowed the demon to exist in the human world, but unless the demon took on a human form – which only succubi and incubi did – demons with physical forms couldn't produce offspring. Only women like Taylor's mother, who had a non-physical demon partner, or women who had an incubus for a partner could produce the next generation of demonborn children. It was a strange system, one that the non-demon-born didn't understand and often reviled, but it was what kept the demons alive.

He shut his eyes and adjusted his wrist under his cheek as he rolled to his side. He was exhausted and worrying about demons was not helping him sleep. He didn't know how he was supposed to fall asleep, and he only had three nights. What would happen if he couldn't fall asleep? He would lose one of his precious nights and waste his first demon season. He heard footsteps and opened his eyes, rolling over to look at the room. It was dark, darker than he remembered. There was a floodlight near their window but it must have gone out. He squinted and could just make out a shadow outside the window. Just someone walking by. No reason for alarm. He closed his eyes and tried again to fall asleep.

"Taylor," a voice whispered. It sounded like his roommate and Taylor buried his head into his arms.

"Not now, Jordan, I'm trying to sleep."

There was a low chuckle that didn't sound at all like Jordan, but when Taylor looked back at the room, it was empty. Jordan stirred restlessly in his sleep. Taylor shut his eyes once again and willed himself to fall asleep. If Jordan hadn't spoken, who had? A demon? He was on the verge of sleep, but he didn't think he was already asleep. He wouldn't be able to think this clearly if he were asleep, would he? He opened his eyes to look again and gasped.

Everything around him was mist. The bed was no longer beneath him; he lay on a soft surface in the ghostlike mist. He stood up, still in his sweats with no shirt. The mist was cool and moist, just like mist ought to be, and it hid his vision almost completely. He held his hand out and could just barely make out its outline. A hand darted through the mist and grabbed his outstretched hand.

Instantly Taylor yanked away from the strange hand, but it was too powerful. He heard that low laughter again and the hand released him, sending him several steps backwards. The mist cleared and suddenly he was surrounded by voluptuous women who had to be succubi. Each varied in skin and hair color, ranging from normal tans and browns to pinks and blues and greens, each wearing a matching gauze dress that revealed more than it covered. He gulped. He had seen succubi before, but never so close, and he was intimidated, embarrassed, and more than a little aroused. They danced around him provocatively and he wondered if they were teasing him or showing off and waiting for him to choose one of them, but they all seemed so similar and despite the pleasure radiating from them, he knew he didn't want one. This was every demonborn boy's fantasy, and he didn't want it.

He turned, wondering if there was a way out of the circle of beautiful succubi, and he saw a lone figure off in the distance. He felt drawn to it, and knew it was the demon who had grabbed him earlier and called his name. He didn't know if they were male or female, but he appreciated that they weren't throwing their sexuality at him like the succubi were doing. He broke through the dancing circle and heard disappointed sighs from the women, but his feet led him straight to the figure. The mist was too thick to see anything more than the vague outline of the figure.

"Who are you?" Taylor asked.

"In time," the figure replied.

Taylor blushed, knowing he had made a mistake. Demons guarded their true names with their lives. Their human partners were responsible for choosing a name for them because their true names could never be spoken aloud. Taylor often wondered what would happen if the human accidentally chose the demon's true name, but he had never heard of it happening.

"You pulled away from me before," the figure said.

Taylor couldn't tell from the deep, sensuous voice whether the figure was male or female, but he wanted to hear that voice talking to him for the rest of his life. This was his demon. There was no denying it.

"You surprised me, that's all."

"You have so many other options."

"I don't want them."

The figure was silent, though Taylor thought they turned to face him. "Who do you want?"

Taylor blushed. He shouldn't do this until he knew more about the demon. You were supposed to talk to your chosen demon first, understand what emotions the demon fed on, come to an understanding about how you and the demon would interact, lay some ground rules for behavior, that sort of thing. But this demon called to him deeply and he didn't want to waste time with any of that. He wanted to belong to this demon whatever that meant, and besides, he didn't think the demon would harm him. They were likely a beautiful woman who would mesh well with him, and perhaps even be able to take on a physical form. Not a succubus, or else she would be with the others, but not a normal demon either. He already knew they were compatible because of the way his heart sang at the sound of her voice, and the only question was whether he would risk joining with her without seeing her.

11

"I want you," he said finally, firmly.

Her hand reached out again to take his, and this time he didn't pull away. Instead, he studied the carefully manicured hands with black nail polish. She had strong hands, and she turned his hand over to expose the birthmark easily. She let out a gasp at the sight of the birthmark.

"This is destiny," she said in a low voice.

She exposed her own wrist and he saw that she also had a birthmark, the same as his down to the hole in the middle. She laid it flat against his and his skin caught on fire. He cried out but she held him still with an iron grip and the burning subsided. He stared at the figure in the mist and two red eyes peered out at him. She pulled her wrist away and his birthmark glittered crimson. Could he have partnered with anyone besides the demon who had the same peculiar birthmark as him?

Then she took a step forward and the mist fell away. Taylor gasped. She was a he.

The demon was quite possibly the most beautiful man Taylor had ever seen. His face was delicately sculpted and his eyes smoldered red above a thin nose and full, dizzying lips, framed by long ebony hair tucked behind his ears. Taylor licked his own lips at the sight and wondered what it would be like to kiss him. He was built, too, with broad shoulders narrowing down to a beautifully tapered waist, and his hands, which Taylor had mistaken for a woman's, had long, elegant fingers with that ebony nail polish. His voice, when he spoke, was low and melodic, and Taylor suspected the demon could speak to him for ages and he would never get tired of listening. But which emotions the demon would feed on? They were compatible, or else he wouldn't be drawn like this and the demon wouldn't have bonded with him, but what exactly would their relationship entail?

"You have many questions," the demon said. "Now that we are bonded, I can see into your thoughts quite easily. I placed a shield on your mind so that no other demons may enter your mind or read your thoughts. Only I can exist here."

"Thank you, I guess," Taylor said. Had other demons been reading his mind before?

"We keep an eye on all of the demonborn," the demon said as if in reply to his thought. "I've been watching you for a while now. I suspected you might be a good match for me, if you could overcome your fears."

"What fears?"

"Your fears of love."

"I don't understand."

"Then you haven't fully understood who I am. Earlier today you were quite thrilled at the thought of me."

Taylor gasped and his cheeks flamed with the same burning as his birthmark as he lifted his hands to cover his face. Had this demon been inside his head earlier in the day without his permission, listening to his thoughts? But what could he mean? Unless he was-

"You're the prince?"

It came out as more of a squeak than a statement, but the demon understood and nodded. He wore a smile like a Cheshire cat.

"You're an incubus!" Taylor continued. "But then why weren't you like the succubi? Why were you alone over here?"

"Because I have other plans for you, plans you will enjoy," the demon said, reaching to caress his cheek. "I feed off your pleasure, and you would not enjoy what they had in mind."

He unintentionally leaned into the demon's caress and then jolted, his already hot cheeks notching another degree.

"But there is one thing we must do in order to cement our relationship. I must feed on you to establish the connection between us."

Taylor shivered. All of his fears about demons came rushing back and suddenly he was terrified that the demon was about to rape him. But the demon cupped his cheeks in his hands and leaned forward towards a kiss. Taylor closed his eyes, frightened that the kiss would lead to more, but the demon brushed his hair away from his face, their lips not meeting yet.

"Just a kiss, my human," he murmured. "Nothing more."

The demon's lips pressed against him and he tried to relax into the strange motion. He had never kissed anyone before and didn't know what to do, but he had seen enough movies and read enough books to know that a kiss was supposed to be a lot more romantic than this.

Then the demon gripped him by the back of his neck and started kissing him in earnest and Taylor moaned against those skilled lips as his knees went weak. Fire danced along his lips and he eagerly opened his mouth, wanting to feel more, wanting to give pleasure and not just receive it. The demon's long tongue wound along Taylor's until his knees trembled and threatened to give way, and he moaned as he hardened in the pleasure. Still the kiss continued, and the demon held him up as he went limp with pleasure, the demon's arms the only things keeping him upright. The pleasure faded into blackness, into bliss, into deep sleep.

Chapter 3

Naming Ritual

Taylor awoke to sticky sheets and a throbbing headache. He looked at his sheets with dismay. Had he actually come from a demon's kiss? He didn't remember that part at all. He balled up the sheets and leapt down to the ground. Jordan was nowhere to be seen, luckily, as he quickly remade the bed with clean sheets. As he moved, he tried to sense the demon, but nothing seemed unusual. Had last night really happened? He glanced at the blood-red birthmark on his wrist. It really happened. It wasn't just a dream. Well, it was a dream, but a demon dream, not a regular dream. He had bonded with a demon. And not just any demon: a prince and an incubus. He grinned, imagining telling everyone about his demon. Then his smile faded. What would people say? He was a guy, and had bonded to an incubus. How could he tell anyone?

He climbed into the shower and as the steam surrounded him in the shower, he was reminded of the mist in the dream and wondered how much control his demon would have. Demons lived inside dreams, but powerful ones could control their humans' perceptions of the outside world. And the ones that took on physical forms could perform magic. Most succubi took on a human form; would his incubus take on a human form as well? And how much energy would that require? More importantly, what would Taylor have to do to produce that much energy?

He sped through the shower and was drying his hair in front of the mirror when he caught a glimpse of someone else in the bathroom. It wasn't unusual, but he hadn't heard the person come in. He reached out and wiped some of the steam from the mirror and jumped at the sight of his demon staring at him. He turned and saw only empty space beside him, but when he looked at the mirror, there he was.

I can appear to you in reflective surfaces, the demon said. *But only to you, and only you can hear me.*

"Great, now people will think I'm crazy," Taylor muttered. "What are you doing here?"

Watching you, the demon said with a grin.

Taylor blushed and tightened the towel around his waist. Had the demon been watching him the entire time he was in the shower? It was unnerving having a demon who was so interested in his body and his sexuality.

You haven't given me a name yet, you know, the demon said.

"Oh, right." Taylor wracked his brain and drew a blank. "I just met you. I haven't found one that suits you yet. Have you had humans before?"

Of course.

"What did they call you?"

The name should come from you, the demon chided. *It's part of the bond between us. But take your time, if you must. I don't want a name you aren't pleased with.*

Another student came into the bathroom and Taylor stopped talking. Luckily, the demon didn't seem to be in a mood to chat either, although he remained in the mirror the entire time Taylor brushed his teeth and hair and prepared for the day. Did the other student, an upperclassman who proudly bore a red birthmark, have a demon in his mirror as well? Taylor returned to his room and dressed quickly, donning a long-sleeved shirt that would cover his birthmark. He should be showing off his new status, but he didn't know how to explain it to anyone so he would keep it a secret for now. Everyone would just assume he was ashamed of not having been picked the first night. No one would know it was actually shame over who he had been picked by.

The demon's displeasure at his thoughts radiated through him, but he couldn't help it. He wasn't ready for the world to know that he was gay yet, and besides, he didn't want to become the enemy of all of those squealing girls from yesterday.

His first class of the day went smoothly, and then he went to eat lunch with Natalie. This would be the first test, because she would be bound to notice that his birthmark was covered and want to know why. Could he tell her about the demon? Part of him wanted to. The thought of finally having a demon thrilled him but now that it was his reality and he had to explain to people that he had bonded with an incubus, the thrill was wearing off.

The cafeteria was noisy, and he scooped up the most edible looking dishes there: a slice of apple pie and some pizza. The apple pie would be good and there were days when it was the only thing he ate, but the pizza was hit or miss. Still, it was better than the other options. He sat at his usual table near the window and watched as Natalie made her way through the line, ending up with the same meal as his. She wore a short-sleeved shirt and a happy smile, and as she drew closer he saw that she held her hand so that her wrist was prominently displayed. Her birthmark flamed scarlet.

A grin spread across Taylor's face. So Natalie had gotten a demon on the first night. That ought to show those girls who made fun of her all the time. Getting a demon so quickly would surely make her more popular, if that was what she wanted. As she made her way across the cafeteria towards him, several upperclassmen stopped her to congratulate her, and she seemed happier than he had ever seen her look before. She finally reached him, took in his long sleeves with a sympathetic smile, and sat down looking for all the world like a queen.

"So tell me about your demon," Taylor said, delighted to be able to

17

ask and also delighted to know that she would be too preoccupied to ask about his night.

"Her name is Ariel."

"Female? That's cool."

"Yeah. She feeds on learning, so the more I study and read and do all the things I love to do, the stronger she'll become. She thinks that if continue my studies, she'll be able to take on a physical form."

Taylor smiled. Those were the sort of things you were supposed to discuss with your demon. He didn't know any of that about his demon, except that his demon fed on pleasure because he was an incubus, and he assumed at some point the demon would take on a human form, simply because most succubi did and an incubus was a lot like a succubus.

"Do you know what form?"

"Not yet. Apparently we'll choose the form together, when it comes time. Oh, it's so exciting. You don't know what it's like, Taylor. She's in my head now, and I can hear her sometimes. It's like having a friend right inside you, all the time."

"That must be nice," he said. His demon felt more like a creeper, stalking him and watching him shower, but perhaps that was the difference between an incubus and a regular demon.

"So did any succubi come and visit you last night?" she asked.

"Actually, yes," Taylor said hesitantly, thinking of the scantily clad demons dancing in a circle around him. "But I didn't want any of them."

"I can't imagine you with a sex demon," she said with a laugh. "They should have known they were wasting their time on you. But remember, you do have to choose someone to be your demon."

"I know," Taylor said. "You don't have to worry about me."

"Well, I've got to get going," Natalie said, tossing aside her pizza. She had devoured the pie, but the pizza just wasn't good today and Taylor had been pushing his around on his plate as well. "Everyone who bonded with a demon last night is supposed to go to a special meeting at 1pm. I guess I'll see you later."

"Have fun."

Taylor waved and waited a few more minutes before leaving. He headed to the bathroom. There was a large mirror there and hopefully some privacy so he could talk to his demon. He needed to find a name for the demon. He kept running through potential names in his head, but none of them sounded right. It needed to be a strong name, for a strong demon, but something he could say lovingly as well. Because as much as the thought made him squirm, there would come a time when he would want to say the name as an endearment.

The bathroom was empty when he entered and he went straight to the mirror, where the demon was waiting for him.

You didn't tell her about me. Anger tinged his voice. *I understand why you aren't telling the others, but you could have told your friend.*

"Once she finds out, everyone will find out. She'll know that I've bonded, and she won't be able to hide it. I just need more time to get used to this."

You don't need more time; you need more courage.

"Let me handle this my own way."

It is a joint decision. You refusing to acknowledge me reflects poorly on me.

"It has nothing to do with you."

"Problems, Taylor?" a different voice said, and Taylor whirled. He hadn't noticed Mr. Hill enter the bathroom. Taylor blushed and stared at the mirror, but his demon was gone. He and Mr. Hill were alone.

"I was just, er-"

"Talking to your demon," Mr. Hill finished. "Let me see your birthmark."

Reluctantly, Taylor pulled up his sleeve. If it were any other teacher, he would have made an excuse and left, but Mr. Hill terrified him. He couldn't disobey. Mr. Hill studied his birthmark for several long seconds, then met his gaze.

"And why is it that you don't want people knowing about your demon?"

"I'm not comfortable with it, that's all."

"You've been raised all your life to be comfortable with a demon, and if you really weren't comfortable, you wouldn't have been able to bond with your demon. Is it a succubus? Is that why you're embarrassed?"

Taylor blushed and stared at the ground. "No, sir."

"Then what is it?"

"He's an incubus."

Mr. Hill's eyebrows rose nearly to his hairline. "You bonded with the prince of demons? That incubus?"

"Yes, sir."

"That is important news, important news indeed. You need to go to the meeting for new demon partners in order to learn how to nurture your bond, because you are going about it all wrong. What is his name?"

"I don't have one yet, sir."

"That is unacceptable. You have been given a great responsibility and a great honor, and you must respect that. You think of a name immediately while we head to the meeting. You will not be allowed to miss it."

"Sir," Taylor said, not knowing why Mr. Hill would care but hoping that there was a shred of empathy in the teacher, "I just don't want everyone to know that I have an incubus. You know, because I'm a guy."

There was a flash of what might have been pity in Mr. Hill's eyes, but his jaw was set. "Guy or not, bonding with the prince of demons is a momentous occasion. You will have a place of honor among the demonborn. Perhaps that will lessen the prejudice that some may feel about you having an incubus for a demon."

Taylor stared at the ground. Mr. Hill was set; there was no way out. He sighed and obediently began thinking of names for his demon while they headed towards the meeting. Gabriel, he thought. Then he could shorten it to Gabe when he wanted to be more casual. It was a regal enough name to please everyone, including the demon, but still with a casual enough nickname so that Taylor would feel comfortable using it.

Will that be my name, then? You don't have to speak; you can just think.

Yes, Taylor thought loudly. *Your name is Gabriel.*

A chill swept over him and he paused. Something shifted inside him, as if the demon were actually changing to fit the name, and suddenly the demon felt much more approachable and human. He was no longer the demon, after all, he was Gabriel, and though it was a slight difference, it felt like something major had been decided.

Thank you, Taylor, Gabriel said. *This will be a good name for me.*

Taylor came back to reality with a start when Mr. Hill placed a hand on his shoulder.

"Did you name your demon? Good. What is his name, then?"

"Gabriel," Taylor said.

Mr. Hill seemed surprised. "Well, that is an interesting name. Either you've been studying your history or you made an unusual choice. Either way, we'll have to watch out for you in the future. You should come talk to me sometime, after your demon has taken form."

Taylor's brow furrowed. He had no idea what Mr. Hill was talking about, and neither did Gabriel. But then they were entering the class-room where about twenty of his peers were seated, and Taylor blushed as Mr. Hill pushed him inside. He took a seat next to Natalie, keeping his eyes down. She stiffened when she saw that his birthmark was red.

"Why didn't you tell me?" she hissed.

He just shook his head. Mr. Hill, in the meantime, went up to the front of the room and exchanged quiet words with Ms. Winde, who was in charge of the meeting. Taylor couldn't hear what they were saying but he knew they were talking about him because Ms. Winde gasped and then looked over at him, causing most of the students to look at him as well. He wanted to shrivel up and die and felt Gabriel comforting him as best the demon could. Then Mr. Hill left, and Ms. Winde gathered everyone's attention back to her.

She began talking about the responsibilities they now had because of their bonds with their demons, and even though Taylor knew he should be paying attention, he began scribbling an apology to Natalie on the back of some of his notes from class. He snuck it to her when Ms. Winde was turned the other way and some of the disappointment vanished from Natalie's face. He would have preferred to talk to her and tell her why he had hidden his demon, but he could tell that the written explanation of his embarrassment at bonding with an incubus was just as reassuring to his friend. She smiled and squeezed his hand, and for a moment the world was at peace.

Then Ms. Winde turned directly to Taylor. "We even have a royal demon in last night's bondings. Taylor, would you like to say anything about your demon?"

Chapter 4

Inside a Nightmare

Taylor inhaled sharply at the question, heat flashing over him as his pulse pounded in his ears. What was Ms. Winde doing? Surely Mr. Hill had shared his reluctance and desire to keep this secret. Then again, that might be asking too much from the dour man.

"Er," he began, reaching to Gabriel for help. He had nothing to offer other than a wave of reassurance.

Luckily, Ms. Winde didn't mind taking over, though he hated her words.

"Taylor here has bonded with the prince of demons," she announced, and there was silence. Then the eyes of the class turned to him and he flinched.

The guys in the class all had the same disgusted look and the girls eyed him with barely concealed jealousy and hatred. Was this going to be his life from now on?

Ms. Winde finished the lesson and released them. Taylor slunk out of the room with Natalie at his side. One of the more aggressive guys in the class made a beeline for him but Natalie stepped between them and shoved him towards our next class, luckily next door. All of our classes were in the same building and he had never been happier as he slid inside. The teacher was already at the front and looked at him with interest. Did he know? Did everyone know? How quickly was this rumor spreading, and who else had Mr. Hill told?

As he sat down, one of the girls in class plopped down next to him with narrowed eyes.

"So you took the prince." Her voice was level and didn't have the same anger as her eyes, but he wasn't fooled. "What gave you the right?"

"You know demons are the ones to choose who to appear to," he said, relying on what they all learned.

Humans were the ones who chose which demon to bond with, but their choices were limited to whichever demons showed up. He could have claimed Gabriel or the succubi, but no other demons had shown up. He suspected Ariel was the only demon to show up for Natalie since she hadn't mentioned a choice. That was the way it usually was. One demon showed up per night, and the human could either choose them or not. No one knew if they talked about their choices with each other beforehand or if it just happened that there was usually one demon per human, but it almost always worked like that.

She sniffed and stood back up. "Watch yourself."

He shivered as she returned to her usual seat and the guy who always sat next to him sat down, eyed him, and scooted the desk slightly further away. His heart sank. They often talked and Taylor considered him a friend, but apparently not anymore.

Gabriel stirred in his mind. *Don't mind them,* he said soothingly. *They'll understand in time.*

He sighed and focused on the lesson, and soon he was heading home. He passed one of the janitors and smiled and waved without thinking, as he usually did. Then he remembered his demon and flinched, not wanting to see her reaction. To his surprise, she beamed at him.

"Congratulations," she said in a warm voice.

He paused. He often stopped to talk to her between or after classes.

They were friendly, but so was the guy from class. Why was she so accepting?

"You don't care?"

"Of course I care," she said. "The demon prince is beloved, and it's been too long since he bonded with someone. You should be honored."

"Even though I'm a-" His voice dropped. "I'm a guy?"

She laughed. "Rumor is the demon prince usually bonds with a man. No one who knows anything will judge you."

That was something. He turned to Gabriel and asked if that were true and felt a shrug.

I prefer men, Gabriel said, and Taylor's cheeks heated. At least he wasn't unusual. Maybe people really would accept him, or at least the people who knew Gabriel's history.

"We're all just glad he chose someone," she continued. "He's very picky. But demons have to bond to survive and he's the demon king's only son, so it's vital he survive."

"Does the demon king ever bond with anyone?"

She laughed again. "No, he learned to live without humans a long time ago."

"How?" He remembered learning that in school, but no one had ever explained it.

"Who knows?" she asked, and he reached out to Gabriel and felt a similar lack of knowledge.

You really don't know? He thought it so Gabriel would hear.

You don't need to think so loudly, Gabriel said with a chuckle. *And no one knows how he did it. It's a mystery. He refuses to talk about it.*

Taylor shivered to think that Gabriel was so closely related to the demon king that they had conversations. It was easy to forget that he was the prince of demons because he felt so approachable now that he had a name. But that was the entire reason people were making such a fuss. He was bonded to the prince of demons, and that made him special in some way. Why had Gabriel chosen him? He reached out to Gabriel and felt nothing. For an instant he panicked, then he remembered that demons often ignored their humans to go about their own business.

Demons who existed only in people's minds could communicate with each other. Taylor's father often left his mother alone for months. That was pretty normal. What would it be like if Gabriel left him like that? As much as he resented having people know about his demon and judge him, he had to admit he would feel abandoned without him. Something about having Gabriel with him felt so right.

The janitor wished him well as she got back to work and he headed to dinner, where he ate alone. Natalie had a night class and he always ate alone this one night of the week, but he had never felt so isolated. Combined with Gabriel's continued absence, it was almost more than he could bear. But right when the pressure became too much, he felt a brush against his mind.

Sorry, Gabriel said, and sent a wave of reassurance. *I had other matters to take care of.*

Don't do that again. Taylor didn't mean to sound so plaintive but he couldn't help it. He never wanted to feel so alone again and now that he had a demon, he shouldn't have to. Another caress.

I won't.

As soon as he was finished eating, he reluctantly headed to his dorm. It was nearly time to go to sleep. He always ate late without Natalie. It wasn't good to go straight from eating to sleep but he was used to it. She never tolerated it and insisted on eating closer to five, but he was perfectly content eating after nine, catching the last minutes of the cafeteria's hours.

As he approached his room, his steps slowed. Jordan would be waiting. How would he feel about this? Their relationship already had so many fractures. Sometimes they were friendly, but every so often that strange look came in Jordan's eyes and he was rude, pushing Taylor away for no reason. Would this be the final straw in their relationship?

Taylor took a deep breath and pushed the door open to see his roommate halfway ready for bed with his shirt and shoes off. His dark hair was mussed and he smelled like sex, and he sneered at Taylor when he entered the room.

"I hear you got an incubus," Jordan said. "So you just keep your eyes off me and we'll be fine."

"I'm not interested in you," Taylor said, turning his back to prove his point.

Jordan grabbed him and whirled him around, clutching him tightly as they faced each other.

"Everyone is interested in me," Jordan said. "I've seen the way you look at me. I just didn't know what it meant before. But you keep your hands off me, understand?"

Jordan leaned closer until he was breathing in Taylor's ear, his bare chest brushing against Taylor's shirt. Taylor was confused and terrified, unsure what the hell Jordan was doing. Then Jordan let go of him and started laughing. He climbed into bed, still laughing, and pulled his covers up.

"Here's hoping for a succubus," he said. "Turn the lights off, will you?"

"Sure," Taylor said quietly, still confused.

He turned most of the lights out, leaving one on while he undressed, did his evening routine with Gabriel watching from the mirror, and got into bed. He clicked the final light off and shut his eyes, wondering what his dreams would be like with an incubus in charge of them. He would never have normal dreams again; they would always be controlled by his demon, even if Gabriel gained a physical form. This was the first night of the rest of his life, and he was nervous. He shut his eyes and counted backwards from ten slowly, willing his body to relax with each number. By the time he was done, he was completely relaxed and he let his mind wander wherever it wanted.

There was mist again, and a single figure too distant to make out. This time, however, there were no dancing succubi. It was just him and his demon.

"Gabriel," he called, and the figure turned to him.

Taylor ran towards him and the figure opened its arms, but when he drew close enough for the mist to part he screeched to a halt. It was Gabriel, but he was drastically different. His eyes and face were the same, but he had two horns curling from his forehead and great ebony wings spread from his back. He wore nothing, but his loin and legs were covered in thick black fur and Taylor could see hooves instead of feet. He stopped, in awe at the transformation and more than a little terrified. He had always known that he would be bonding with a demon, but the demons he had seen were always domestic animals or people. He had never truly realized that he would be bonding with a creature that served the night and was as inhuman as this.

Gabriel still held his arms out as if inviting Taylor for a hug, and a flash of pain crossed his face when Taylor refused to come any closer.

"You should know my true form," he said.

His arms closed and crossed over his chest almost as if he were protecting himself. Guilt flooded through him. He hadn't meant to withdraw from his demon and he took a few steps forward. A whiff of sulfur filled his nostrils.

"You surprised me, that's all," Taylor said. "I wasn't expecting this. If you gain a physical form, is this what you'll look like?"

What would he do if Gabriel said yes? He couldn't imagine going through life with a full-fledged demon following him around. The non-demonborn would freak out and he would never be accepted in regular society. It was hard enough living outside demonborn society with a red-eyed demon, but one with wings and furry legs would be impossible.

"I will appear as human as you, except for my eyes, as you know," Gabriel said. "Only in this realm can I be my true self."

Taylor caught a thread of wistfulness in that last comment and realized that Gabriel, like Taylor, was used to living a lie. Gabriel had to lie to fit in with the other demons and the humans, and Taylor had to lie to fit in with the other students. They had more in common than he might have believed.

"I understand," Taylor said. "I'm sorry. I was just surprised."

He took a few more hesitant steps and raised his arms, and Gabriel enveloped him in a hug, even folding his wings around them securely. It was strange but comforting to be held by a powerful creature like this and he felt like a piece of precious china being carefully cradled by a bull. Gabriel was so powerful, but he was being so gentle with Taylor and it would never be otherwise. Gabriel would always protect him. It was part of their bond.

"Thank you for accepting me," Gabriel whispered. "Not many have. My last human insisted that I wear a human form at all times and went into a pure panic the one time he saw me like this."

"You've had many humans, then?"

Somehow Taylor didn't like to think that his demon had been bonded to others before him. Gabriel was his first, and he wanted to be Gabriel's first as well. But Gabriel was probably thousands of years old and had bonded to dozens of people before, so his jealousy was useless and misplaced. Still, he couldn't get rid of it.

"I have been waiting for someone special. Perhaps you will be him. Perhaps not. I've learned not to get my hopes up."

"What do you mean, special?"

"It's hard to explain, and I'm not going to try."

Something about his voice indicated that this was the end of the conversation and Taylor looked up at Gabriel, with his curling horns and blood-red eyes. He truly appeared a prince of demons, but the smile on his face belied the terror that his appearance would otherwise provoke. Taylor had nothing to fear from him. Gabriel lowered his head to Taylor's and he raised his head up so that their lips met for the second kiss in Taylor's life. His hands traveled around Gabriel's waist and gripped him firmly as Gabriel's tongue gently intruded between Taylor's lips. Taylor more than allowed it, he pressed against Gabriel and invited the demon in, wanting to experience the same bliss he had felt last night. He wanted to be Gabriel's someone special.

His mind grew dizzy and faint as the demon fed on him through the kiss, but this time he recognized the feeding and fought to remain conscious despite the urge to fall asleep under the demon's power. He wanted to experience the entire kiss, beginning to end, not just the delightful beginning. Gabriel brushed a strand of hair out of Taylor's face and pulled away for a moment.

"You are much stronger tonight, darling. I think you might be ready for more. Shall we see?"

His heart leapt and he nodded eagerly. Gabriel kissed him again on the lips, then let his kisses travel across his cheeks and nose and finally down to his neck. Taylor moaned in pleasure as Gabriel mouthed along his neck, and then Taylor realized he was naked. He surely hadn't been naked a minute ago, but now, wrapped in the demon's wings with his body pressing against his hairy legs, Taylor was completely nude. Panic set in as memories of his childhood flooded over him. Gabriel must intend on having sex with him in his demon form. Taylor didn't want to have sex with any form, but he was far too weak to even budge the powerful demon physically. But his emotional distress was obvious, and Gabriel wasn't immune to his needs.

"What's wrong, darling?"

"I don't want to do this."

"You did a minute ago."

"That was before I thought that you were gonna... that you were..."

He couldn't say it, couldn't make it a reality.

To his surprise, Gabriel laughed, a gentle, chiding laugh.

"Oh, darling, I would never do anything to you that you didn't want. I'm not allowed to. I have no intention of bedding you tonight. But I will touch you, with your invitation. I've been longing to touch you and kiss you and stroke you ever since I first laid eyes on you."

Taylor flushed. What exactly did Gabriel meany by touch? He remembered his childhood, how that started with watching, then touch, then more. Gabriel had already watched him in the shower this morning. Now he wanted to touch. He might say it stopped there but would it? He inhaled slowly. He shouldn't jump to conclusions. Kissing Gabriel felt good. Maybe touch would feel good too.

"You won't... I mean, we won't have sex?"

"There are many kinds of sex," Gabriel said. "But this is all new to you. Why don't you just relax, and remember that I won't do anything without your express permission. Can we agree to that?"

"I guess."

He wanted Gabriel, but he was afraid of what he was getting himself into. Still, he knew that demons had rules they had to follow and if Gabriel couldn't do something without his permission, then Gabriel would follow that rule. It gave Taylor some control over the situation and made him feel considerably better. Because he really didn't want to stop now, not when Gabriel was making him feel so good.

"All right," Gabriel said. "Then let's start this again."

Chapter 5

Limited Form

Gabriel picked up Taylor easily in his strong arms and Taylor blushed, feeling like a girl in the romances he sometimes read when no one was around. His handsome demon carried him until the mist around them solidified into a beautiful bedroom suited for the prince of demons. The four-poster bed was made of blackened wood that seemed to be four trees growing from the floor itself as their branches intertwined in the canopy overhead. The bed itself was covered in black satin sheets and looked incredibly inviting, and Gabriel let him look his fill before gently resting Taylor down on the silken sheets.

"What a beautiful place you have created," Gabriel said.

"I created it?"

"With the power of your fantasies. This realm is very sensitive to the needs and desires of humans, and with me in it as well, I can make sure that all of your fantasies become a reality."

Taylor's blush spread as he thought of some of his darker fantasies, the kind that involved him and Gabriel engaged in things he wouldn't dare mention. An image flashed through his mind of him sprawled on this bed with Gabriel inside of him, both panting and thrusting together as Taylor's entire body was filled to the brink with pleasure. Taylor shook his head to rid it of that image; maybe in time he would be ready for that, but not yet. He barely knew his demon, after all, and he certainly wasn't ready for sex. Sex was something that other people did, not him.

Gabriel wore a grin when Taylor finally made eye contact and Taylor realized that he must have seen that flash of a fantasy as well, and could read Taylor's deepest fantasies with ease. It was frustrating, having a demon who fed off what Taylor considered off limits and completely private, but at least Gabriel didn't say anything about it. He respected the illusion of privacy, even though they both knew it was just an illusion. But was it really the worst thing in the world if Gabriel knew what he wanted? Right now the thought of sex was terrifying, reminding him too strongly of his childhood, but in time he would want it, wouldn't he? Just as he had chosen Gabriel's name to have an endearing nickname, he had to keep the future open to any possibilities.

Gabriel laid Taylor down on the bed and climbed on top of him, gently pressing him into the pillows just as Taylor fantasized about the first time he heard that there was a prince incubus. It felt incredibly good to lie underneath him and feel his hard body above Taylor's and know that he was protected. This was nothing like his memories. Gabriel stroked his arms and his shoulders, then kissed him thoroughly. Taylor melted under him and was grateful that the bed cushioned him, because his whole body went limp with desire. Already he was growing hard, and Gabriel was aware of it because the demon allowed his torso to sink against Taylor's and rub together in a most delightful way. Maybe this was what Gabriel had meant by touch.

Taylor gasped for air when Gabriel finally released him from the kiss, but Gabriel's lips continued traveling down his body, down his neck to his shoulders, then his chest, and Taylor moaned as his lips locked on one of his nipples and playfully flicked it with the tip of his tongue. It felt like he was on fire as he kept pushing dark memories from resurfacing. This was completely different. Gabriel played with the other nipple as well and Taylor realized both nipples were erect, just as he was becoming below. It was odd how perfectly Gabriel could arouse him, but he suspected Gabriel was reading his body language and also his mind to see what he liked and what he didn't like and act accordingly. It was odd to know that the demon was inside his head, but the pleasure was worth it.

Then Gabriel lifted off him and his penis sprang erect without the weight of the other man keeping it down. A flash of embarrassment flooded over Taylor, but Gabriel looked at his penis in awe, as if at a delicacy, and Taylor knew he hadn't done it to embarrass him. One of Gabriel's hands snaked around his length and began stroking him, and Taylor gasped and clutched the silk sheets tightly. It was incredible. Gabriel knew exactly where to touch, exactly what to do and how fast to stroke, and Taylor tossed his head and felt as though he were going to burst. This had never happened before.

"Gabriel," he cried. "I can't hold on."

Gabriel grinned, as if pleased with himself for bringing Taylor to the brink so quickly. He leaned over as if to place his mouth on Taylor's penis and Taylor flinched. Gabriel was going to finish him with his mouth? He wasn't ready for that. Gabriel felt the flinch and backed away, but his hand kept stroking. Gabriel smiled at him as if to reassure him that the demon would respect his wishes, and then his hand motions grew complex and Taylor's head spun from pleasure. He could barely breathe, and then everything exploded. He was vaguely aware of Gabriel cradling him in the black bed before sleep took hold of him.

When he awoke, his sheets were once again ruined. He needed to come up with a better solution. Once Gabriel took form, of course, this wouldn't be a problem, but in the meantime he couldn't keep changing his sheets every day. He balled up his sheets and leapt down from his bunk, nearly running into Jordan, whose back was to him.

"Sorry," he said.

Jordan turned with a smirk on his face. Taylor suddenly realized there was another person in the room, a woman. A woman with fire-red hair, red eyes, and wearing a flimsy red gown. A succubus, one of the same ones who had danced around Taylor that first night. She was exceptionally beautiful, even more so when she was by herself and not surrounded by other equally beautiful succubi. And she held Jordan's hand tightly.

"You got a demon," Taylor said, slightly out of breath. The succubus was so pretty he was having trouble thinking around her. He felt Gabriel's annoyance in the back of his head and he tried to pull himself together. He couldn't, after all, admire someone else's succubus while he had a beautiful incubus of his own.

"Yes," Jordan said proudly. "And she's already taken form. This is Callan."

"Pleasure to meet you, Callan."

"We've met before, young one," she said in a smoky voice. "I know you remember."

"Yes, of course, but I didn't really meet you, I more just... saw you."

Jordan shook his head. "I don't get you, Taylor. How could you possibly give up a succubus like Callan? She's incredible. But she's mine now, and nothing will ever change that."

The succubus smiled at him as if at a child and Taylor remembered that demons were virtually immortal as long as they fed on willing humans, so Callan would not be Jordan's forever, as Jordan seemed to think, but only for a short time during the demon's life. Still, it was all of Jordan's life. Taylor wondered what Gabriel thought about him. Was he just one more blip in an immortal life, or would his relationship with Gabriel actually mean something? Gabriel had said he was looking for someone special; could Taylor be that person? Gabriel was oddly silent inside his head and Taylor wondered if he were even here, or if he had wondered off somewhere else again. But he wouldn't do that, would he? Not after Taylor asked him not to. A vague pulse from his demon. Gabriel was nearby but might not be monitoring him carefully.

"It looks like you and your incubus are compatible," the succubus said, gesturing to the sheets that Taylor held with increasing embarrassment. "Why hasn't he gained his form yet?"

"I don't know," Taylor said. "There's no rush, is there?"

"Not really," the succubus said. "But it is the mark of a strong relationship. I knew as soon as I laid eyes on Jordan that he was the one for me. I feed off him so easily," she added, stroking Jordan's hair.

Jordan grinned.

"Well," he said, "Let's give Taylor some privacy. I need a shower, and I think you need a snack."

Taylor blushed as the two left arm in arm. Were they really going to have sex in the shower? Or could the succubus feed from other pleasures besides sex? He knew it varied from succubus to succubus and wondered what kind Callan was.

He remade the bed again and changed into clothes. It was Friday, so he only had Mr. Hill's class in a couple of hours, and then people with new demons were expected to attend an afternoon class on securing the bond between human and demon. He had time to do some laundry, so he piled up his basket with clothes and sheets and headed to the laundry room. Luckily, the laundry room was empty and there was a mirror at one end. He put his clothes in two of the washers and went to the mirror. Gabriel was waiting for him.

"Why haven't you taken on physical form yet?" Taylor asked.

I haven't been able to get enough energy from you yet, Gabriel answered. *You shy away every time I get close.*

Taylor thought of the previous night, how he had backed away from letting Gabriel suck him off. Was that what was needed to give Gabriel form? Why?

I must experience your pleasure more directly, Gabriel said, answering his unasked question. *Feeding through my hands is indirect and while it gives me strength, it isn't enough to give me form. I need to feed on you directly to gain a form.*

Taylor hopped up on one of the washers and stared at Gabriel's face in the mirror. Gabriel looked a little tired. Perhaps feeding through his hands was making him weak. Taylor didn't want to be the cause of his weakness, but he was so afraid of what would happen if he actually gave in and allowed Gabriel to do what he wanted. But what was he afraid of, really? Everyone already thought he had slept with Gabriel, or would in the near future, so there were no problems with rumors: the rumors were already there. It was a personal thing, a personal value that he was afraid to break. How would he be able to look at Natalie, at his mother, if he gave in to pleasure and let his demon do what he wanted? That was it, the giving in to pleasure. All of his life he had denied himself pleasure because he had been the outcast, not worthy of normal pleasures, but now here he was being forced into them and even though he knew he needed to accept pleasure into his life, he balked.

"Excuse me," a voice called, and he turned to see Natalie come in the laundry room with a stack of clothes. "Do you mind?"

"No, I'm just talking to my demon," he said, hopping off the washer and helping Natalie sort her laundry into piles for the washers. Together, they were using all of the washers and he hoped no one else came in and got mad at them.

"I'm sort of surprised he isn't here in person," Natalie said, looking around as if waiting for Gabriel to show up.

"What do you mean?"

"I mean with the demon season almost being over and all. Ariel and I talked about it and we're going to try for this year, but she thinks it'll probably be next year before we succeed. But most succubi and incubi gain a physical form their first season."

"What do you mean? Can't he gain his form anytime?"

A flash of annoyance from Gabriel, but apparently the demon was content to let Natalie scold him because he didn't say anything.

"Didn't you listen to the lecture yesterday on our demons? Demon season is when the gateway between our world and theirs is the most open, and it only lasts for three nights. This is the only time that demons can come through to bond with a human, and it's the only time they can come through and take on a physical form. The rest of the time they're trapped in their own realm, only able to communicate and feed through dreams."

Taylor's eyes widened. He only had one more night to give Gabriel a physical form. Why hadn't Gabriel pushed him before? Why hadn't Gabriel forced him into sex in order to gain a physical form?

Because, Gabriel said inside his mind, *Then you would never trust me and more than anything I want your trust. I believe that tonight will be our night and I will gain my form.*

"Gabriel thinks it'll be tonight," Taylor said in a somewhat shaky voice.

He remembered what Mr. Hill had said about how being chosen by the prince was an honor. What people would think if he couldn't give that prince a physical form? They would turn against him and he would be alone again, shunned by his whole society. Even his parents would be disappointed that he had been given this wonderful opportunity and blew it because of his fears of intimacy.

"Don't be so afraid," Natalie said. "Incubi feed on love and pleasure, not on worry and doubt. You just have to relax and trust him."

"I'll try. What about your bond? What happens if you can't give her a physical form?"

"We've discussed it, and I'm all right with a demon living in my dreams. She gave me a preview of what that would be like yesterday and it was quite an experience. It was like having a friend with me at all times. As much as I want her to take on a physical form, I really wouldn't mind having her with me all the time."

"I wonder what it would be like to have Gabriel in my head all the time," Taylor mused. "He mostly stays silent, like he doesn't want to bother me."

"That's not like a demon at all," Natalie said. "You should ask him for a preview of what it would be like if he didn't take on a physical form. Maybe that would help inspire you when it comes time to give him your energy."

Taylor blushed. She said it so easily, as if she had no idea what was involved in giving Gabriel his energy. And to be fair, she didn't. With her demon she just had to educate herself and take joy in learning new things. With his demon, on the other hand, he had to learn how to love a body he often felt at odds with and overcome his fears of sex. He could easily envision himself having sex with Gabriel in the future, but only in the distance future. The road to that future, unfortunately, was a big blank and he was not eager to get started.

Silently, he asked Gabriel a question in his mind. *What do you think? Could you give me a preview of what you would be like if you don't get a physical form?*

Gabriel chuckled. *I can do that. It will certainly inspire you, I think, because I am not the kind of demon to be kept inside someone's mind. But you have too many fears. Tonight I will gain my form, and you will want to cooperate. Believe in it.*

I do believe, Taylor thought. *But just in case, let me see what it's like.*

As you wish, darling.

Chapter 6

Demons in the Head

The day seemed to be going normally with Gabriel's thoughts occasionally intruding into Taylor's mind. Gabriel was quick to notice inconsistencies in people's behavior and had a negative view of most of the students on campus, but he genuinely liked Natalie and the whole time Taylor and Natalie talked, he remained quiet. Once the laundry was done and Taylor had returned it to his room, he headed out to class thinking that having a demon in his head wasn't nearly as much of a distraction as both Natalie and Gabriel had indicated.

Mr. Hill began rambling about complex mathematical equations as usual and Taylor suddenly realized that he could talk to Gabriel during class instead of sitting and being bored. But when he tried to reach Gabriel, he realized with shock that Gabriel was already there, in the real world, sitting underneath him. The desk chair had vanished and instead Taylor was sitting on Gabriel's lap. He looked around to see if anyone noticed, but everyone was paying attention to Mr. Hill.

Don't talk, Gabriel warned, *And don't draw attention to yourself. Just think things if you want me to hear them.*

What's going on? Taylor thought. *I thought you didn't have a physical form.*

I don't, Gabriel said with a chuckle. *I'm simply manipulating your mind into thinking that I'm here right now. No one else can see me or hear me. But this is what you wanted, isn't it? You wanted to talk to me? Well,* and he leaned so that his breath trailed across Taylor's ear, *You got it.*

Taylor shivered. There was something sensual about the way Gabriel was holding him. Then Gabriel's arms wrapped around his waist and slid under his shirt.

Demons need to eat, you know, Gabriel said, and then planted his mouth on Taylor's neck in an open-mouthed kiss as he started sucking his flesh.

Taylor jumped in surprised as Gabriel's finely manicured fingers reached his nipples. How could no one see this? But as he looked around, no one noticed anything out of the ordinary. Mr. Hill continued to blather, Natalie desperately took notes, and the other kids passed notes or sat with glazed eyes. Taylor took a deep breath. Gabriel's lips on his neck and his fingers on his nipples were having a large effect on him and his heart rapidly sped up. He could almost feel his heartbeat in his penis as it built in rigidity. He would not get a boner in the middle of class.

But that's what I want, Gabriel whispered. *I want to feed on you in front of all these people, in this oh so public place, and feel how turned on you get by it.*

Taylor's face suffused with color. He was turned on, and partially by how public this was. The question of what would happen if he were found out hung over his head but he cared less and less as his body shifted into a higher gear of pleasure. His breathing became forced as he tried not to pant for breath. Gabriel wasn't doing anything different, just fingering his nipples and sucking on his neck, but he was lighting on fire. He took a deep breath and tried to calm down. This wasn't going to end well. But his body had a mind of its own now, and there was nothing he could do to stop it. He looked around again at the other students, still surprised that none of them noticed anything out of the ordinary. He was sweating, breathing heavily, yet none of them seemed to care, not even Natalie.

A ruler slammed down on his desk. Taylor gasped and stared up at Mr. Hill, who stared at him with knowing and merciless eyes.

"Mr. Taylor," Mr. Hill said. "And this goes for everyone in the class. None of you are allowed to feed your demons during class. It is rude to me and to your fellow students. What do you have to say for yourself?"

Taylor swallowed hard. He was sitting on a desk chair again; Gabriel had vanished but Taylor could feel him nearby, amused by this turn of events. Taylor tried to calm his body down, knowing that everyone was now looking at him and at least some of them could guess what had been happening. Natalie was looking at him with an I-Told-You-So expression and for once he agreed: Gabriel needed his own body so he couldn't pull stunts like this anymore.

"I'm sorry, Mr. Hill," Taylor said, his voice shaky from residual lust. He just hoped Mr. Hill didn't make him get up and leave because he was still hard. Mr. Hill's eyes dropped to his crotch and he hesitated.

"I'll let you remain for the rest of the class period, but this is the last time this happens, do you understand?"

"Yes, sir," Taylor said, infinitely grateful that he wouldn't have to leave class with a boner for all the world to see.

Mr. Hill walked away and Taylor instantly turned inward to Gabriel, who was still amused and showed no sign of remorse.

You almost got me in a lot of trouble, Taylor yelled.

I'm an incubus, Gabriel said with a mental shrug. *I need regular feedings. When I have my true form it will be much easier to feed from you but if I live inside your head, I have to take whatever I can get, and I was feeling like a snack.*

I'm not a snack!

You're just mad that you got caught.

I'm mad because you made me miss this whole assignment.

Oh, if that's all, Gabriel said, and suddenly Taylor's right hand started moving of its own volition. Gabriel must be controlling it, and it was frightening to have a body part moving without his control. His hand scrawled out a formula in handwriting that wasn't his, and when he studied the formula, suddenly everything Mr. Hill was talking about made sense. It was like all of the missing pieces of the puzzle snapped into place and Mr. Hill's roundabout, elaborate teaching method was boiled down to a single equation.

Taylor's mouth dropped open, but he snapped it shut before Mr. Hill could see. His hand returned to his control and he started taking notes again, but only half-heartedly. Now that he saw the equation that everything boiled down to, it didn't make sense to learn Mr. Hill's lessons. He wondered how Natalie would react when he showed her the equation. He felt Gabriel's pleased smile in his mind.

You take pleasure in helping others, the demon said. *I enjoy that. I feed off that as well, you know, though it isn't nearly as filling as physical pleasure.*

Well, no more physical pleasure until we're alone, you got that?

If I don't take form tonight, you should expect me to feed on you when I want, not when it is convenient for you, Gabriel warned. *But for right now, I'll wait until we're alone.*

Taylor shivered. He needed to get Gabriel into a form. There was no way he could last a year with Gabriel sending him into an aroused state whenever the demon wanted. But he understood that Gabriel grew hungry and the demon was only partially aware of what Taylor was doing, so unless Gabriel eavesdropped on everything in his life, there was no way to guarantee that Gabriel's feedings would come at good times. And Taylor wouldn't survive with Gabriel being that close to him. He needed space to breathe, and he suspected Gabriel did as well. They were both independent types who happened to be reliant on each other to survive.

Class was finally dismissed and Taylor took the equation over to Natalie. Mr. Hill left with the students and they were alone in the classroom. For some reason, Taylor didn't want Mr. Hill to know that he had found an equation that simplified the course. It was forbidden knowledge, after all, ill begotten goods from a demon.

"You'll never guess what Gabriel gave me," he said, holding the equation tightly.

"After getting you in trouble, I'm glad he gave you something. I thought you were going to explode your face was so red."

Taylor blushed again at the thought of the confrontation, but his confidence in the equation overcame his previous embarrassment.

"Yeah, I need to talk to him about that. But his apology was well worth it. I give you: the answer to this class."

He laid the equation before her. At first, her eyes squinched together and he wondered if she could read it properly, but then her eyes widened and her mouth dropped open. He could practically see the wheels spinning in her head.

"Gabriel gave it to me. It explains everything Mr. Hill's been teaching us this entire semester."

"I know," she murmured.

Her eyes kept getting wider until they looked wild and her mouth was still open. Crimson flushed her dark cheeks and a dazed look crossed her face. She went limp without warning and Taylor leapt forward to keep her from collapsing to the floor, easing her fall and fanning a notebook at her face to help her breathe better. But she was breathing, and she seemed fine, just stunned. Then Gabriel warned him to step back and he did, reluctantly.

A paw appeared in her mouth, then another, and her mouth widened to inhuman proportions. A large ginger cat escaped the gaping hole that was Natalie's mouth and as soon as the damp creature was out, Natalie's mouth returned to its normal size with no damage done. The cat meowed loudly and butted her head against Natalie, who blinked and stared at the creature.

"Ariel?" Natalie asked in a hoarse voice.

The cat meowed again and curled up on her chest. She was an enormous cat, far larger than the domestic cats that Taylor had seen but an average size for a demon cat. He stared at Natalie in shock. He had actually witnessed the birth of her demon's physical form. It was awe-inspiring and a little gross, too. He wondered if Gabriel would emerge from his mouth as well. Gabriel was oddly silent on the matter, but perhaps Gabriel didn't know.

Natalie tried to sit up and failed, and Taylor knelt beside her and helped her to a sitting position.

"Are you okay?"

"I feel so weak, like everything was sucked out of me."

"I think it was," Taylor said. "You just gave all of your energy to create a physical form for Ariel, it might take you time to recover."

"It was that equation," she said. "Everything just fell into place and I felt so overwhelmed with joy and knowledge and it just happened. We didn't plan it like that."

Ariel settled on her lap and purred. Natalie laughed.

"I can still hear you in my mind. Good. I was worried I'd never be able to talk to you again now that you're a cat. Taylor, Ariel says I need a doctor to check on me. Can you go and get one? I'll wait here with her."

"Are you sure I shouldn't wait with you?"

"Ariel can protect me," she said with confidence.

The cat grinned and displayed a full set of sharpened teeth, and Taylor laughed and backed away with his hands up.

"All right. I'll be back with a doctor."

He raced to the nearest nurses' station and told them what happened. They seemed surprised that it had happened during the day, but all of them knew exactly what to do. Two nurses followed him back to the classroom. One of them examined Ariel while the other knelt beside Natalie and checked her vitals.

"A clean forming," she said. "You look perfectly healthy. Some-times the demons will accidentally draw on the wrong body systems and we'll see deficits or even missing body parts, but your Ariel knew what she was doing. We'll take you back to the hospital for observation and to rehydrate you a little, but you should be fine in a day or two."

"I have classes," Natalie protested.

"It's Friday," Taylor pointed out. "Aside from that meeting today, we don't have anything for a few days."

"And you don't need to go to the meeting, not since your demon has taken form so well," the nurse added. "The two of you already have a great bond between you. But you," she said, turning to Taylor, "You will need to go to the meeting. It's starting soon, I believe. You don't want to be late."

"I just want to make sure Natalie's okay."

"I'm fine," Natalie insisted. "Go to the meeting and maybe you can give your demon form, too."

"I hope so."

Inwardly, he wondered if he would even be able to stand the demon if Gabriel didn't take on a physical form. Today had not gone well for him, and if today was a preview of life with an incubus in his head, he didn't want it. He would do anything to get Gabriel his own body. He just hoped it wasn't too late.

Chapter 7

Blocking Memories

When Taylor finally returned to his dorm that night, he was exhausted and ready for sleep even though he knew he wasn't likely to get any. But there was a rubber band around his doorknob, a signal he and Jordan had set up in jest when they first moved in together. Jordan had used it once before to signal that he had a girl inside, and now he was no doubt using it to signal that he and his succubus were getting it on.

Taylor snapped the rubber band angrily. He was tired and just wanted to lay down and sleep, even if that sleep brought arousing dreams. Plus, this was his last chance to give Gabriel his physical form and he didn't want to spend half the night waiting for his roommate to finish up. He would need the whole night to feel comfortable enough with Gabriel to finally allow Gabriel to feed on him fully.

Taylor wandered through the dorms and was stopped by his RA, a friendly guy who was one of the few people Taylor felt comfortable around. His attitude hasn't shifted after learning about Gabriel and Taylor appreciated it.

"Why aren't you asleep?" The RA put his hands on his hips in disapproval.

Taylor explained the situation and the RA's lips tightened. "He should be more considerate of your needs. You need the room more than he does. Well, you're in luck. We have a couple of spare rooms for similar situations and you're more than welcome to use one."

He led Taylor down a few hallways into a part of the dorm he had never been, then unlocked a door with a special key from his keychain. He removed the key and handed it to Taylor.

"That's the only key to the room, so no one will interrupt you. Keep it as long as you need it, within reason. A day or two, probably. Return the key to me when you're done. You'll find clean sheets in the dresser and an attached bathroom, so you don't have to go down the hall for that. There's not much in there, but it's better than nothing."

"Thank you so much," Taylor said, gratitude filling his heart.

He could feel Gabriel's relief as well, and he hugged his RA briefly as he took the key and entered the room. It was simple, just a bed and a dresser, not even a desk and no window. There was a mirror above the dresser, however, and a door to an attached bathroom which none of the other dorm rooms had. The bathroom looked spotless, but that wasn't what held Taylor's attention. He stripped down to his boxers and got out some clean sheets. As he made the bed, he kept looking at the mirror where Gabriel stood. Gabriel occasionally stretched out his arms as if longing to help Taylor, but they were in two different realities. Not for long, Taylor hoped, but his fears were beginning to rise.

Why don't we talk first? Gabriel asked. *I don't want you to do this because you feel you have to. I want you to want this.*

"I do want you," Taylor said. "You know that, don't you?"

Of course. But there's still something holding you back. Something hidden in your mind so tightly that even I can't read it.

Taylor looked down at his hands, then sat on the newly made bed. "Something happened to me. When I was a kid."

Gabriel appeared to sit down as well and leaned forward, cupping his chin in both hands and giving Taylor his full attention. Taylor blushed.

"I don't like talking about it."

But you must, if you want to move on from it.

Taylor took a deep breath. "There was a demon hunter."

Gabriel hissed, then apologized and gestured for him to continue.

"She knew my mother somehow. She was interested in me. She thought my birthmark meant that I had a chance at a normal life, a life without demons. You know, because my birthmark isn't the same as everyone else's. I think my mom was also afraid that I would turn out normal, so she let the demon hunter teach me about the non-demon-born world. We would have long sessions together, just me and her. But that wasn't what we talked about."

He swallowed hard. "She started by wanting to look at my birthmark, then she wanted to see my whole body to see if I looked like a demonborn or a human. I did what she wanted. My mom trusted her, you see, and she was an adult. At first she just looked at me. Then she began touching me, first my arms and legs, then... then other places."

Taylor stared at the ground, unable to risk looking up at Gabriel. He had no idea how the demon would react. There had been some pleasure in those touches from the demon hunter and it would kill him if he looked up and saw that Gabriel was getting enjoyment from this story. He risked a quick glance up and Gabriel's eyes were wide with horror. Feeling reassured, he cleared his throat and continued.

"After the touching, she showed me videos of humans together and said that's what humans did, and if I wanted to be a human I should do it with her. I didn't want to be a human, I wanted to be demonborn, but she was an adult and I didn't have much of a choice. I cried afterwards and she told me to act like a human."

What stopped it?

"It happened quickly, in a matter of weeks, and my father – the demon – wasn't paying attention during that time. When he returned to my mother and discovered that she had let a demon hunter close to me, he forced the demon hunter to leave. But he never knew what she had done to me. I never told anyone... before now."

I can't believe your mother let a demon hunter alone with you, especially when you were just a child, Gabriel said, and Taylor could hear the anger in his voice. *And a dangerous predator at that. All demon hunters are dangerous, but she was doubly so. What was her name?*

"Yolette," Taylor whispered.

Gabriel's eyes flashed fire and he rose from his sitting position. *I know this demon hunter. Her family has been hunting me for centuries now. For her to hurt the one that I am bonded to, even before I was bonded to you, is inexcusable. If I ever meet her again-*

"But we won't, will we? Meet her again, I mean? You'll protect me from her?"

Gabriel calmed down and turned to Taylor with outstretched arms. *Of course I will protect you. And I promise you that no matter what that witch has done to harm you, what I do will wash away all of her poison.*

A tear fluttered at the edge of Taylor's eye. It was exactly what he needed to hear. He didn't want Gabriel to deny that Yolette had done anything, and he didn't want Gabriel to exaggerate its importance. Gabriel was doing exactly the right thing by saying that their love could erase the ill that had been done to him as a child.

Now, my darling, Gabriel said, *Lie down and fall asleep so that I may hug you properly and start reclaiming your body from that witch's grasp. Because it is your body, not hers, and it is about time you celebrated it instead of hid from it.*

Taylor smiled a wavering smile and laid on the newly made bed, pulling the covers under his chin. He counted backwards from ten and everything shifted. The coarse cotton sheets were suddenly silk, and when he opened his eyes, he was looking at a living canopy of black wood. He was back in his fantasy of the demon prince's chambers and Gabriel lay on the bed next to him.

"Oh, Gabriel," he murmured, and clutched the demon to him as he let his tears spill. Over a decade of repressed pain exploded from him and Gabriel cradled him through it all, patting his head and murmuring soothing things until Taylor managed to get a hold of himself. While in reality his nose would have run up a storm and his eyes would have drenched the sheets, in this dream his tears fell without leaving a trace and his nose wasn't stuffy at all. A benefit of weeping in dreams, he thought as his sorrow and pain lessened.

Gabriel kissed his eyes and licked the tears from his cheeks, then kissed his lips. He tasted salty, like tears, and Taylor opened his mouth to embrace the taste and chase it further. He barely noticed the horns curling from Gabriel's forehead or the thick fur covering his groin and legs, but he did idly notice that he couldn't see Gabriel's penis under the fur and he wondered what it looked like. Still, that was a matter for another time. He wasn't sure he could make that much progress in a single night.

Gabriel's kisses grew intense, and the demon's hands began plucking at his body, teasing and arousing wherever they landed. Just as the demon had started a fire in him earlier in the day during class, he was starting a fire now, only now it was permissible and Taylor didn't have to worry about hiding his emotions. He could enjoy this to his heart's content. He didn't even have to worry about his memories anymore; they were out on the table and he could now move on and create new sexual memories.

Taylor wrapped his arms around Gabriel's waist and pulled him close, then let his hands play with the fur along his backside. He was extremely muscular under the fur and Taylor wondered what he would look like when he finally took form as a human, without the fur. Gabriel's kisses began traveling down his body again and Taylor's penis hardened in anticipation. By the time Gabriel nibbled at Taylor's nipple, his penis jerked against his belly, eagerly awaiting a touch of some sort. Taylor was still frightened at the thought of someone touching him, but Gabriel would never hurt him and always had his best interests at heart. After all, Gabriel couldn't feed if Taylor wasn't enjoying himself. The thought gave him courage.

Gabriel played with his nipples a bit more, then his hands closed around his penis and Taylor grunted at the sudden pleasure. Those strong, elegant hands knew exactly what to do just like last time and as they stroked him, he flailed against the sheets in helpless ecstasy.

"Gabriel," he called, knowing his time was coming.

But whereas before Gabriel had been pleased at his quickness, this time Gabriel grinned and wrapped his hand around the base of Taylor's penis, squeezing hard. The urge to come spiked, then decreased rapidly and Taylor knew he would be able to take more pleasure before his orgasm. He was still panting for breath and he didn't know whether he was glad that the experience would continue, or angry that Gabriel had manipulated him so skillfully, but either way he knew his orgasm, when it occurred, would be better than anything he had experienced so far.

Gabriel lowered his head to Taylor's penis and Taylor held his breath, unconsciously remembering Yolette doing the same, her tongue seeking out his tip and wrapping around it in a way that made him feel funny inside. Gabriel set Taylor's head on his tongue, then slid his penis into his throat and Taylor nearly screamed with pleasure as his penis was transported into the tight, hot, wet confines of Gabriel's throat. Gabriel moved on him, rocking back and forth and creating a rhythm that had him grunting and practically howling, and then his penis was back outside and Gabriel was wrapping his long tongue around his penis and stroking it, focusing especially on the thick vein on the top of his penis that was extremely sensitive. Then he was back in Gabriel's throat experiencing ecstasy and he did let out a brief scream, praying that this was still a dream and no one would hear him.

His balls were heavy and began to tighten, and he wouldn't be long. He was on the brink of something magical, something Yolette had never given him, something only Gabriel could give him. He murmured Gabriel's name to warn him about his impending orgasm, and Gabriel took him in his throat again. Was Gabriel going to swallow him? The thought caused his penis to twitch and he shifted uncomfortably as the pressure in his balls continued to build. He just needed something, some touch, to push him over the edge.

Then Gabriel lightly ran his teeth over the vein on his penis and the world exploded. Vines of pleasure spurted out of him, and Gabriel sucked out even more. For several long, blissful moments all he felt was Gabriel's tongue drawing him out, extending his passion while his entire body was locked in an orgasm. Then his balls expended themselves and he went limp. Gabriel sighed in pleasure and crawled up his body to kiss him on the lips with a mouth that tasted of cum.

Taylor's mouth went numb with the kiss, then it opened wide, wider than it ever had before. Gabriel reached inside his mouth with his hands but instead of going into his mouth, he seemed to vanish. Taylor's mouth stretched further and suddenly Gabriel's head and shoulders were traveling through his mouth, and then his entire body was sliding through Taylor's wildly extended open mouth. When Gabriel's wings and hooves were completely through, something changed in his mind, some wall close off that had previously been open. He opened his eyes and realized he was awake again, and Gabriel was beside him.

Gabriel was damp, and completely naked. He was in human form, as he had promised, with no wings, horns, or hooves. It was the first time Taylor had really seen him naked and he couldn't help but look at the demon's penis. It was beautiful, a rosy pink color, and perfectly sized – about eight inches, not too large, but by no means small. Gabriel grinned as if he were aware of the examination and he stood up, showing off his body further.

"What do you think?" he asked, turning around so Taylor could admire his buttocks as well. They were perfectly sculpted and Taylor longed to run a hand down his curves.

"Beautiful," he managed.

Talking was hard, but then again, if Gabriel's emergence was anything like Ariel's, he had just come out of Taylor's mouth. He felt completely drained, like everything in him had been tapped out and it took all of his strength just to lie still and keep breathing. He wondered if someone would call the doctor for him, or if he could just stay here until he recovered. Natalie would worry about him if he didn't show up tomorrow, but no one else would really notice that he was gone. And she was recovering for the next few days as well, he realized. She might not notice.

"You need a doctor," Gabriel said, and Taylor wondered if he were reading Taylor's thoughts or if his need was just obvious. "I used all of your energy to take on this form, but you'll be pleased by it. This is the most powerful form I've ever taken and it will serve both of us well. I'll get someone to look after you."

He headed towards the door.

"Wait!"

Gabriel turned back.

"You're naked. Wear my clothes, at least."

Gabriel grinned. "I'm an incubus. I'm used to humans feeling lust towards me."

"You're my incubus. I don't want anyone else feeling lust for you," Taylor snapped, then blushed.

But it was true. He wanted to be the only one with access to his beautiful incubus and he didn't want Gabriel displaying his goods to the entire campus.

"As you wish," Gabriel said, then picked up Taylor's clothes.

The jeans and long-sleeved t-shirt were snug, which served to emphasize the strong muscles of Gabriel's chest and legs, but they were better than nothing.

"And bring the key," Taylor added.

"I will, but keys don't matter to me. I can unlock any door with the touch of my hand. Now lie still and get some rest – real rest – while I find a doctor to look after you."

"Wait," Taylor called again.

Gabriel again turned back, this time with an eyebrow raised and an amused expression on his face.

"I'm beginning to think you don't want me to leave."

"I don't," Taylor admitted. "Will you kiss me before you go?"

A gentle smile lit Gabriel's face. He knelt beside the bed and stroked Taylor's hair from his face, then he kissed Taylor softly. It felt different in real life than in a dream, more real and infinitely better even though it was short. He could still feel Gabriel feeding through the kiss and the desire for sleep washed over him. Would he always become tired when Gabriel fed on him? Or would he eventually get used to it? Either way, he wasn't complaining. He had successfully given his demon form, and he deserved a bit of real rest. He suspected that once he woke up, his life would be forever changed and quite a bit busier than he was used to, so he might as well rest while he had the chance.

Chapter 8

New Reality

Two lips pressed against his as he started coming out of a deep slumber, but he couldn't feel Gabriel feeding off him. The lips vanished quickly, almost so quickly that he wondered if they had been there at all, and Taylor opened his eyes to see why the kiss had stopped.

Jordan stared back at him. Gabriel was nowhere to be seen. Taylor squinted. No one else was in the room and Jordan's cheeks were flushed red. He knew Jordan couldn't have kissed him; had he imagined the kiss?

"You're awake," Jordan said. "How long have you been awake?"

"What do you mean?"

Jordan fidgeted nervously but Taylor's response must have calmed him because he suddenly regained his usual composure.

"Everyone's been waiting for you to wake up, that's all," Jordan said. "We've all been taking shifts since you fell asleep."

"Everyone? Who is everyone?"

"Me and Callan, Natalie and Ariel, a couple of professors, the doctors, and of course Gabriel."

"Where is he?"

A sudden longing to see Gabriel washed over Taylor. They had just met, but he was bonded to the demon and already he couldn't imagine life without him. It was part of the demon bond, but it felt like more than that. It felt like they understood each other on a deeper level. Maybe it was because he told Gabriel about Yolette and he had never trusted anyone else with that knowledge. Maybe it was because he fully trusted Gabriel with his body and mind in order to give the demon form. But he felt closer to Gabriel than he had ever felt to anyone else in his life, even his friends. Even Natalie, though he hated to say it.

"He's talking to the president of the college," Jordan said. "I don't know if he'll be able to sense if you're awake now or not. Everyone says he has a really powerful form, so he might be able to tell. Either way, you'll see him soon."

Taylor sat up and held a hand to his head as his senses blurred. Jordan was at his side in an instant, holding his shoulder to help him remain upright. Jordan's touch was gentle, not what he would have expected from his roommate.

"I'm sorry about the other night," Jordan said. "I didn't realize you would need the room. I guess I just got caught up in Callan and didn't want you to intrude, and forgot that you would need the room too."

"It's okay," Taylor said. "It worked out for the best."

Something about the way Jordan said the other night bothered Taylor, however. He frowned.

"The other night? Wasn't that just last night?"

Jordan hesitated, then patted Taylor's shoulder.

"You've been asleep a long time. It's Sunday evening."

"What?"

Taylor nearly leapt out of the bed. He did swing his legs off the bed and attempt to stand. Sunday evening? He fell asleep on Friday and woke up on Sunday? How much energy had Gabriel taken from him? Would that happen again? If Gabriel were in such an energy-intensive body, would Gabriel have to continue feeding off him and keep him weak just to keep that body functioning? Why hadn't anyone woken him up earlier?

It made sense now that people had been watching him in shifts, and he wondered what they all thought. Gabriel better have a super powerful body to cost Taylor a whole weekend, he thought, scowling as he remembered the paper he needed to write and the exam he had planned on preparing for. Would his teachers be flexible? He could imagine Ms. Winde being understanding, but someone like Mr. Hill would be utterly inflexible. That man had no more compassion than a toad. Well, he had let Taylor stay in class when Gabriel had fed on him, so maybe he had a shred of compassion. But he had also told Ms. Winde about Gabriel and now everyone looked at him with that blend of hate and jealousy.

Jordan helped him stand up and take a few wavering steps. He was dressed only in his boxers but he didn't feel embarrassed, since Jordan was his roommate and had seen him in boxers before. For some reason, though, Jordan blushed when he stood up and was keeping his eyes on Taylor's face, as if he were embarrassed. But there was nothing to be embarrassed about. Taylor suddenly remembered Jordan's odd words the other day when Jordan had insisted that Taylor was interested in him and wondered if Jordan still thought Taylor was interested. Jordan probably had some issues with homophobia that he was still working out and felt awkward around a half-naked gay guy. Taylor was just glad that Jordan cared enough to help him. It meant that they would be able to have a friendship after all, even after Jordan's careless actions lately.

Taylor walked to the bathroom and shut the door. He stared in the mirror and felt a pang of regret as Gabriel's face didn't materialize beside his own. From now on, he would be alone in mirrors, but it was for the best. He relieved himself and wondered if he had been holding it in for two days or if doctors had done something to help him go while he was unconscious. The idea made him uncomfortable and he pushed it aside. He washed his hands in scorching hot water that helped to wake him up and felt wonderful compared to the relatively cool air. After drying his hands, he took a deep breath and opened the door.

Jordan was waiting, and now so was Natalie and Ariel. Taylor blushed and looked around for clothes, remembering too late that he had given his clothes to Gabriel to wear. He was fine being half-naked around Jordan, but Natalie was a different story. She didn't seem to care, however, and was actually carrying some clothes for him.

"Here, I brought you these," she said, handing him some jeans and a clean shirt.

He took them into the bathroom and changed quickly. He probably could have changed in front of her, but it felt rude and oddly provocative to get dressed in front of such a large audience. When he emerged from the restroom this time, fully clothed, Callan had joined the party as well and was clinging to Jordan's arm.

Ariel marched up to Taylor and wound between his legs, purring slightly, and he reached down to scratch behind her ears as he would any other cat. She batted at him slightly as if reminding him that she was a demon, not a pet, then rolled onto her back as if asking for a belly rub. He hesitantly stroked her belly, wondering if she was just trying to get his hand into a vulnerable position to attack. But she seemed to enjoy the attention and after a few seconds she meowed and rolled back over, retreating to her original position by Natalie's feet.

"She says you've recovered," Natalie said. "I was so worried about you. It took me a full day to recover, and everyone's been saying how powerful Gabriel's body is, no one knew how long you'd be out."

"Well, I'm fine now," Taylor said, but he kept glancing at the door, waiting for Gabriel to come in.

The succubus stroked Jordan's arm. "Gabriel has not taken on a form in some time and was quite out of practice. Those of us who have more experience can reduce the costs to our humans. Jordan was only out for a few hours."

Jordan grinned, but there was something off about him. His eyes were filled with desire, but that desire dampened when he looked at his succubus, not light up. Oddly, when he looked at Taylor he seemed the most alive. Very bizarre, but Taylor didn't have time for mysteries. He wanted Gabriel, here, now.

"I suppose Jordan told you where Gabriel is," Natalie said. "A message was sent to him immediately and he should be back here pretty soon."

"Thanks. Not that I don't want to see you guys."

"I understand," Natalie said. "We'll keep you company until he arrives, though. How are you feeling?"

"Fine," Taylor said. In truth he felt more than fine. He felt great. He had given his demon form and survived, and he felt as though he had more than enough energy to share with his demon. "Did you finish your paper?"

"Yeah," Natalie said. "I think Ms. Winde will push the due date back for you, though. The whole campus knows you've been in a coma."

"What?"

"It's because you bonded to the prince. That's a really big deal," she explained. "Rumors about you are flying. I've tried to stop the crazy ones, but it's not going to be the same when you go back to class. People know you now, and a lot of people think they can earn favor with the demons if they befriend you."

"Gabriel's the one they should befriend, but he's here now, not in the demon's realm. I don't know if he even has power there anymore."

"He's the demon prince, Taylor," Natalie said with a hint of annoyance. This was probably material that had been covered in a lecture he hadn't paid attention to. "Even though he entered this world fully, he left behind a shadow of himself so that he can return anytime he wants. No other demon can do this, not even the princesses."

Taylor pondered this. He remembered the feeling of a wall closing in his mind and he knew that Gabriel had cut himself off from the other realm, the realm where the demons lived. Gabriel would exist fully in this realm until Taylor died. When that happened, he would be like a ghost, trapped in this world with no body and no one to connect to until the demon season began again and he could escape back through the veil dividing the realms. But if he had left a shadow in the other realm, then he could pass back and forth between realms even when the realms were closed. Taylor's death, in that case, would be of little importance because Gabriel could immediately rejoin the other dimension.

It hurt to think that Gabriel might already be planning for Taylor's death, but he was glad that Gabriel wouldn't be trapped between realms. Demons who were trapped often became twisted and were one of the reasons demon hunters had formed among the humans. The demonborn even tolerated many demon hunters because they only targeted the twisted demons and left the good ones alive, but any demon hunter who set their sights on a good demon was likely to die quickly at the hands of the demonborn who watched out for such things. Taylor thought of Yolette, who was hunting Gabriel. She would have many enemies among the demonborn. Taylor's mother must have mistaken her for one of the good demon hunters, but she was evil to the core. He shivered.

"Are you alright?" Natalie asked, wrapping an arm around his shoulders and leading him back to the bed. "Maybe this is too much exertion for you."

"No, I'm fine," he insisted. He didn't want to admit that it was his fears that were troubling him, not his physical condition.

Ariel meowed knowingly and hopped on his lap as he sat back down, curling up and purring. He stroked her and wondered if she was already planning for Natalie's death. Human lives must seem so brief to the immortal demons. If the demons didn't need to feed on humans, would the demons even bother with humans at all? He thought of the demon king, who didn't need to feed on humans, and realized the answer to his question. People spoke of demon princesses and occasionally the demon prince, but there were almost no stories of the demon king, at least not stories that involved humans as well. The demon king remained in his realm and never interacted with humans at all if he could help it. His sole purpose in life seemed to be creating new demons to replace those killed by demon hunters or starved to death due to lack of human contact. Those were the only ways demons could die, and they did die, but the demon king always replaced them.

Taylor thought of his incubus, the demon prince. Supposedly the demon king had made a single demon in his likeness, a demon prince, who had all the powers of the demon king but, unlike the demon king, was still reliant on humans to survive. Why had the demon king created him? The many princesses were not made in the demon king's likeness, Taylor knew from his studies; they were simply powerful demons who earned the demon king's favor through acts of bravery, courage, or loyalty. But the demon prince was different. Gabriel was different. He was not a simple demon, and Taylor would have to remember that. After all, his transition to a physical form had wiped Taylor out for days when it had only left his friends weak for hours. Gabriel was definitely different, and it was up to Taylor to find out how.

Chapter 9

Gabriel's Return

"Taylor," a new voice said from the doorway and Taylor knew he lit up like the sun at the familiar, husky voice. Gabriel.

Taylor dropped Ariel off his lap and rushed past Natalie to lunge into Gabriel's arms, and the demon welcomed him with a tight hug that squeezed out all of his fears and doubts. Gabriel kissed the crook in his neck but didn't try to kiss him on the lips and Taylor wondered if he thought Taylor was too weak to feed on. Taylor wished they could kiss without feeding, but feeding was still the primary reason they were together. Taylor was Gabriel's food source. A beloved food source, hopefully, but a food source nonetheless.

"May we have some privacy?" Gabriel asked, stepping carefully into the room with Taylor still wrapped around him.

Natalie and Ariel wished them luck and left, and Jordan eyed them jealously before Callan whispered something in his ear that elicited a naughty grin and had both of them scooting out quickly. Gabriel kicked the door closed and locked it, still keeping one arm around Taylor.

"I was worried I took too much of you," Gabriel said. "You slept for so long. Yet you were beautiful when you slept, and I knew you were in no pain."

"I didn't even realize I was sleeping. I didn't have any dreams."

"I wanted you to rest, so I sent you into a very deep, healing sleep without dreams."

Taylor sighed and leaned his head against Gabriel's chest. "Did you feed on me while I was asleep?"

Gabriel stiffened. He appeared unsure as to what to say, then he shrugged. "Yes," he said. "I had to keep my body functioning. I knew it would prolong your sleep, but I need sustenance. This body is very costly."

"What are the costs? How will you need to feed on me?"

"Twice a day, I'll need to kiss you on the lips. The rest of the day, any casual touches will help keep me going. Even brushing your hair gives me energy," he added, brushing back Taylor's hair as he spoke. "I gain energy from every touch that brings you pleasure, but I gain the most energy from touches that reach inside you. Your mouth, for example," and he brought his head down to Taylor's, who opened his mouth in preparation for a kiss that didn't come.

Taylor pouted. "I have so much energy," he said. "Please feed on me."

"If you wish," Gabriel said, sounding almost out of breath.

His lips lowered onto Taylor's and then parted, and Taylor dove inside his demon's mouth to stroke and feel the mouth that he was beginning to know as well as his own. Gabriel's tongue invaded his mouth and he loved the long strokes Gabriel was giving him. He wondered what it would be like to suck Gabriel's penis. Then he blushed at such a thought. Still, it would likely happen at some point, so what was the shame in imagining it?

He imagined Gabriel's perfect body beneath him as his hands slid to Gabriel's waist and he came face-to-face with the man's beautiful flushed penis. Taylor would caress it with his tongue, just as Gabriel had done, and then slide it down his throat the way Gabriel's tongue was sliding down his throat right now. He didn't know if he would be able to get all of it, but he would certainly try. He could almost imagine

Gabriel's helpless pants as he lost control and cried out in ecstasy, an ecstasy caused by Taylor.

Their kiss broke apart and they both nuzzled each other, breathing heavily.

"I can still see into your mind when we are locked physically like that," Gabriel said with a hint of amusement.

Taylor stiffened and pulled away from Gabriel. "You mean, you saw-"

"I look forward to the day when you are brave enough to do in reality what you have no problems doing in your fantasies."

Taylor stared at the ground furiously. He had no idea that Gabriel would have been able to see what he was envisioning. The demon should have announced that ability sooner. Then again, Taylor should have expected something like it. It was foolish to have sexual fantasies while kissing an incubus and think the incubus wouldn't notice.

"Don't be ashamed," Gabriel said, placing a finger on Taylor's chin and forcing his face upwards until their eyes met. "What you imagined was beautiful and natural. I plan to make it come true for you when you are ready."

"I'm not used to having people sharing my fantasies," Taylor admitted, feeling less embarrassed.

"All of your fantasies that I have seen are glorious," Gabriel said, gesturing to the room around them. "Your fantasy of our bedroom in the other realm is beautiful, and so are the things you want to do there. There's no shame in any of it."

"But how are we going to do any of it?"

"What do you mean?"

"I mean, I have a roommate. Who has a succubus, no less. I'm not the type to leave a rubber band on the door and kick him out."

"Ah, yes, I was going to tell you about our living arrangements when I arrived, before we were so wonderfully distracted. Why don't we sit down."

Gabriel escorted Taylor to the bed and pulled Taylor onto his lap. He had never sat on anyone's lap before, not since he was a child at least, and it was strange. He felt like he would crush his demon but Gabriel seemed so content to have him there, he allowed himself to relax and enjoy the position.

"You're right, having a roommate will not do," Gabriel began. "I was just speaking to the president about our new apartment. You know the on-campus apartments? We will be moving into them immediately. No roommates, just us."

Taylor's jaw dropped. The on-campus apartments were every student's dream. They were brand new and had beautiful, large kitchens and enormous bathrooms. They were built for decadence and had a price tag to go with it. They were also reserved for upperclassmen, graduate students and professors who wanted to live on campus and walk to work rather than commute from the nearby neighborhoods, since parking was a major issue on campus.

There were scholarships available to help pay for the apartments, but they were highly competitive since nearly everyone wanted to live there. Aside from the dorms, which were on campus, there were no other neighborhoods within walking distance and the shuttle was notoriously late, so after the required year in the dorms, students were almost forced to get a car, or at least get a friend with a car. Taylor had hoped to get an apartment but was also saving up his money for a scooter, which would be enough to take him back and forth to school and also to the grocery store even if he couldn't go out on the highway with it.

"How did we get an apartment?" he asked. "How will we pay for it? I mean, I can get a job, I guess, but demons aren't allowed to work and I wanted to focus on school, not working full-time on top of being a student full-time."

"The college will pay for it," Gabriel said while waving his hand as if to dismiss the matter. "They are honored to have the demon prince on campus and they understand that I require a certain level of comfort that only the apartments provide."

"And me? They're letting me go too?"

Gabriel laughed, a soft, husky laugh. "What good is an apartment to me if you aren't there? The apartment is for you, darling, I just follow you. Surely one of your friends mentioned that your position in this college is changing. You were just another student before. Now you are bonded to the prince of demons. Many things will change for you, some for the better, some for the worse. You must be prepared to face all of the changes."

"What changes for the worse?"

Gabriel's mouth twitched into a frown. "Demon hunters, primarily. I will protect you, but you must always be on guard when you are around humans. You can never tell who is human and who is a demon hunter."

Taylor's mind fled to Yolette. Would she come after him again? Would he be able to face her if she did? Taylor trembled, and Gabriel's arms wrapped around him as Gabriel rocked him in his lap.

"She will never touch you," he whispered as if knowing exactly where Taylor's mind had gone. "I will always be here to protect you."

"You weren't here when I woke up," Taylor said, trying not to sound accusatory.

"You were safe with friends, and as soon as I felt you awaken I came running. I was across campus at the time, and even in this body I can't shift places the way I can in the other realm. I have to move through space and time just like everyone else—I can just do it a lot faster."

"You felt me wake up? So you can feel me?"

"Yes," Gabriel said and kissed the top of his head. "You are like a gentle whisper in my head, and when you sleep you are like a quiet song. Everything about you is delicate and beautiful."

Taylor blushed and smiled, pleased by the description. He wasn't used to being called delicate, since he was pretty well-built and had a generous helping of muscle, but that word coming from Gabriel felt right.

"As long as you're with me, I'll get used to the changes," he said, hoping it was the truth.

He was actually frightened at the thought that people on campus would know him now. It was weird enough when the cleaning lady said congratulations; having the entire campus know about him and Gabriel would be even more awkward and strange. But the benefits would surely outweigh the costs, he figured. For every uncomfortable moment at school, he would be able to dream about his beautiful apartment when he finally went home. That was a fair exchange. And Gabriel would accompany him for most of the day, so he would have some back up if things got too uncomfortable. Gabriel seemed to be a natural at talking to people and as the prince, he must be used to getting a lot of attention so he could help deflect the attention away from Taylor.

"Well, then," Gabriel said. "Let's go pack up your stuff and start moving."

"Now? I have a paper to write, and a test to study for."

"I've spoken with all of your teachers," Gabriel said. "You will not be attending school tomorrow and you've been granted extensions on the paper and the exam."

"Mr. Hill is letting me take the exam late?"

Taylor stared at Gabriel in shock.

"He suggested it. Now," Gabriel patted him on the back to encourage Taylor to stand up. "Shall we get going?"

Taylor thought of the look Jordan and Callan had exchanged before they left the room.

"What if Jordan and Callan are in there? You know, together or something?"

"They are elsewhere," Gabriel said. "I informed Callan that she would need to leave the room alone for the next few hours while we packed, and she'll obey. I don't know where they are, but they aren't in the room. Taylor, I want you to be careful around her."

"You think she'd hurt me? She's a succubus, she doesn't feed off pain."

"I don't think she'd hurt you, no, but she has some game afoot. Jordan wasn't the best match for her by a long shot, but he is the only male on campus with a clear connection to you."

"She's trying to get to me? But I didn't want her. Is she mad that I didn't want her?"

"I suspect her true intentions have to do with me, not you," Gabriel said. "I've known her for a long time and things haven't always gone smoothly between us. I doubt she'll try anything that would harm you, but just—be wary around her. She may try to trick you or mislead you."

"All right," Taylor said, wondering if he would be able to tell if a succubus was lying to him and wondering what Gabriel was worried about. Did Callan know things about Gabriel's past that Gabriel was ashamed of? And what had caused the friction between them in the first place? Taylor almost looked forward to seeing Callan now to have some of the mystery cleared up, since he knew not to trust her.

Taylor stood up. "Should I remake the bed?"

"Let the RA take care of that," Gabriel said. "I want to be moved into the apartment by tonight, and it's already getting dark."

"You're sure in a hurry."

Gabriel grinned. "This is our first night together after demon season. The first night I will truly be able to experience my human form."

Taylor stopped, fears crashing around him. What did Gabriel expect from him? He wanted so much to cast aside his doubts and follow through with his fantasies, but fear and doubt were too strong and he knew he wouldn't be able to do what Gabriel wanted to do. He wouldn't be able to go all the way, not tonight, no matter how special tonight was.

Instantly Gabriel embraced him.

"You have nothing to worry about, darling," he murmured. "All I want from you tonight is for you to touch me in this human body and help me feel its reality. We will hold each other, touch each other, and nothing more. I would never pressure you, surely you know that."

Taylor let out a slow breath and wondered why an incubus had chosen him when he had so many strong fears about sex. But perhaps incubi were more interested in pleasure than in sex. That was at least the case in this incubus, and Taylor needed to stop panicking every time intimacy was brought up. Gabriel was going at his pace and would never rush him. Touching was permissible—more than permissible—and he shook himself to rid his mind of the lingering fears. He would pack up his belongings, move to the new apartment, and then he and Gabriel would lie together in bed and he would be able to explore his demon's new form as thoroughly as he desired.

Chapter 10

King Bed

T heir new apartment was a dream, just like Taylor had imagined it. Packing was a dream, too, since Gabriel hired a moving company to help them. Taylor just had to put things in boxes and the boxes were taken to his new apartment, even put in the proper rooms when he discovered that he could label the boxes and get such incredible service. The apartment was fully furnished, but Gabriel assured him that they would be buying nicer quality furniture once they had a chance. Everything looked pretty nice already, but he wasn't complaining. Gabriel was a prince, after all, and clearly used to living like one. From Gabriel's comments, he gathered that Gabriel's last human had bought an entire castle for the demon; he was glad that Gabriel was willing to settle for an apartment even if Gabriel upgraded every item in the place. And really, as long as neither of them had to pay, what was the harm?

Despite his skepticism about the furniture, Gabriel was impressed by the kitchen, especially when Taylor showed him the fridge and the microwave, which hadn't been invented yet the last time Gabriel was in the human world. Taylor hid his glee when Gabriel caught sight of the large whirlpool bathtub and the possibilities almost visibly flashed across the demon's face. There was also a large shower, and Taylor allowed his fantasies to run wild as he imagined Gabriel pressing him tenderly against the wall as he penetrated him. Gabriel must have caught a glimpse of that fantasy because his eyes sparkled and he smiled a knowing half-smile, but for once Taylor didn't feel ashamed. Perhaps he was getting used to having a demon read his innermost thoughts.

Most of his boxes went to the closet and the bathroom, since he had very little else, but he had a fair share of kitchen utensils and some pillows that clashed terribly with the elegant sofa. They would have to go through all of Taylor's things and decide what to keep and what to toss, but that could wait until the morning. As soon as the moving people were finished with his boxes and his main necessities like his toothbrush and pajamas were unpacked, Gabriel picked him up and carried him across the threshold to the bedroom, a magnificent room with a king bed. He felt like a bride on his wedding night and felt a familiar suffocating anxiety, but he reassured himself that they were only touching tonight. Nothing more. And boy, was he eager to touch Gabriel and feel the body that the demon had created and everyone was saying was so powerful.

Gabriel laid him on the bed and began peeling off Taylor's shirt. Taylor blushed and tried to help, but Gabriel tutted at him and insisted on stripping him. His shoes and socks were next, then his pants. His boxers revealed a hardening mound in his groin as the slow stripping was getting him hot, and when Gabriel slid his hands beneath the waistband of his boxers Taylor moaned inadvertently. Gabriel pulled his boxers off and breathed a sigh of awe as he released Taylor from the confines of the boxers. Taylor bobbed up in an embarrassing manner but oddly Taylor didn't feel embarrassed, because he knew Gabriel wanted this to happen. Then Gabriel began to strip.

The first thing Taylor noticed was that Gabriel was wearing new clothes. Somehow, the demon had acquired black slacks, a white shirt, and a black jacket. It looked so natural on him that Taylor hadn't even noticed before. He wondered when Gabriel had the time to go shopping, but then the jacket was off and Gabriel set it delicately on the chair, and the white shirt was so thin he could see some of the muscles underneath. Gabriel kicked off his shoes and socks—again, when had he had time to buy them—and then began unbuttoning his shirt.

Taylor's mouth went dry as Gabriel peeled back the material to expose a handsome, pale chest inch by excruciating inch. He wanted all of it, now, and he could tell by Gabriel's grin that his need was apparent. He was hard, and he leaned forward and fought the urge to jerk himself off as he watched Gabriel finally finish unbuttoning himself and pull one shoulder back to reveal a gloriously smooth shoulder that needed to be kissed. Then the other shoulder was revealed, as was the chest below and the dusky nipples that were standing erect in the cool air. Taylor ached to touch him and claim Gabriel as his own, but Gabriel wasn't even halfway done.

With the shirt off, Gabriel let his hands travel slowly down his body, caressing himself until he reached the button on his pants. He unbuttoned it and then unzipped himself, and let his pants fall to the ground. He wore nothing underneath and the sudden exposure made Taylor dizzy with desire. Gabriel's penis hung beautifully, a rosy peach, perfectly formed and the perfect length, between two powerful thighs that Taylor itched to caress. His legs were perfect all the way down, and his feet were beautiful, with perfectly formed toes that Taylor had the sudden, irrational urge to suck. He knew some people got off sucking toes and he had never expected it of himself, but now, seeing those plump little toes, he wanted them in his mouth.

Gabriel stood before him now completely exposed and nude, and Taylor looked his fill. But as much as he enjoyed the view, he was eager to get on to the next part, the touching. He wanted to feel this incredible body and know for sure that it was real, because at the moment he had a horrible fear that it was all a dream and couldn't possibly be real life. Things like this didn't happen to him, and until it was within his grasp, he wasn't sure he would believe it.

Then Gabriel walked over to him with graceful strides and put his hands on Taylor's shoulders, pushing him backwards on the bed. He helped Taylor scoot up so that his whole body was cushioned on the king-size bed, and then Gabriel swung one leg over his prone body and straddled him. Gabriel's penis brushed against Taylor's painfully erect one and Taylor cried out at the sudden pleasure. Gabriel brought his head down and kissed Taylor, who returned the kiss with a ferocity that surprised even him. He was turned on as he had never been in his life.

As they kissed, Taylor let his hands travel across the broad expanse of Gabriel's back, caressing and soothing him. Gabriel's groin pressed against his and he maintained a slow grinding rhythm that had Taylor out of breath and desperate for air in no time, but the kiss continued and Taylor grew dizzy. His energy drained into Gabriel but he had plenty to spare; the grinding motion produced so much raw energy he knew Gabriel could drink from him for hours and he would never run dry. Gabriel broke away from the kiss and sat up, still keeping up the rhythm below. Taylor's hands slid to his chest, to his nipples, to the belly that, oddly enough, had a belly button. He had heard that demons didn't have belly buttons but perhaps Gabriel added one to this body to fit in better. He caressed the belly button and followed the trail of hair below, to where the pleasure was spiking.

Gabriel was barely hard and his eyes widened. Was he not turned on by this? Did he not like Taylor for some reason? Then again, Gabriel had plenty of experience with sex and probably wouldn't be close to coming after such little stimulation. Still, it was a surprise and Taylor felt put out to know that he wasn't arousing his demon as much as his demon was arousing him.

"You are doing everything right," Gabriel murmured. "It just takes me longer."

Taylor's unpleasant surprise must have been obvious, but he had other concerns, primarily feeling his demon's beautiful body and trying to provoke more from his demon. He let his hands slip to Gabriel's backside and squeezed the powerful buttocks. They were perfectly formed, just as they had been under the fur in his true shape. He wondered if anyone had ever penetrated Gabriel, or if Gabriel was always the top as he was likely to be in this relationship. Gabriel rubbed against him especially closely and Taylor moaned and shut his eyes. He wasn't going to last much longer with the constant rubbing and pressure, but he wanted to feel everything.

His hands traveled down to those lovely thighs and he caressed the insides of the thighs, hearing Gabriel's breath stutter and knowing he had found a sensitive region. He tickled the area and Gabriel huffed in laughter and leaned his head against Taylor's.

"Little imp," he said. "You must be the demon here."

Taylor continued to stroke those thighs and he felt a response in Gabriel's penis as he hardened while continuing the steady rocking against Taylor. So this was his weak spot, Taylor thought, feeling victorious. But then Gabriel pushed against him hard and his balls seized up and a feeling of inevitability came over him. He cried out Gabriel's name and his body spasmed, blasting outward from his penis as pure bliss crashed over him and a pleasant fuzziness fogged his senses. When he returned to his senses, there was sticky cum on both their chests and Gabriel looked extremely pleased with himself.

"Shall we try out the shower?" he asked in an innocent voice.

Taylor laughed.

"I'm exhausted, but we do need to get clean."

"I won't try anything," Gabriel said, kissing Taylor's forehead. "You need your strength. You've just given me an amazing meal and now it's time for you to rest, after we bathe."

Taylor smiled, but he was disturbed by the thought that their intimacy was nothing more than a meal to Gabriel. It meant something to Taylor, something important, but to Gabriel it was just an amazing meal. Would he ever get over the feeling of being used? Would Gabriel ever come to see him as more than a meal? He didn't have any answers, and it was too troublesome to think about now with the memory of the orgasm so close at hand. He would take a shower and lather up his beautiful incubus and try not to dream of things that could never be.

Chapter 11

Essential Meetings

"Good morning."

Taylor stretched, a smile curving his lips as he opened his eyes to see Gabriel's blazing red eyes watching him. Normally it would be unnerving seeing a demon so close, but this was his demon. Those crimson eyes would only look on him with compassion.

"Morning, Gabriel."

The demon leaned close and kissed his cheek and Taylor's cheeks flushed with heat at the gentle, sweet gesture. Then Gabriel rolled out of bed and Taylor eyed his naked form. Then he realized he was naked and flushed. They had gone straight from the shower to bed and he hadn't even realized he hadn't gotten in pajamas. Had he really slept naked?

He supposed there was nothing wrong with sleeping naked, but what if something happened in the middle of the night? He would have to stumble into his clothes before figuring out what was happening. What if there were an emergency and people came in? Or what if there were a thief? He would be completely naked and defenseless.

Then he took a deep breath and studied his demon with a soft smile. If something happened, he had Gabriel now. There was no need for fear or panic. Gabriel would take care of him. Taylor slid out of bed and tried not to feel too self conscious as he went to the bathroom.

When he returned, Gabriel had an outfit laid out for him and he blinked. It was his nicest outfit, a suit that he brought just in case he needed to do any job interviews or something where he would need to impress people. It was buried in the boxes of clothes. How had Gabriel found it?

"What's this?"

"We'll be meeting a lot of important people today," Gabriel explained. "You need to look good. I've asked for a tailor to take your measurements so we can get you something better, but this will do for now."

Taylor narrowed his eyes at the implied insult to his nicest outfit. It was by far the most expensive clothing he owned and he had saved up for it. And it wasn't good enough? Well, Gabriel was no doubt used to having the finest of everything, he reminded himself.

"Speaking of clothes, where did you get yours?" He started getting in his suit, pulling on the pants and shirt.

"The tailor already took my measurements," Gabriel said, and reached out to button Taylor's shirt, their fingers tangling together. "And he had some clothes on hand."

"I can do this," Taylor said with a laugh, and Gabriel withdrew to let him finish buttoning. "I'm glad you were able to get clothes so quickly. They look good on you."

"I know." He glanced up to see Gabriel's sly smile and flushed. The demon must be able to sense the lust he felt at the sight of Gabriel in those finely fitted clothes. He hadn't wanted anyone else to see Gabriel naked and lust after him, but the clothes, while they covered him completely, were just as seductive. Still, Gabriel was an incubus. He would be irresistible no matter what he wore.

As soon as Taylor finished dressing, he went to the mirror to brush his hair a final time. Gabriel went with him this time and tousled his light brown hair.

"Hey!"

Taylor glared, though he was amused by the gesture.

"I'm just helping," Gabriel said in an innocent voice, his scarlet eyes projecting sincerity. Just the slight tug of a smile on his lips revealed his true intentions as Gabriel smoothed his hair back down, sliding his fingers through the curls and caressing him in a distinctly seductive manner.

Taylor was about to scold him when his eyes widened. "Are you feeding?"

Gabriel paused. "Does that bother you?"

No wonder the demon was touching him so much. Gabriel had said he needed touches throughout the day. He should probably get used to this type of thing.

"You can touch me," Taylor said. "But maybe not right now. Don't we need to go to breakfast?"

"All right," Gabriel said, letting his fingers run though Taylor's curls down to his neck, which he caressed before releasing him completely. Taylor finished brushing his hair back into a semblance of order, though his hair was always a bit unruly. He stared at himself in the mirror. He looked good, but compared to Gabriel he was a disheveled mess. How could he ever compare to an incubus?

"You look wonderful," Gabriel said, smoothing the edge of his collar. "But I can imagine you looking even better in clothes designed to fit you and show off that body of yours."

Would that make that much of a difference? He studied Gabriel's clothing in the mirror. It did fit him quite well, even if wasn't specifically tailored yet. Maybe he really would look better in clothes designed just for him. It was such a foreign concept. He wasn't poor exactly, and his mother did her best to get him everything he would need, but he never splurged the way some of his peers did. He remembered the other boys in class taking expensive trips to the coast. He was invited once and naively agreed.

As soon as he arrived, he realized everything was going to cost way more than he expected. He skipped meals because they were so expensive, his stomach grumbling in protest, and stayed at the beach house while they went on expensive outings, instead walking along the beach feeling left out and unbelievably poor. No one even noticed anything. They thought he was on a diet, and just tired so he didn't want to go on the outings. They were oblivious to the costs because they were raised on that kind of extravagance and he knew he never wanted to be that uncaring of other people that they couldn't even recognize he was starving because he couldn't afford the food.

He didn't want to become one of those boys, but surely a few extravagances wouldn't hurt. And really, he would never be that blasé about someone else's wellbeing. If he saw someone skipping meals he would ask why and offer to pay for them. It was only right. But somehow none of the rich people he had ever met thought that way. What was Gabriel like? Was he generous with his wealth? Taylor hoped so. He would have to see. So far they hadn't been in a situation where it was put to the test but he was curious. Was Gabriel generous or greedy?

"We meet with the president of the university first," Gabriel said, and Taylor jolted.

"What?"

"I told you, we'll be meeting important people today. It should be fine. Try not to be intimidated and let me do the talking."

Taylor nodded. The first part would be difficult but he had no problems letting Gabriel take over the conversation. He glanced at the mirror again.

"I look good enough?"

Gabriel leaned to kiss the nape of his neck. "You look beautiful."

"Even though my clothes aren't great?"

Gabriel chuckled and punched his arm in a friendly manner. "That will make you more beautiful, but you're still beautiful to begin with. You'll make a good impression."

He glanced at his watch. "We'll talk to him first, then have breakfast. Is that all right?"

Taylor wasn't hungry, so he nodded. He often went hours after waking up before eating. Sometimes he didn't eat at all and his first meal was lunch. He ate most meals with Natalie and she was good to make sure he ate enough, but he didn't mind putting off breakfast.

Gabriel led him out of the apartment and Taylor locked the door and put the key in his pocket, pushing away the disbelief that one of these apartments actually belonged to him. This was his new reality. All of the things he had only dreamed about were now his. He shyly reached out to Gabriel, who took his hand readily. Gabriel was his, the apartment was his, and it was more than he ever expected.

When they arrived at the President's house, there was a tailor waiting to take Taylor's measurements and he worked quickly, finishing before the President even saw them. The tailor promised to have a wardrobe finished for both of them within the week so they could dress properly. He looked at Taylor's current outfit with some disdain and seemed about to say something until Gabriel stepped between them with an icy glare.

Then they were ushered into the President's office. The President was an imposing man in his sixties, with thick hair so pale it was hard to tell if it was white or blonde, and a sharp nose that dominated his face. He exuded confidence and Taylor stood up straighter. Gabriel placed a hand on his shoulder as if sensing that this man intimidated Taylor, or perhaps the demon sensed that the President was disappointed in Taylor. Taylor could feel the disappointment in the way the President's eyes flicked up and down his body before settling on his face.

"You must be Taylor," the President said, walking forward and extending his hand. "Please call me Samson."

It was his last name, Taylor noticed, already feeling on uneven grounds. He accepted the handshake and the man's forceful hand nearly crushed him. He didn't know if Samson always shook hands like that or if he was trying to make a point, but he attempted a strong hand-shake in return and was rewarded with a slight nod from Samson.

"I understand you are a first-year student here," Samson continued. "And you managed to bond with Gabriel in your first demon season. Congratulations."

"Thank you," Taylor said, not knowing what else to say.

"We take our responsibilities to the demons very seriously. If there is anything that you need, do not hesitate to ask. We are honored to have you and the demon prince on our campus and we will do our best to make both of you comfortable."

"Thank you," Taylor said again, almost wishing Gabriel was inside his head again so the demon could tell him what to say. Luckily, Gabriel was standing right beside him and had no problems taking over.

"Your generosity is overwhelming, and we will be sure to let you know if we need anything," Gabriel said, squeezing Taylor's shoulder as if to reassure him. "Your campus honors us with its kindness, and we shall make sure word of its generosity reaches the demon realm."

Samson smiled, and there was an edge of mercenary delight in it. Was he doing this only so that his campus would be more appealing to other demons? Taylor didn't know, but it didn't really matter, not as long as Samson kept his word and continued to protect and cater to him and Gabriel. Not even him so much as Gabriel, since it seemed that Gabriel was far more high maintenance than Taylor.

"There is the issue of demon hunters," Gabriel continued. "We spoke of them earlier. I want all visitors to the campus screened. Have you had time to put something into place?"

"Yes, about that," Samson said as his lips twisted. "We have an open campus and anyone can walk in. We have tight security, but we can't close our campus completely. It just isn't feasible. I've doubled the security and made sure that the areas where you and Taylor will be are completely secure, but the campus itself cannot be made one hundred percent secure."

A chill went down Taylor's spine. So Yolette could just walk onto the campus anytime she pleased?

"What would be involved in closing the campus?" Gabriel asked.

"We would have to build a fence around it, or something like that, and it just isn't possible given the landscape and size of the campus. There are always ways for people to slip in, so even if we were to build some sort of structure to channel people, there would still be danger. I think the best solution is to simply stay in the areas where you live and have classes, because those areas are secure, and whenever you have to leave, come to me for a protection detail."

Gabriel nodded. "If that's the best you can do, then we'll accept it. Taylor? Does that sound acceptable to you?"

"Sure," Taylor said hesitantly.

It didn't sound great, but he did understand that the President couldn't just cut off outside communication for the entire campus just because the demon prince lived there now. There were so many hiking trails that led off campus, and so many ways to get on and off campus aside from the roads, that it would be nearly impossible to track them all. But as long as the areas where he and Gabriel spent their time were safe, perhaps the rest didn't matter as much.

He didn't like having his mobility limited, however, and he wished there was some way he and Gabriel could be safe wherever they went. A security detail would help, but would they be able to prevent demon hunters from finding them? Would they be able to stop Yolette?

The questions kept running through his mind long after they left the President's office and made their way towards the faculty lounge, where Gabriel informed him that they were scheduled to meet with his teachers. Taylor was halfway there before he realized that they were meeting with his teachers, and he had no idea why.

"I won't be able to go to classes with you," Gabriel explained as they walked.

"What do you mean? I thought you wouldn't leave my side."

"Have you ever seen a succubus in a classroom? Any demon in human form is asked to wait outside because we can be too distracting, and that includes incubi. Even me. Most succubi go to an area on campus set aside for them and hang out during the day, but I plan to wait for you outside your classes so that I can see you as soon as possible and walk you to your next class."

Taylor smiled, pleased by the thought. He hadn't ever seen a succubus in a classroom but he always assumed it was the succubus's choice and not a school policy. But it did make sense, and if Gabriel were in class with him he would be distracted. Maybe not as distracted as he had been when Gabriel was inside his head, but distracted just the same. And the other students would probably be distracted as well with an incubus nearby, especially all of those girls in love with the idea of an incubus prince. They might even try to steal Gabriel from him, though he doubted that would work. Gabriel seemed pretty attached to him despite Taylor's shortcomings. And once bonded, a demon was stuck with their human for better or worse.

He knew there was an area on campus reserved for demons and he, like every other student, was extremely curious about it. Most demons went there sometimes, not just the succubi, and it was rumored that they had all sorts of demonic entertainment and humans brought in for feedings and everything else a demon could want. Taylor was glad Gabriel wouldn't be going there, since it had the vibe of being a seedy, underhanded sort of place where demons went when they wanted to escape the morality of living with humans. In all probability it probably wasn't as sketchy as it sounded, but he was still happy Gabriel was avoiding it. He was also pleased that Gabriel wanted to spend more time with him, even if it was just the few minutes between classes.

They arrived at the teacher meeting and his palms sweated. Mr. Hill was there, looking somewhat annoyed, and Ms. Winde, looking serene as always, and his two other teachers as well, Mr. Fischer and Ms. Salazar. All four turned to look at him when he entered and he froze. He had never been the focus of all four teachers' gazes before and it was terrifying. Luckily, Gabriel was with him and Gabriel wrapped his arm around Taylor's shoulder and guided him into the room and into a chair. He and the teachers were sitting in a circle now, but he couldn't help but notice that the teachers were all in comfortable teachers' chairs and he and Gabriel were in the student desks.

Mr. Hill began. "I suppose Gabriel has already told you that he won't be in class with you. Well, that's true for every class you take at this university. We do not allow demons in human form into the classroom."

"I understand," Taylor said in a small voice, cowed by the presence of all four of his teachers.

"I plan on waiting outside your classes," Gabriel explained. Gabriel was holding Taylor's hand and Taylor was grateful for the contact. "I don't want to disturb you or your students."

The teachers nodded, though Mr. Hill exchanged a glance with Ms. Salazar. What did that mean? Then Ms. Winde leaned forward.

"You'll need to talk to us individually about how to make up the work you've missed this weekend," she said. "We will all be very flexible," she added, shooting a glance at Mr. Hill, who rolled his eyes and nodded.

"You also need to get back into our classes as soon as possible," Ms. Salazar said. "Even though you're adapting to a new way of life, I think you'll find that having the structure of classes makes everything easier, not harder."

"Yes," Mr. Hill said. "Classes create structure and structure is exactly what you need right now."

Taylor nodded. "Yes, of course. I won't take any more days off. I want to get back to my classes."

Mr. Hill began discussing how to make up the test for his class. Taylor was impressed that he was even allowing him to take the test late; having a prince for a demon was truly a lifesaver for this class. He thought of the equation Gabriel had given him and knew that for once, he might actually pass the test as well. Then Ms. Winde explained her late paper policy and he nodded again, inwardly dreading the next week. He would be writing two papers, it seemed, the one he needed to make up and the new paper she had just assigned. But he could do it.

The other two classes didn't have any assignments that he had missed, but both had upcoming deadlines and he was going to be busy preparing for more tests and papers while trying to make up the other test and paper. It was going to be a busy week, but perhaps having Gabriel there for moral support would help.

As soon as the teachers finished explaining his new role in their class, Gabriel stood up.

"Thank you for your time," he said. "Taylor will see you tomorrow."

He gestured for Taylor to stand and Taylor obeyed, and then they left the classroom. He heard the teachers begin talking to each other as soon as they exited the room and was tempted to stay behind and listen, curious as to what they were talking about.

"They're talking about us," Gabriel said quietly, leaning so close to Taylor that his breath brushed against Taylor's ear. "And how unusual it is for an incubus—or succubus—to wait for his student instead of leaving for the day."

"Will you be bored waiting for me?" Taylor asked, worried that he was causing his demon undue stress or boredom.

"No," Gabriel said. "I've spent decades of my life doing nothing but waiting, and compared to that, an hour or two is nothing. Besides, I doubt I'll be alone. I suspect many students will come and try to talk to me while I'm waiting."

Jealousy flared in Taylor's heart. "But you won't talk to them, will you?"

Gabriel laughed. "Of course I'll talk to them, my jealous darling. But you come first in my life. You know that. You are my partner. You have nothing to fear."

Taylor ducked his head. "I guess. I just can't figure out why you chose me."

Gabriel smiled and kissed his hand. "There is no one else like you, Taylor. I've had many partners, but no one like you. You are kind, loyal, loving, and I'm honored to have bonded with you."

Taylor's cheeks were on fire, but a pleased smile lit his face. He still didn't understand why an incubus would choose someone like him when so many other men were more than willing to have sex with a gorgeous demon like Gabriel, but he was thrilled that Gabriel thought so highly of him. He wrapped his arm around Gabriel's waist and pulled the demon close as they walked back to the apartment, ignoring the judgmental looks of the students that they passed. Let them judge. Taylor would never be ashamed of his incubus again.

Chapter 12

Swarmed

As soon as Taylor entered the classroom the next morning, students swarmed him. Students who hadn't spared him a second look all semester clamored for his attention or else craned their necks to see outside the door where Gabriel waited. Natalie wasn't in this class with him, unfortunately, and the crush of attention completely overwhelmed him. He smiled at the people trying to talk to him and attempted to be polite, but it was a struggle when everyone was talking to him at once and some of the questions were outright vulgar—how did it feel to have sex with an incubus, was it true that the prince of demons was an exceptional lover, what did he have to do to give his demon form. He blushed at those questions and focused instead on the people asking questions he felt he could actually answer.

He was grateful when Ms. Salazar called the class to order. She had to call it to order three times before everyone settled in their chairs and stopped talking, and even then he could feel eyes on him. He saw pity in the teacher's face as she started lecturing but as usual in her class, about twenty minutes in they broke into small groups. Normally, they choose their own groups but today she selected groups for them and he hoped that she had done a good job picking people to be with him. As he scooted his desk to join the three other students, he was pleased to see that none of them had asked him inappropriate questions and one of them hadn't even pestered him with questions at all. Ms. Salazar had chosen the groups well and he smiled at her.

They worked on several questions about the reading that Taylor had stayed up late finishing. It was about education and how the education system ought to work as opposed to how the education system did work and he found it fascinating. It brought to light a lot of the problems he had with schools and he was surprised that teachers knew about the problems with teaching and were trying to fix them. He just assumed all teachers were alike and taught the same way, though his college experience was starting to change that view as all of his teachers were so dramatically different from each other.

He realized about halfway through the activity that he was the only one talking in his group. The girl who hadn't bombarded him with questions before class was writing the answers, but the other two were just looking at him in awe. He was used to doing all the work in groups —he was usually the only one who had done the reading—but he wasn't used to being looked at like that. He stumbled to a halt in the middle of one of his answers and the girl writing the answer looked up in surprise.

"What's wrong? I totally agree with what you're saying," she said.

"It's just, I'm doing all the talking," he said. "What do you guys think?"

The other girl fluttered her eyelashes. "Oh, I completely agree with you. Whatever you say is right."

"Yeah," the guy said. "Definitely."

"Did you guys do the reading?" Taylor asked.

"Yeah," the guy said, but the girl shook her head. The guy shrugged as if embarrassed that he did the reading. "It was really interesting."

"So what did you think about banking education?" Taylor almost felt like a teacher trying to pry knowledge out of his classmate's heads and wondered if this was what it felt like for teachers. If so, he had a whole new level of respect for them. It was hard getting them to even acknowledge that they read, let alone share what they thought about the reading.

"I thought it was a pretty cool way to think about education," the guy said. "And we need to change it, like the author says."

The girl in charge of writing scribbled something down.

"That was the last question," she announced. "We're done!"

With her usual flawless timing, Ms. Salazar appeared at their group.

"Finished? We'll be working for about five more minutes, so just relax until then."

They nodded and she left. Then all eyes turned to Taylor and he blushed. 'Relax' might not be the right word.

"So what's it like having the prince as your demon?" the other girl asked.

"I imagine it's just like having any other demon, except he's in human form and can talk and be more independent," Taylor said.

"What was it like when you choose him?" she asked.

He blushed and noticed the red mark on her wrist.

"What was it like you when you found your demon?" he countered. Everyone had been asking him this question, but he still didn't know if his experience was normal or unusual because he hadn't heard about anyone else's experience, not even Natalie's.

The girl didn't seem perturbed by his question at all and smiled happily. "I fell asleep and woke up on an island with a woman dressed in a robe of a million colors. We started talking and I realized she was a demon, and she was compatible with me. We talked about what our relationship could be like and I realized I wanted her in my life, so we bonded. What about you?"

Taylor thought about his experience, starting with the circle of succubi and ending with his kiss, and hedged. Luckily, just at that moment Ms. Salazar called for everyone's attention and they began talking about their answers as a class. There was no more time to talk and soon they were dismissed. When Taylor left, he was again surrounded by students wanting to talk to him, but not as many and he soon saw why—they had rushed Gabriel.

Gabriel handled them with a cool demeanor, ignoring most but choosing a few to smile and respond to—Taylor would have to find out what criteria Gabriel used when determining who to talk to—but Gabriel's main attention was on Taylor as he pressed through the crush of people to reach his demon. He took Gabriel's hand and the two of them headed to the cafeteria to eat with Natalie, still surrounded by people. If this continued, he would never get any privacy and poor Natalie would get caught up in the madness as well.

As he turned up the hill towards the cafeteria, Gabriel steered him towards the apartments instead. He didn't protest; Gabriel must want some time alone and they could always order food. He had three hours until his next class. But he didn't like the thought of abandoning Natalie like this. He tried to tell Gabriel but he didn't want to say anything for fear that the crowd around them would hear and swarm Natalie instead.

The crowd finally thinned as they approached the apartments and when they entered, Gabriel firmly kept everyone else out. As soon as they were safely inside the building, Taylor glanced in the direction of the cafeteria.

"Poor Natalie," he said. "Is there any way to get a message to her?"

"I'm already here," she said, and he turned and saw her in the foyer of the apartment building with Ariel at her side.

"I can talk to Ariel," Gabriel explained, "And I didn't think we'd have any peace at the cafeteria. Now, please, come upstairs and let's order some lunch."

Taylor followed his demon up the stairs and Natalie was awed by the apartment. She hadn't seen one of the campus apartments before, since they were so exclusive, and it was infinitely better than the dorms. Everything was neat and sparkling and new, and it was fabulously furnished even though Gabriel wanted even newer things. Ariel took it in stride and hopped onto the couch with a meow before curling up and purring. Natalie perched beside her and Taylor glanced at Gabriel. The demons didn't need food but the humans did.

"Should we order something?" Taylor asked. "It's sort of expensive to get delivery here but I know they come to the apartments."

"Money is not an issue," Gabriel said. He pulled out a wallet and handed a credit card to Taylor. "The President gave me this. He said it would cover anything we wanted. Apparently it's currency now?"

Taylor took the credit card as he explained how it worked to Gabriel. He didn't have a credit card of his own yet. He had a debit card but his balance was always so low he had to track his spending carefully. His mother would help with money if he asked, but he wanted to be self-sufficient. He wasn't comfortable with the idea of credit for small things. If he didn't have money for something, it was probably something he didn't need. But he could already tell Gabriel would have expensive tastes and he wondered what the limit was on this card and who exactly was paying for it.

Taylor pulled out his laptop and Gabriel was immediately curious, showering him with questions as he pulled up the site for the place that delivered from local restaurants. It wasn't a national company; it was a local place but they were the only delivery service that came to this campus. Not everyone was entirely comfortable with the demonborn and while the restaurants had no complaints, the drivers sometimes did. Most of the drivers at this company were themselves demonborn so it was never an issue.

Gabriel was transfixed by how the mouse worked but Taylor finally got him to look at the actual menus. He and Natalie liked the nearby Thai restaurant and they got it on special occasions, but there was also a good pizza place and a variety of other foods. Even though Gabriel wouldn't be eating anything, he was curious about the various foods, especially the Thai food, so Taylor checked with Natalie before ordering their usual combo of pad thai and red curry. Technically the pad thai was for Taylor and the curry for Natalie, but they almost always ending up sharing.

This would be the second time this month they'd be ordering out, and he wondered if this was going to be a regular thing since the cafeteria would be unmanageable for a while. He hoped everything calmed down soon and he could sink into obscurity again. Somehow, though, he doubted that would ever happen with Gabriel as his demon. He glanced at Gabriel, who smiled reassuringly at him as if he knew Taylor were uncertain of his future. He was happy, he decided. Gabriel was worth all the inconveniences in the world.

Chapter 13

Reciprocal Pleasure

"You're taking a shower?"

Taylor turned to see Gabriel entering the bathroom and blushed, covering himself even though there was no real need. His demon had already seen everything, but it was habit.

"You don't mind, do you?"

"I'd love to take a shower with you."

"I can take it alone." Taylor's heart pounded as he thought of what might happen if they showered together, of the fantasies he had of Gabriel pushing him against the cool tile and entering him, the water slicking their bodies... He shook his head sharply. Had Gabriel seen that? The demon was grinning.

"I just want to shower with you," Gabriel said. "That's it. Unless you want more," he added with a wink.

"All right," Taylor said, and Gabriel began stripping off his fine clothes. Taylor watched for a moment, then turned the water on. At the dorms it sometimes took several minutes for the water to heat up and once it did, it quickly became scalding. When he and Gabriel showered last night, the water came out hot right away and stayed stable the entire time. Even so, Taylor tested it cautiously and waited before getting in, not wanting to burn himself as he often had at the dorms.

Gabriel came up beside him and leaned to test the water.

"Is this the temperature you like?"

Taylor tested the water as well. He hated really hot showers and would rather take a cold shower than have steaming hot water. But if Gabriel wanted hotter water, he would adapt.

"We can make it hotter if you like," he offered.

"If this is what you enjoy, then I also enjoy it," Gabriel said. "I want to know how hot you like your water in case you ask me to start the shower or bath for you."

"You don't have to do that."

"I might want to," Gabriel countered, and Taylor shrugged.

"Yeah, I don't like super hot water. This is perfect."

Taylor held his hands to cover himself as he sidled by Gabriel into the shower. His incubus had seen him naked before, of course, but he was still shy about his body. Gabriel had no reservations about his body and got in the shower with him, standing behind him. Taylor drew in a sharp breath as Gabriel wrapped his arms around Taylor and pulled him tight. He thought of all the things Gabriel might do and he imagined Gabriel coaxing him into spreading his legs, allowing the incubus deep inside of him, thrusting against him until he exploded. He trembled. He wanted it so badly but not yet. He wasn't ready yet.

Gabriel kissed his cheek, then let his hands explore Taylor's body. He grabbed soap and a loofah and began cleaning Taylor, keeping him in his arms. Taylor relaxed into the soothing, sensual touch. Gabriel cleaned everything except his penis and when he was finished, he finally ran a soapy hand along Taylor's hardening length and Taylor sighed in pleasure. The slick movement of Gabriel's hand along his growing, dripping cock was unbelievably good.

Gabriel licked the water cascading down his neck, his long tongue flicking Taylor's skin, teasing him, making him moan. Taylor turned his head and Gabriel kissed him. As Gabriel's tongue mapped his mouth, the incubus continued to stroke him and his heart raced until it felt it would burst. His mind went dizzy with pleasure and he could feel Gabriel feeding on him. He arched his back and cried out as Gabriel flicked his wrist and he burst into an explosion of pleasure and satisfaction. Gabriel continued to kiss him and stroke him slower and slower as he came down, and finally Gabriel cleaned up the mess. When Taylor was completely clean and limp from the orgasm, Gabriel turned him in his arms. The water ran down Taylor's back as he gazed at his beautiful incubus.

"Will you clean me?" Gabriel asked in a husky voice.

Taylor imagined doing to Gabriel what Gabriel had done to him and his throat closed up, not from fear but from desire. There was some fear to it, though, as he nervously began cleaning Gabriel's body. He barely used the loofah, preferring to use his hands on the soft skin and hard muscles. He was just as thorough as Gabriel had been, though he blushed as he ran his hands across Gabriel's ass and tentatively ran a hand down his crack. Gabriel grinned and spread his legs a little and Taylor's heart thudded erratically. He let his fingers continue forward to graze against Gabriel's balls and felt Gabriel respond. While Gabriel wasn't hard yet, he was well on his way and Taylor couldn't hide his pleasure as his lips curved into a smile.

He remembered how much Gabriel enjoyed having his inner thighs stroked and soon Gabriel was completely hard, though Taylor hadn't touched that beautiful cock yet. He was certainly admiring it, though, and couldn't help the visions that flashed through his mind with searing intensity. Kneeling before Gabriel and taking that cock into his mouth. Lying in bed with Gabriel over him, being penetrated as Gabriel moaned in pleasure. Bending forward as Gabriel took him from behind, pushing up against his incubus in a rhythm of pure lust. Taylor was getting hard just thinking about the possibilities and he finally, hesitantly, touched Gabriel's penis.

Gabriel let out a soft moan. Encouraged, Taylor wrapped his hand around Gabriel and stroked lightly. Gabriel grew harder underneath his hand and he stroked again, more firmly. Gabriel moaned again. Very pleased now, Taylor began stroking Gabriel, trying to imitate what

Gabriel had done to him. He wasn't as good and he was probably making a lot of mistakes, but Gabriel was enjoying himself thoroughly. Gabriel was panting soon and Taylor himself was completely erect and starting to long for release himself.

Then, unexpectedly, Gabriel turned and took Taylor's cock in his hand, rotating them so Taylor couldn't access the demon's cock anymore. Taylor was startled but Gabriel was stroking him now and he could barely think from the pleasure. It was a matter of moments before his pleasure peaked into the second orgasm of the night, his incubus drinking in his pleasure as he cried out and his knees went weak.

As Taylor returned to his senses, he noticed that Gabriel wasn't aroused anymore. Had he come as well? There were no signs of it, but he must have. He couldn't go from that state of arousal to this without coming. Gabriel finished his own cleaning and then helped Taylor out of the shower, patting him dry and kissing him constantly before leading him to the bed. Taylor pulled towards the dresser to find pajamas, but Gabriel wrapped an arm around his waist and forced him into the bed.

"I want to feel you while we sleep tonight," Gabriel whispered. "No cloth between us."

Taylor's mouth went dry. Last night, their second night together, had been fairly uneventful. They had gotten into bed and though Gabriel cradled him all night, that was it. He briefly dreamed, but in his dream Gabriel had kissed him and held him, then there was a restful darkness. Even though demons controlled the dreams of their humans, they always let their humans get plenty of true rest. It was part of the bond between them; if the human died from exhaustion, after all, then the demon wouldn't be able to feed. Taylor knew that throughout history there were demons who kept their humans awake day and night, but it never ended well. Those were the types of demons that demon hunters targeted, and generally the demonborn let them.

Taylor relaxed against Gabriel, feeling his silky skin pressing up against his back as Gabriel spooned him. He could feel Gabriel's cock pressed against his ass but he felt safe that Gabriel wouldn't try anything right now. He was getting more confident about what Gabriel would and wouldn't do and somehow admitting what Yolette had done to him made him more comfortable with himself. He wanted Gabriel to help him recover and erase her from his mind. He shut his eyes and thought of how good it felt to bring Gabriel pleasure.

"Why did you stop me, Gabe?" he asked sleepily. "I wanted to feel and see you."

Gabriel stroked his shoulder silently for a moment.

"I didn't want you to be disappointed," Gabriel finally said.

"How would you possibly disappoint me?"

There was another long silence, then Gabriel sighed.

"I can't orgasm."

Taylor laughed in disbelief, then turned to look at Gabriel. It was ridiculous that an incubus, a demon who fed on sexual pleasure, was incapable of that pleasure himself. But Gabriel looked deadly serious and his laughter petered out.

"Are you serious?"

"Yes," Gabriel said, brushing a strand of hair from Taylor's forehead. "All other pleasures are available to me, except that."

Taylor stared at him, puzzled. He knew—all the demonborn knew—that demons couldn't experience love, but he had never thought that would extend to pleasure. He hid a flicker of disappointment that Gabriel would never love him, but this was something all of the demonborn had to come to terms with. Their demons enjoyed them, sometimes adored them, but couldn't love them. No one knew why, but there had never been any exceptions. The pleasure, though, seemed odd.

"Is it just you, or other incubi too? What about succubi?"

"Just me," Gabriel said, looking away. "But it won't be permanent. When I find the right human, it will happen. Father assured me. I've never found them, though. Perhaps you will be him, but perhaps not. I've been disappointed before and I can't let myself hope."

Taylor stared at him, then snuggled into his chest. He had never wanted anything as much as to be the one who made Gabriel come. It was such a bizarre, foreign desire for him but he desperately wanted it. He wanted Gabriel to feel as good and complete as Gabriel made him feel.

"How will you know if I'm the right human?"

Gabriel kissed the top of his head and held him tightly. "We'll see."

Not a very reassuring answer but he was pleased that Gabriel hadn't ruled him out. Taylor was still a potential. Of course, Gabriel probably wouldn't have bonded with him if he didn't think Taylor had that potential, but he hadn't ruined things yet. He ached with the need to please his incubus but Gabriel kissed him again.

"Sleep, my darling," he whispered. "You need your strength."

Taylor snuggled closer to him and let his mind relax. He counted backwards from ten and soon was sound asleep in the arms of his incubus. There were no dreams, though he was aware of the passage of time and vaguely able to think as the night passed. It was a pleasant, deep sleep and he was just aware enough to be able to enjoy how soundly he was sleeping. He wondered idly if Gabriel were feeding on that enjoyment and hoped he was. He wanted Gabriel to see him as more than food but if he were going to be food, he wanted to be good food.

As time flitted by in a pleasant blur, he wondered at what Gabriel had said. He knew Gabriel was different. Special. The demon king's only son, made in his image. The only prince. He had assumed that everything about Gabriel would be better because of that. After all, why would the demon king give him any weaknesses? Did that mean the demon king was incapable of pleasure? He wasn't sure, and he wanted to know how Gabriel would know if he were the one. He wanted to be the one and if there were something he needed to do, he wanted to know about it so that he could do it. Gabriel probably knew that, though, and wasn't going to tell him for precisely that reason. He wanted Taylor's authenticity, not Taylor's need to please.

But how would Gabriel find out if he could experience pleasure if he stopped Taylor from trying? It felt odd trying to coax an incubus into pleasure when most of his interactions with Gabriel were Gabriel coaxing him into the same. But if Taylor were being forced to come to terms with his sexuality, then Gabriel needed to do the same.

He drifted in and out of consciousness throughout the night and then the world solidified around him. He expected to be awake but he was lying in his fantasy bed, the ebony silk sheets cradling him pleasantly with Gabriel wrapped around him. Was he supposed to be here? Shouldn't he be in the real world, not the dream world?

"You're in the right place," Gabriel said, amused. "I wished to speak with you more before you woke up. I know my words have distressed you, despite the sleep I tried to give you."

"You didn't distress me," Taylor said, turning in Gabriel's arms to face him. "You just gave me a challenge."

Gabriel's lips twitched into a smile. "A challenge?"

"Yes," Taylor said. "One I intend to win."

"So you want me, then?" Gabriel asked, his voice smoky with desire. "You want to be mine, absolutely and completely?"

Something in the way he asked made Taylor shiver and almost pull away, but belonging to Gabriel was exactly what he wanted.

"Yes," Taylor said, but it was a whisper.

Gabriel kissed him softly.

"You are the sweetest human I have ever bonded with," he said. Taylor beamed. "I hope you are the one. But you mustn't take it as an insult if you aren't. It isn't in my control. I don't want you to worry, and I don't want to cause you pain."

"You could never cause me pain. As for worrying, though, well," he paused, thinking of what Natalie had said about him worrying too much and grinning. "I think that's just in my nature. You'll have to get used to it because I worry about everything."

Gabriel grinned in return. "I wouldn't want to change your nature, then," he said, caressing Taylor's cheek. "Your nature is what makes you so delicious."

Taylor wondered if he meant that as a compliment or as a description. He was food to Gabriel, after all, but he hoped Gabriel meant more. He kissed Gabriel cautiously and the incubus responded fiercely, blowing past every worry in Taylor's mind. He gasped when they broke apart, his body revving into high gear.

"Don't I have to wake up soon?"

"Not until I let you," Gabriel said playfully. "Do you want to leave right now?"

Taylor's body gave him his answer as he kissed Gabriel. He didn't want to leave his incubus, not now. Gabriel kissed him and stroked him, but after many, many kisses, he did pull away. Taylor moaned in disappointment and Gabriel tapped his nose with a wink.

"Now I let you wake up," he said. "And when I'm ready for more, you'll be ready too."

"You are a demon," Taylor muttered, and Gabriel laughed and kissed him one last time. Then the world faded and he woke up in his real bed, Gabriel still curled around him. He relaxed against his incubus and knew that when Gabriel was ready, he wouldn't refuse.

Chapter 14

Past Indiscretions

C lasses were a disaster again, with students tripping over themselves to talk to him and bombard him with questions. They were worse with Gabriel. Gabriel had thought ahead to pack a lunch since they didn't get a long break for lunch and they hid in an unused classroom. Natalie was at class but Taylor didn't mind the extra time with his demon. Still, when his classes were over, Taylor needed time alone. He tended to be a solitary person and all of the chaos was absolutely draining. Even Gabriel's presence was a little much, though he hated leaving his demon.

As soon as he and Gabriel were back in the apartment lobby, he took the demon's hand.

"Gabriel, would you mind if I went on a walk?"

"Alone?"

He nodded, and Gabriel squeezed his hand. "You'll stay safe?"

"Of course," he said, though the thought of danger chilled him. He would be careful to stay in the populated areas of campus even while he found solitude.

"Come back soon." Gabriel leaned to kiss his cheek and Taylor was grateful for the permission. Gabriel could probably tell he needed time alone to hold onto his sanity, because being surrounded all the time was really getting to him and as much as he loved being with Gabriel, he just wanted space to breath.

He headed to the biggest hiking trails that made a loop in the woods between the two sides of campus. It was all firmly within school grounds and ought to be safe. As soon as he was just out of sight of the brick buildings where he spent the day, he leaned against a tree and shut his eyes. Silence. Just the occasional sound of the forest as squirrels leapt from tree to tree and birds called to their mates. Another sound intruded on his awareness. Footsteps. He tensed, but they were coming from campus and in a moment Jordan turned the corner and waved at him.

"Hey Taylor, Callan wanted to talk to you in our room. Your old room, I guess," Jordan said. "She said you'd be out here."

"Why?"

"I don't know," he said with a shrug. "But it sounded like it was really important that you get there fast."

"Okay," Taylor said, mystified. Gabriel had warned him about Callan, but he didn't want to turn the succubus down completely. He would go, see what she had to say, and be on guard the whole time. Gabriel had said she wouldn't hurt him, after all, just that she might lie to him. And he was curious what she would say.

He arrived at his old dorm and felt a flash of sadness that he didn't live here anymore. He had some good memories from his room, doing homework while Jordan played games in his chair, and he wondered how Jordan felt now that he was living alone. Jordan always liked having a roommate, even though they weren't exactly friends outside of the room, and he was glad Jordan had Callan to fill Taylor's place. Not that her new role was anything like Taylor's role had been, he thought with a blush. She was more like a girlfriend, and Taylor was definitely just a roommate.

He heard voices inside and paused. He recognized the voice. It was Gabriel. He hesitated before going in. What were the two of them talking about?

"Of course I haven't told him. Why should I?"

"Don't you think he deserves to know about your habit of sleeping with other people while being bonded to a human?"

Taylor's mouth went dry. His heart thudded loudly in his ears. Gabriel sleeping with other people? Is that what Gabriel didn't want him to know, why Gabriel warned him against talking to Callan? He thought of Gabriel's actions immediately after being formed, when the incubus was prepared to stroll through campus searching for a doctor while completely naked. Gabriel certainly didn't have any shame, and was used to people feeling lust for him, as he had said then. But did that mean that he occasionally slept with those other people? Taylor's hands trembled.

He had known, of course, that Gabriel had lots of sexual experience. More than lots. But somehow Gabriel always made their experiences seem unique and special, as if the two of them were the only people in the world. But if Gabriel were sleeping with other people while he was bonded to Taylor, he wouldn't be able to stand it.

"Hush, you bitch," Gabriel said in the angriest voice Taylor had ever heard from him. "Taylor is close enough to hear. Or was that your plan?"

"He should know that you come to me when your humans are too busy to satisfy you. Or will you deny it?"

Taylor's head spun once again. If he was too busy or unable to satisfy Gabriel, would Gabriel search for food elsewhere? Would he turn to Callan? It seemed unlikely, since Gabriel warned him about Callan so strongly, but perhaps the reason he hadn't wanted Taylor and Callan to talk was because Callan was his usual booty call. Tears threatened to spill down his cheeks as he thought of the sweet words last night as Gabriel spoke of the one person for him and suggested that it might be Taylor. But he also remembered that Gabriel hadn't wanted him upset if it wasn't him. If he wasn't the right person, would Gabriel turn elsewhere?

The door to the room opened suddenly and Gabriel marched out to sweep him up in a hug, but he barely felt it. Was Gabriel his demon, or was Gabriel a demon who happened to be bonded to him? He didn't think he could bear it if Gabriel grew bored of him and all of his complicated sexual past and turned to Callan, who was more than happy to satisfy him sexually. Taylor caught a glimpse of Callan's face through Gabriel's arms and she smiled triumphantly.

Then Gabriel started dragging him away, stroking his hair and wiping the tears from his face. Gabriel's fury made itself known in the strength of his arms as he practically yanked Taylor towards the exit of the dorms. They passed a few students who stared at them curiously and Taylor kept his head buried in Gabriel's chest so no one could see his tears. When Jordan appeared before them, though, Gabriel cursed under his breath and suddenly everything moved in slow motion. Jordan slowly raised his hand in greeting but Gabriel was pulling Taylor by so quickly Jordan's hand had barely moved by the time they passed him, and Taylor blinked and looked back to see Jordan still raising his hand as they passed him in the hall. They zoomed outside and everything was still in slow motion, with Gabriel lifting Taylor in his arms and carrying him towards the apartments. Even the air seemed still, and everything was unnaturally quiet. They arrived at the entrance to their apartment, and then everything jumped forward again. Noise returned, and the air ebbed and flowed like usual in the warm breeze. Taylor was stunned and his tears had dried.

"How did we get here?" he asked, looking around in shock as Gabriel opened the door and pulled him inside.

"I told you that I can move through time and space differently than most people," Gabriel said. "When you're with me, you can too. I wanted to get back here without anyone else interfering. We need to talk."

Callan's words came crashing back and he sniffed and turned his back on Gabriel.

"I don't know what there is to talk about. We clearly have different ideas of what this relationship will be like. So you just do whatever you want, and I'll make sure you get fed."

Taylor practically spat out the last words, angry that he was nothing more than a food source to Gabriel. It had bothered him ever since he bonded, and now that insecurity was coming out in full force. He had always known that he was just a food source, nothing more, but he tried to read romance and interest in Gabriel's actions, especially after last night. He had invented an entire relationship between them that simply didn't exist. Gabriel wasn't interested in being exclusive, obviously, and Taylor couldn't expect it of him. After all, why would he stay loyal to Taylor, of all people, with all of his holdups and problems? Why would Taylor possibly be the right person for the prince of demons?

"You're not just food, Taylor," Gabriel said, but Taylor knew he was lying. Gabriel had bonded with him in order to feed from him, no other reason.

"I can see your thoughts, you know," Gabriel continued, reaching out to stroke Taylor's back. "Your insecurities. You don't need to have them. You're not just food to me."

"Of course you'd say that. You'd say anything to put me in a good mood so I'll be more likely to feed you. I have to be enjoying myself for you to feed, so you have to keep me happy."

"That's not true," Gabriel said. "Or it's not entirely true. I care about you. I want you to be happy for your own sake."

Taylor shook his head. "Then why do you sleep with other people?"

"I would never sleep with anyone else while bonded with you, Taylor," Gabriel said. "Our relationship is different. It's closer than any I've ever had before. I respect you, and I would never turn to another."

"Then why did you do it before?"

Gabriel sighed and sat on the corner of the couch. Taylor turned to face him. Gabriel's face settled into sad lines as he spoke.

"Many of my partners have been married. People used to marry at your age, you know. I would come second in their lives. Very few were willing to let me feed on them while they were with their loved ones. So they had very little pleasure left over for me, and I had to turn elsewhere to survive. I grew lonely, too, and in those times I would sometimes turn to a succubus for companionship. We can't feed off each other and I can't truly experience pleasure, as you know, but I needed touch. I needed someone to care. Callan was the one I spent the most time with, though I despise her. But she was always there, waiting for me, ready to help me get through the hard times when my bonded human was ignoring me and neglecting my needs."

Gabriel looked up at Taylor. "But you would never do that. You actually—care for me. No human has ever cared for me before. I don't think you would ever abandon me or neglect me, therefore I would never need to find food elsewhere to survive. Most of my humans wanted as little to do with me as possible, but I find I can't be apart from you and you don't seem to mind. Perhaps in time, when the novelty of having a demon wears off, you won't want me around, but so far you have given me what I've always dreamed of: a home."

Taylor's eyes filled with tears again, but this time they were tears of love. He knew from his history classes that the demonborn didn't used to be proud of their status and many demons starved to death before the demonborn gathered together to form a society. People who were demonborn in the old days used to see their demons as curses and often neglected them or even tried to kill them. He had assumed that the demon prince would be treasured, but it didn't sound like it.

And the way Gabriel described their relationship was just right. Taylor did care for him, and would never neglect or starve him. And he would never grow weary of having Gabriel at his side, though a few short breaks might be needed. He never would have guessed that Gabriel had insecurities as well, and hopes and dreams, but he was honored to have given the demon something that he wanted and created a real home for Gabriel. He only hoped he could live up to all of Gabriel's standards.

He thought of Callan and tried to imagine being so lonely that he would turn to her for comfort, but he just couldn't imagine it. Still, Callan was beautiful and no doubt had used some of her succubus charm to lure Gabriel to her. He wondered why Callan was trying to drive a wedge between him and Gabriel now by revealing this information. If Gabriel hadn't been completely honest and his explanation so sincere, Taylor likely would have been furious at the demon and kicked him out, temporarily at least. Perhaps she was hoping that Gabriel would go back to her for comfort, as he had before, but he knew that Gabriel wouldn't go to the demon who had wrecked his relationship. Callan had to have some greater plan.

"I forgive you," Taylor said quietly, stretching his hand towards Gabriel in a forgiving gesture. "I understand and it's all right. I know you won't hurt me. The past is the past, and we have to make our future together."

As he spoke, he thought of his own past and Yolette, and how he and Gabriel were building a future on that trauma as well. The past held so many problems and misjudgments and horrible things, but none of it mattered when they were together. He would never say it out loud, but he loved Gabriel. He wistfully wondered if someday the feeling would be returned, though he knew from all of his lessons in and out of the classroom that love was the one emotion denied to all demons. No matter how much they cared for their humans, it was never love. Taylor's heart clenched as he saw the relief in his demon's eyes, and the happiness that worked across Gabriel's beautiful face. Gabriel stretched out his hand and took Taylor's, and pulled him into his lap. Taylor was starting to get used to sitting in Gabriel's lap.

Gabriel kissed him gently on the lips, then again with more pressure. Taylor opened his lips to give Gabriel access, and the demon's long tongue flicked inside his mouth and began caressing the interior. Taylor grabbed Gabriel's shoulders as the kiss grew more intense and dizziness spread through his limbs as his energy was sucked out of him into the kiss, but he was determined to save his strength and not let Gabriel drain him with a mere kiss. They finally broke apart and Taylor gasped for air.

"You're so much stronger than you were," Gabriel murmured, kissing his neck. Tingles ran along his skin where Gabriel's tongue caressed him as he continued to kiss his way down Taylor's neck to the collar of his shirt.

Taylor wanted to enjoy his incubus, but even as Gabriel lifted up his shirt so the kisses could continue, Taylor found himself wondering how many times Gabriel had done this before and if Gabriel would ever do this with someone else. The thought hurt and he shied away from Gabriel's hands, carefully keeping his shirt down. Gabriel had given a beautiful apology but the hurt was still there, and it would be a while before he was truly comfortable with his demon again.

Chapter 15

Forbidden Knowledge

Taylor luxuriated in the feel of a body next to his as he returned to consciousness, mind filled with remnants of his dreams. A journey; a quest. He led a party of thieves searching for an ebony earring with the power to save the world. They finally found the earring but one of the thieves sprouted wings and flew away with it, and the loss pierced him even as the sense of adventure flooded over him. He wanted to linger in this half-sleep and Gabriel would let him. The demon curled around him and he tried to remember the details.

"Good morning," Gabriel finally murmured. It must be time to wake up. "Did you sleep well?"

"I dreamed," Taylor said sleepily. "Was that you?"

"Your mind was filled with such beautiful images; I didn't want to interfere."

"But you've interfered other nights?"

Gabriel let out a huff of laughter. "Do you normally dream every night? This is the first time your mind has wanted to create its own reality."

"I guess not."

In truth, Taylor almost never remembered his dreams. He thought back to the adventure that lingered in his memory, but the details already slipped from his grasp. A quest for... something. And when they found that something, something else happened. What was it? There was something important about it, about the person who did something when they found whatever they were looking for. But he couldn't remember, so he sighed and sat up.

Gabriel leaned against his back, kissing his neck.

"This week has gone well?"

"I didn't know having a demon would be like this," Taylor said.

"Any plans for the weekend?"

Taylor blushed. Exactly one week ago, Gabriel took form and Taylor fell into unconscious, wasting their first weekend together. This time, nothing would stop him from being with his demon. They ought to do something fancy, but he was so exhausted from catching up in his classes all he could think about was sleeping in and watching tv. Really, he was still trying to get back on track in Ms. Salazar's class. She didn't give many tests but when she did, they covered everything. He needed to know the subject in and out before he felt comfortable taking her tests.

"Not really. Do you mind?"

Gabriel kissed him again.

"Anything that makes you happy, makes me happy."

He leaned back against his demon, who held him tight for one minute before pushing him forward.

"You need to get up. Hopefully your dreams gave you a deep enough sleep. I know I kept you up too late last night."

Heat crept up Taylor's cheeks as he stood up and went to the bathroom. Last night, Gabriel spent hours seducing him, arousing him, before finally taking him in his mouth as he had a few times before. In the week since Gabriel was formed, the seductions delighted him each night, but he was always hesitant to go farther. After Callan's words, he didn't want to go beyond touching, but soon he was begging Gabriel for more. Still, he wasn't ready to go all the way and have actual sex.

Somehow that crossed a line he wasn't ready to cross. Not yet, anyway. Only I n his fantasies.

"You only have one class today, right?"

Gabriel tousled his hair as he emerged from the bathroom and he groaned.

"Do you have to do that every morning?"

His demon grinned. "You look cute disheveled."

"So I shouldn't redo it?"

"You don't have to. You look good."

Taylor went to the mirror and stared at himself. He did look good. Maybe he would let it stand for today and see if anyone commented, for better or for worse.

"All right. And yes, just one class today."

Ms. Winde sent out an email last night. Since today was just covering old material in preparation for their next paper, she assigned a series of videos to watch and canceled class. He wondered if something happened to inspire the sudden decision, if for some reason her cheerful demeanor cracked and she didn't want to be around students. Maybe a family emergency, or maybe the emergency was hers. She didn't say anything in the email, only that class was canceled and they should watch the videos and be prepared for discussion on Wednesday. He wouldn't pry.

Taylor sat at the table as Gabriel poured his cereal and brought it to him along with the milk. He liked being the one to pour that. He hadn't ever stated that preference but Gabriel knew, just as Gabriel knew all about breakfast. He rarely looked into Taylor's mind, preferring to ask him things instead, but he had, with Taylor's permission, learned about the basics of the modern world. Now he navigated the kitchen with ease, and the computer as naturally as one born to it.

Gabriel never explained why he was so hesitant to look into his mind, but Taylor wasn't going to question it. It was strange enough having Gabriel read his desires; having him in his mind, watching his thoughts and emotions, would be too much.

Soon he finished and Gabriel took his bowl and rinsed it out as

Taylor tied his shoes and hefted his backpack. At first Gabriel tried to carry that but Taylor liked carrying his own things. He wanted to do something by himself.

"Ready for the day?" Gabriel wrapped an arm around his waist and pulled him close for a kiss. Taylor responded, their tongues intertwining for a long moment before he slowly drew back.

"We'd better get going."

Taylor reluctantly agreed.

Gabriel sat down to wait outside as usual as Taylor entered. Two girls crowded at the door to stare at the demon while Taylor sat beside Natalie. Things were getting better, but even so one of the more persistent guys sat in front of him and immediately turned around.

"Anything new happening?" he asked, and Taylor bristled at the implied familiarity in that question. He barely knew the student, but he felt like he had the right to inquire about his life and imply that he already knew everything up to today.

"No," Taylor snapped, and turned to Natalie, who smiled sympathetically.

Mr. Hill began the class before anything else happened and as class continued, he noticed the teacher eying him more than usual. Dread pooled in his belly. He had retaken the missed test on Wednesday and Mr. Hill promised to have the results today. Surely he hadn't failed. Now that he had Gabriel's equation, the questions were remarkably easy. Had he really done so badly that Mr. Hill was looking at him like this?

He tried to ignore the teacher's scrutiny and look like he was paying attention, but he didn't need to take notes anymore. Instead, he doodled and passed the occasional note to Natalie. She also didn't need to take notes and he wondered if they could place out of the class since they already knew the end result of the class, the equation that Mr. Hill's rambling explanations inevitably led to. As class came to a close, Mr. Hill gestured for him to stay. Natalie waved at him with a sympathetic expression as he waited nervously by the front desk.

When everyone was gone, Taylor glanced towards the door.

Natalie would have told Gabriel that the teacher wanted to talk to him, but he didn't like leaving Gabriel alone for so long. Mr. Hill took out the test Taylor had taken and held it, not showing it to Taylor but just looking at it for a long moment.

"Did you get this test in advance?" Mr. Hill asked.

"What?"

"Did you get the questions in advance and have your demon help you with the answers?"

Taylor stared at him in shock, barely able to process the accusation. Mr. Hill thought he plagiarized the test?

"I would never steal a test," he said. "Why would I? My grade in this class is pretty much set. I doubt a couple good test scores would affect it too much."

Mr. Hill handed him the test. He had scored an 88, which didn't seem high enough to warrant a plagiarism talk.

"You would have scored higher but you made careless mistakes," Mr. Hill said, pointing to one spot marked with red pen. "Like here. Your addition was off, and here you divided wrong."

"Then why would you think I cheated?" Taylor asked, puzzled and embarrassed that he did basic addition wrong. "If Gabriel were helping me, he wouldn't have let me make those mistakes."

"The only time anyone has ever scored this high is when their demon does the work for them," Mr. Hill said. "How did you get the right answers?"

Taylor blushed, thinking of the equation Gabriel had given him. Maybe after learning the equation the other students were sworn to secrecy and that was why he automatically blamed his demon. And Mr. Hill was right that Gabriel had helped him, but he didn't think it was plagiarism, not really. Gabriel hadn't helped with any specific problems; he just taught him the guiding equation.

"How do you know another student didn't teach me the equation?" Taylor asked, not wanting to acknowledge that it was in fact his demon who had helped him.

"What equation?"

"The one this class is about," Taylor said, gesturing to the board that had symbols scribbled all over it. "The one you're teaching us. The problems are easy once you know the equation. Why do you teach it like this?"

Mr. Hill's eyes widened and his lips parted. He started to speak, paused, and licked his lips. "Your demon couldn't have given you the equation."

"Why are you ruling out other students?" Taylor asked, still wanting to protect Gabriel.

"The other students don't know the equation," Mr. Hill said. "I don't know the equation. No one does. The purpose of this class is to figure out the equation. All of the demons know it but while they'll help humans with problems, they don't share the actual equation with us. Did he really teach it to you? Will you show me?"

His voice was strained and there was a desperate glint in his eye, and Taylor was taken aback. Had Gabriel taught him something that humans weren't supposed to know? If so, was he allowed to tell others? Gabriel hadn't minded when he told Natalie, but would he mind if he told Mr. Hill? Uneasy, he glanced towards the door and wondered if he should ask first.

"Gabriel might not realize the equation is hidden," Mr. Hill mused, glancing at the door as well. "The last time he was in this world, people knew the equation. But the war that killed his last human partner also wiped out a great deal of our knowledge, including that equation. We've spent a hundred years trying to relearn it. Please, Taylor, if you know it, you must tell me."

"Why haven't the other demons told you? You said they knew it," Taylor said nervously. "I mean, why hasn't your demon told you if you really want to know? What does that equation even mean, anyway? You've never really told us."

"It's the equation that holds the key to a demon's power," he said, and Taylor drew in a sharp breath. "People used that equation to calculate how powerful each demon was, and even before they took form, how powerful they could potentially be. They could calculate how much energy a demon needed to survive. I admit, it was abused in those times. Some people would calculate the minimum energy a demon could survive on and give them nothing more. But it was mostly used to help. Do you really know it?"

"Gabriel gave me an equation that solves the problems you give us," Taylor said. "But I need to check with him before sharing it. I didn't realize no one knew it."

Mr. Hill's brow creased. "Taylor, he'll likely forbid it. Please, you must share it. You're the only human who knows what used to be common knowledge."

"If the demons haven't shared it, maybe they have their reasons," Taylor countered. "You said it was used against them. Maybe they don't want humans knowing it."

"You will ask him, though?" Mr. Hill said. "You'll emphasize how important it is for us to know?"

"I don't understand why it's important, but sure, I'll ask," Taylor said, puzzled once more.

"Why did he teach you the equation, Taylor?" Mr. Hill asked. "Was it to help you with the test?"

"No," Taylor said, some of his indignation returning. "I studied for that on my own. It was, well, um, when he fed on me in class. I was mad because I couldn't pay attention and that was his apology."

Mr. Hill stared at him in shock, then started laughing. "He gave it to you in apology? The most sought-after equation in our society and you got it in exchange for a few moments of discomfort in my class?"

Taylor blushed. "I was pretty mad at him."

Mr. Hill shook his head in amusement. "Well, if he told you for that, he might let you share it after all. He's not like the others, that's for sure."

"Yeah," Taylor said, thinking of Gabriel's inability to truly experience pleasure and his quest to find the right human. "Definitely not."

"Do you know what he is?" Mr. Hill asked, curiosity brimming in his eyes. This was the most relaxed Taylor had ever seen him and it was very odd.

"What do you mean?"

"He's not an incubus, despite the common rumors," Mr. Hill said. "Anyone who's studied him knows that, and I wrote my dissertation on his history."

"What are you talking about? Of course he's an incubus. He's called himself an incubus," Taylor said. "You called him an incubus too!"

But Gabriel was distinct from the succubi, he had to admit.

"He acts as an incubus for the most part," Mr. Hill acknowledged. "He may think of himself as one. But a true incubus is solely interested in sexual pleasure. They choose their partners based on that partner's willingness to feed that pleasure. He has never done so. Often his partners seem wildly unsuited for a pleasure demon. Do you think you're a good candidate for an incubus?"

Taylor blushed again, knowing it was true. He wasn't suited for a pleasure demon. There were many, many others who would be far better partners. Demons always chose the easiest human to bond with, the one most likely to feed them, and if Gabriel fed on sex, then Taylor was a terrible partner. That wasn't why Gabriel bonded with him. Gabriel was helping him overcome his resistance to pleasure and in time he would be a good partner, but demons weren't known for their patience or for tolerating human weakness. Mr. Hill continued.

"He rarely partners, which is highly unusual for an incubus or succubus. There are only four known incubi, but they operate just like the succubi. It's rare for them to go more than a decade between partners, but the demon prince frequently goes over a hundred years. An incubus would not do that."

"Well if he's not an incubus, what is he?" Taylor asked.

Mr. Hill shrugged. "No one knows. There's an entire branch of demonology dedicated to studying him. Scholars will reach out to you —and him—before long. I'm lucky to have such direct access, though I would never bring this up with him."

"Why not? Wouldn't it be easier to just ask him what he is?"

"Demons give up their secrets as easily as they give up their true names," Mr. Hill said with a laugh. "He won't tell you if you ask. He probably won't lie to you, but he'll hedge or distract you. He won't answer, though."

"So you wrote a paper on him, and researched him, and you don't want to talk to him?" Taylor said skeptically. "Even if he doesn't answer your questions, you don't even want to try?"

"I am not a student to swarm him with questions," Mr. Hill said. "If the opportunity arises, I would be honored to speak with him. Otherwise I am content to speak to you, who are far more likely to give me actual information."

"I'm not going to share my demon's secrets if he doesn't want me to."

"But you might share things you don't think are secrets," Mr. Hill said with a satisfied smile. "That's enough."

Taylor huffed, his fingers tightening on his test as he promised himself that he would never talk to Mr. Hill about anything, ever. It was odd to have negative emotions about a teacher like this. Normally he dreaded certain teachers, including Mr. Hill, but the main emotion he felt was respect. His respect for Mr. Hill, however, was rapidly dwindling. Mr. Hill must have sensed it and seemed amused, not upset, by Taylor's open resentment of his interference.

"Do ask Gabriel about the equation," he said. "You did agree to ask, after all."

Taylor nodded, since he had indeed agreed. Then he thought of what Mr. Hill said right after he bonded with Gabriel, when he picked his demon's name. Mr. Hill was surprised by the name and told him to talk to him later. Well, this was later.

"Mr. Hill," he began cautiously, and the teacher gestured for him to continue. "You said there was something about the name I picked, Gabriel."

Mr. Hill grinned. "I doubt even he understands the significance of that name. It's something only a few scholars know about, though historically it's extremely important. If you want to know more, however, I'll need some sort of exchange of information. Ask him about the equation and when you tell me his response, I might tell you more."

Taylor glared. How could Mr. Hill keep knowledge hostage like this? He was a teacher; weren't teachers supposed to teach? But he agreed and Mr. Hill excused him before turning to the whiteboards to start cleaning them off as he did after every class. Taylor headed into the hall where Gabriel was surrounded by a crowd of mostly girls. Even though they knew Gabriel was interested in men, they still flung themselves at him.

He observed Gabriel deftly dealing with the crowd, still singling some people out using some unknown criteria. Had Gabriel really taught him an equation that helped him calculate a demon's power? If so, then he had no idea how to apply it. He would ask Gabriel about it but he wouldn't push. And until he had Gabriel's permission, he wouldn't even mention it to anyone else. He would make sure Natalie did the same.

He pushed through the crowd and Gabriel beamed at him, and when he came close enough, Gabriel kissed his cheek. Incubus or not, Gabriel definitely fed off his pleasure. He would ask about that, too. So many questions for his beloved demon, and for once the sting of Callan's word wasn't there as he observed the girls doing the best to entice him despite Taylor at his side. Gabriel was his, and wouldn't stray. He was a fool for thinking so, and if he had any control over it, he would become Gabriel's one and then Gabriel would never need another.

Chapter 16

Bold Steps

"Is there anything you want to do tonight, darling?" Gabriel asked as Taylor slurped up some soup.

Rather than order out yet again, Taylor insisted on making his own dinner despite his limited cooking skills. While Gabriel seemed shocked that Taylor would even consider heating up some ramen and calling it a meal, he hadn't stopped him. He did read the ingredients and look vaguely appalled. Gabriel frequently took advantage of the labeling on food to see what exactly Taylor ate. He explained that he used to watch his humans cook, so he knew a lot of recipes, and it was strange seeing everything premade. He hadn't ever seen something like instant soup, though, and clearly didn't entirely approve. But Taylor loved the salty broth and tangled ramen noodles.

"Um, maybe we could watch something," Taylor said shyly. This was their first relaxing night together and he probably should have planned a fancy meal and event, something more like a real date, but he was so exhausted he hadn't bothered. Gabriel probably would have no problems planning something like that but since Taylor didn't really want to go out, he hadn't asked.

"A movie?" Gabriel asked with keen interest, and Taylor grinned.

Gabriel knew all about the modern world now, but he hadn't experienced it for himself. They occasionally had the tv on while Taylor did homework but he didn't want to get too distracted catching up in his classes, so it was limited even though Gabriel was curious.

"Yeah," Taylor said. "Why don't you pick one out? I like everything."

"You don't want anything in particular?"

"I want something you pick," Taylor said, and Gabriel reached out to take his hand and squeeze it.

"I'll pick something you enjoy," Gabriel promised.

As they snuggled together on the large sectional, Taylor had to admit that Gabriel had chosen well. It was a romantic comedy he hadn't seen before but had gotten good reviews. Romantic comedies were his hidden pleasure, since as a guy he wasn't supposed to like movies like this. But he did, just as he liked reading romance novels when no one would notice. He loved romance of all sorts. Maybe that was why Gabriel bonded with him. He had so many problems with sex, but he desperately wanted romance. Maybe that was the sort of pleasure Gabriel fed on. He leaned against his demon and glanced up at him. Gabriel was staring at the screen with rapt attention but the instant Taylor gazed at him, he turned and smiled.

"Do you need anything?" Gabriel asked, and Taylor shook his head and nestled against him.

Gabriel's arm slung around him as he curled up and leaned against his strong demon, enjoying the feel of his body as the characters broke into a passionate argument, pledging to hate each other forever even as they cast desperately desirous looks at each other.

Everything was so dramatic and as the plot unfolded and it grew more and more ridiculous and the humor shone through clearly, Taylor found himself giggling with Gabriel, tightening his hands against Gabriel's shirt in worry, and glancing at him shyly when the characters at last confessed their true feelings. This time Gabriel didn't look at him; his attention remained on the screen and there was longing in his eyes. Did he want someone to confess their love as the main character was doing? Did he want love? Was he capable of wanting love? Taylor pushed the thought aside. It wasn't time to worry about love, not now. Now was time to enjoy his incubus.

The movie ended and Gabriel kissed his forehead as the credits rolled.

"Did you enjoy it?"

"Of course," Taylor said. "Couldn't you tell?"

"Yes," Gabriel said with a grin. "I hope you don't mind."

That meant that Gabriel had fed on his enjoyment during the movie and while the thought was a little disturbing, it didn't bother him as much as it once might have. He wanted Gabriel to feed on him. He wanted to please his demon and give him sustenance. He loved that Gabriel fed on his pleasure because that meant Gabriel wanted him to be happy. He tilted his head and Gabriel kissed him gently.

It seemed like no one in his life ever tried to make him happy the way Gabriel did. His parents helped him, and loved him, but his father was a demon and his mother, though she would do anything for him, often didn't know what was going on in his life. She knew he faced discrimination because of his birthmark but though she had always comforted him as a child, there was nothing she could do to change it. Natalie was great but she was her own person, too, and while they spent a lot of time together and he loved hanging out with her, and she made him happy, that wasn't her goal. She was herself and he loved her for it. She didn't deliberately do anything to make him happy, or at least not usually. There were exceptions, of course. She was good at cheering him up. But she was just a good person. Gabriel was different.

As they kissed, he was drawn into the kiss as Gabriel fed deeply. Everything Gabriel did was intended to help Taylor. Demons were usually quite dedicated to their humans, safeguarding them and ensuring that they were in the proper mindset to provide food. That meant different things to different demons, of course, but it usually involved their well-being. And for Gabriel...

Taylor squirmed in the kiss, his body lighting up as sparks of pleasure scattered through his body. Gabriel wanted him happy, wanted him pleased, wanted to make him feel good and cherished and loved. He was still getting there with the sex, but it seemed that Gabriel wanted more than just sex. He had to, since he had picked Taylor. Did that mean he wasn't truly an incubus as Mr. Hill had indicated?

Taylor broke off the kiss reluctantly, out of breath. Gabriel stroked his cheek and cradled him.

"Gabriel, what are you?" Taylor asked. "What do you feed on?"

"I'm an incubus, you know that," Gabriel said with a laugh. "I feed on your pleasure."

"Just sex? Or other pleasure, too?"

Gabriel seemed puzzled by the question. "I feed off all your pleasure, but I told you before. Physical pleasure is what I need to survive. Touching your body, inside your body, is what I need to maintain this form. Are you worried by that?"

"I'm not worried," he said. "It's just… if that's true, if you need physical pleasure, why did you pick me?"

"You are special," Gabriel said, kissing his neck and leaving a spark of pleasure. "There is no one like you."

"There's no one like you, either," Taylor said. "You're not like the other demons."

"How many demons do you know?" Gabriel asked with a smile. "I'm different, but no more different than any demon is from the others. We're all unique."

"No, you're special," Taylor said.

"You're right," Gabriel said, his voice dropping into a husky whisper. "I am special, because I'm yours."

Taylor grinned and kissed him, delighted by the response. Gabriel's hands stroked his body and soon they were naked on the sectional, the soft suede of the pillows cool against his bare body as he leaned into his demon's arms and the kisses seemed endless. He was uncomfortable, though, because they were right by the door. No one would come in, but he didn't like feeling so exposed.

Without a word, Gabriel scooped him up and carried him into the bedroom, resting him on the bed gently and then straddling him. Taylor

121

was already hard and Gabriel was responding, but as usual he was slower. Taylor reached out to stroke his legs and wondered why Gabriel enjoyed the touch so much. Was he just sensitive there? In his true form he had hair there, he considered. Maybe he enjoyed the touch because it was so different than his true form. Feeling bold, Taylor sat up and pushed Gabriel onto his back. He lowered his head to Gabriel's thigh and kissed that sensitive spot. Gabriel moaned softly and Taylor locked his lips on his skin, working his tongue along the tender muscles as Gabriel clutched his head and tangled his hand in his hair.

Gabriel was truly hard now as Taylor worked his way along his inner thigh, coming closer and closer to that beautiful flushed cock. He glanced at it and blushed. He thought about putting it in his mouth and as he swirled his tongue against Gabriel's skin, wondered what it would taste like. Was he ready? He focused on Gabriel's other thigh, still keeping close to his cock. Could he do it? Did he want to do it? He did, if he were honest with himself. He wanted to try it. He didn't think he would disappoint Gabriel even if he was hopelessly inept. Gabriel's hand in his hair tightened as he moaned again. Was he ready for this?

He lifted his head from between Gabriel's legs and hesitantly grasped his cock. He had touched Gabriel like this before. It was familiar, reassuring. He stroked Gabriel and felt a tremor along Gabriel's body. He leaned forward, extending his tongue, and let the very tip of his tongue tentatively explore the shaft of his penis. He tasted musky, fresh, and clean. Enticing. He let his tongue trace up and down the shaft, drawing closer until his entire mouth caressed the side of his penis and he moved his head up and down as Gabriel made a whining sound that had his heart pounding. Gabriel was losing control. Could he get Gabriel to come if he tried hard enough? Would Gabriel let it get that far?

He sat up again and caressed the head of Gabriel's cock, tasting the droplets running from a barely noticeable slit as he traced his tongue along every contour, every bit of flesh. He tasted so good. Taylor remembered how Gabriel seemed to swallow him and he opened his mouth, lowering himself onto the massive cock below him. Gabriel tensed, his hand tightening again, as Taylor let his cock fill him as much as possible. He could barely get more than an inch into his mouth and was disappointed with himself, though from Gabriel's panting he knew it was enough. He licked around the shaft, trying to moisten it further to help it slide down his throat, then tried again. He got more and it was delicious being filled like this.

He kept trying, using his hand to stroke Gabriel's length as he played with him, caressed him, sucked him, trying to do to Gabriel what Gabriel had done to him. And then, Gabriel gently pulled at his hair as if asking him to stop. Taylor ignored him, wrapping his hand more tightly, inhaling more of the gorgeous cock. He must be nearing his limit and that meant he might be close to coming, and Taylor wanted him to come.

"Taylor," Gabriel said in a gasping breath. "Please stop."

Taylor ignored him again, even when Gabriel pulled at him more forcefully. He was determined to make Gabriel come. Nothing would stop him.

"Please, Taylor," Gabriel moaned. "You're hurting me."

Taylor let up a little, glancing at Gabriel. His eyes glittered red in the dark lights and his expression was one of pleasure, but there was an edge of pain. Taylor withdrew his tongue, but kept stroking him with his hand. Was it really hurting him to do this? How could pleasure hurt a pleasure demon?

"Taylor, it's too much," Gabriel said, shifting under him. "Please stop."

Taylor released him and Gabriel curled towards him, sitting up and panting, then immediately flipped them so Taylor was suddenly on the bottom with Gabriel over him. Gabriel kissed him fiercely, then let his kisses trail down his body. He was already on fire, though Gabriel's pain had cooled him somewhat. It took only the huff of breath against his cock before he was completely ready again and as Gabriel took him deep in his throat, Taylor bit back his moans and writhed on the sheets, enthralled by the touch of his demon.

Gabriel, as always, knew exactly what to do, exactly what to touch and how, exactly how to manipulate Taylor's body until he couldn't stand it anymore and he grabbed Gabriel's head the way Gabriel had grabbed his, only he used it to thrust against his demon as his hips bucked uncontrollably. Gabriel's tongue wound about him and then he tipped over the edge, his pleasure splashing through him and against him and within him, washing through him and exploding as he cried out.

Soon he was cradled in Gabriel's arms again, body still shivering with pleasure. Gabriel was still half-hard, he could feel, but his demon didn't seem to want anything more and Taylor was too exhausted to give him anything. He was drained and he knew Gabriel had fed deeply from him. He could feel Gabriel's satisfaction and happiness, see it in the smile on his lips and the gleam in his eyes. Even though Gabriel hadn't come, he was pleased and that was enough, for now.

Someday, Taylor would coax him into going farther and allowing himself to lose control the way he urged Taylor to lose control. Someday, he would coax him into an orgasm. But in the meantime, he was just pleased that his demon enjoyed him so much and beyond pleased at how bold he had been and how far they had gotten. Suddenly his other fantasies seemed more like reality and the visions flashed through his mind—lying in the bed facing Gabriel as the demon penetrated him, kneeling as Gabriel took him from behind, straddling him in the large bathtub as the water splashed around them—and Gabriel chuckled softly, no doubt sharing those images.

"You're incredible," Gabriel said, kissing him gently. Taylor could barely feel him feeding through the kiss.

"I love you, Gabriel," Taylor said without thinking. Then he blushed and pulled away. Gabriel wore a sad expression and was silent, though he tucked Taylor against him.

"I know," Gabriel finally said. "You know I- demons can't- it's not my choice, Taylor. Maybe you're the one, but I won't know until later."

Taylor nodded and nuzzled against him, embarrassed by his outburst. Of course Gabriel couldn't respond with love. Demons couldn't experience love. The one emotion barred them. Then

Gabriel's words filtered through his embarrassed disappointment. Gabriel thought Taylor might be the one, but wouldn't find out until later. Did that mean Gabriel would be capable of love if he were, in fact, the one? What had to happen before it was later and Gabriel would know for sure? He ached to fill the void in Gabriel's life, to give him pleasure, to make him feel love. When would he know if he succeeded in his challenge or if he had irrevocably failed?

"I'm sorry," Gabriel said, kissing him again. "Do you want to sleep? Do you want dreams?"

"Just sleep," Taylor said slowly. "Unless you want to hold me. I like feeling you hold me when we sleep."

"Anything, darling," Gabriel said. "I'll take care of you."

Chapter 17

Coming Out

"Hey, Taylor," a familiar voice called as he and Gabriel were leaving for a walk. It was Jordan, and he approached them with an apologetic look on his face. Callan was nowhere to be seen but Gabriel's fists were clenched, his tension obvious.

"Callan's not here," Jordan added. "I'm sorry about what happened, Taylor. I didn't know why she wanted to talk to you."

Gabriel narrowed his eyes. "What did she tell you after you sent Taylor to her?"

"Just that Taylor overheard you fighting with her, and got mad," Jordan said. "I'm sorry. I guess I thought all demons got along."

Taylor considered him. He seemed quite sincere and to be honest, Taylor had also thought that all demons got along until he had seen Gabriel and Callan arguing and heard that Gabriel wasn't fully accepted. Demons were far more complex than they were taught in school and he wondered why they weren't warned about it.

"It's all right, Jordan," Taylor said, though he knew Gabriel wasn't entirely pleased by excusing what had happened. Jordan had caused the first—and hopefully only—major fight between them and Gabriel clearly didn't want Taylor forgiving him, but Jordan had been his room-

126

mate for a long time, and a friend in many ways, too. There was no need to hold a grudge.

"Um, can I talk to you?" Jordan asked, then glanced at Gabriel. "Alone?"

Taylor wondered what he could possibly want that he didn't want Gabriel to overhear. Was it safe? What if this were another ploy by Callan to break them apart? Gabriel was clearly having similar thoughts. But really, was there anything he could learn that would separate him from his demon now? He remembered the taste of Gabriel against his tongue, the helpless cries his demon made, and how desperately he wanted to please Gabriel. He wasn't about to abandon his demon now, no matter what he learned. He hadn't solved Gabriel's challenge, after all. He hadn't made Gabriel come.

"I think that's fine," Taylor said slowly, as Gabriel's expression darkened. But Gabriel didn't question him or refuse. He just squeezed Taylor's hand.

"I'll be nearby if you need anything," Gabriel said, and headed in the direction of the apartments.

They were on the outskirts of the campus, where Taylor liked to take walks even before the demon season. Jordan had walked with him here a couple of times, but never seemed especially interested in it. This time, though, Jordan gestured to the path as if inviting him to keep walking. The area was completely safe. Because he liked this area, Gabriel had specifically requested that it be guarded and the president of the university assured them that nothing would get past his guards in this area, not even an innocent hiker who stumbled on the wrong path. They couldn't close off the entire campus, but they could and did close off this little corner.

They walked for several minutes in silence, and Taylor glanced at his former roommate. Jordan kept shooting him nervous glances and it put him on edge. Had Jordan lied? Was there someone out here? Was Callan out here, waiting to tell him more things to damage his relationship?

"I am sorry," Jordan finally said. "She said you got mad at Gabriel. I didn't mean to do anything that would hurt your relationship with a demon. I know how important it is to you that you got a demon."

Taylor flushed, thinking of his deformed mark. Jordan's attitude towards him had changed when he first glimpsed it, but he had overcome that. Taylor had even talked to him about it once, expressing his fears that he wouldn't find a demon. It was a casual conversation and he hadn't thought that Jordan would remember it, but clearly he did. Taylor was touched that such a small thing made an impression on his roommate. Sometimes it seemed they had nothing in common and Jordan didn't like him at all, but at other times, like this, it seemed like they were truly friends.

"It's okay," Taylor said. "Gabriel and I talked, and we're fine now."

"Oh," Jordan said, sounding almost disappointed. Was that not the response he had hoped for? Had he wanted a more resounding forgiveness?

"So how are you and Callan doing?" Taylor asked. He realized suddenly that if Callan was offering herself to Gabriel, the link between her and Jordan might not be great. He had been so focused on his own demon and their relationship, he hadn't realized that his roommate might be having problems.

"We're good, I guess," Jordan said. "It's a little odd having a succubus, to be honest. When we linked, we talked for a long time about what she would need from me, and what she could give me."

"I'm surprised you didn't just jump at the first succubus who walked by," Taylor said, thinking of Jordan's boasts and taunts before and during demon season.

Jordan laughed, but sounded uncomfortable. "I didn't mean a lot of the things I've said to you in the past, Taylor. I'm sorry about a lot of things. I didn't know how you'd react, so I pushed you away. Now I wish I hadn't."

"What do you mean?" Taylor asked, puzzled, and Jordan pulled him to a stop.

There were dense trees around them and the fog lay in heavy swathes along the path. The air was misting, with nearly invisible flecks of water melting into his exposed face and hands as the air around them oozed oversaturated moisture. He wondered if it would rain later, or if the moisture would remain like this, trapped in a cloud of mist along the ground. He preferred outright rain to misting, but he got soaked either way and they needed to start heading back.

He was about to suggest turning back when Jordan caught his hand. Too surprised to pull away, he stared in shock as Jordan took his hand and raised it to his lips, kissing it before folding it between both of his hands. What was Jordan doing? What was he thinking?

Jordan smiled at him cautiously and Taylor was puzzled and a little angry.

"What is this?" he asked, pulling his hand away. Trying to, at least. Jordan kept a tight grip on him. "Is this some kind of joke? I know you're not comfortable with me being gay, but do you really have to go this far?"

"It's not a joke," Jordan reassured him hastily. "I just... I mean, you've been such a good friend and I didn't think you would understand. And then I found out you'd bonded with an incubus and I felt dumb for not telling you earlier, for not trusting you."

Taylor stared at him in shock. Was he really saying what Taylor thought he was saying?

"Are you... gay?" Taylor asked in disbelief. "But you had a girlfriend for, like, a really long time."

"And when I was with her, she was all I wanted," Jordan said. "I love women. I love seeing them, touching them, having sex with them. But I like guys, too, for different reasons. Why can't I like both? They're so different, and I like both."

"I guess, that means you're bisexual?" Taylor said, his mind whirling. Although Taylor had always passed himself as straight, he never felt interest in women, or at least not sexual interest. He could recognize the beautiful women, and there were some he felt attached to, like Natalie. He adored her, but sex never crossed his mind when he thought of her.

What would it be like to be attracted to both men and women? Did that mean Jordan liked everyone he met? Or did he have types like most people did, certain characteristics he was drawn to? Was it the same or different in the men and women he liked? He said men and women were different; was he attracted to different types of women than men? Jordan's last girlfriend had been quite petite, with long blonde hair. Callan had a fairly similar appearance. But Taylor was heftier, with brown hair. If Jordan was attracted to Taylor—and that kiss on the hand implied as much—then maybe he did look for different things in men and women.

"I don't really want to put a name on it," Jordan said, looking down. He was still holding Taylor's hand. "If I give myself a label, then it's making it real. I've always been able to consider myself straight because I only date girls, and I've never done anything with guys. I just... ignore those feelings and focus on the feelings I have for women. But when I found out you were gay, I..."

He ducked his head and finally released Taylor's hand.

"I just wanted you to know. I won't do anything. I don't want anyone to know. Just you."

"I-" Taylor paused, unsure what to say. "Thank you, Jordan. Thanks for telling me. But are you sure you're okay with Callan? I mean, with all women, but especially her as a succubus?"

"It's not that I don't like women," Jordan said. "I do. I love having Callan. She's great. And she knows I like you. She doesn't mind, because I also like her. I guess... there's something wrong with me, isn't there."

His voice hitched and Taylor quickly patted him on the back.

"No," he said firmly. "There's nothing wrong with you. You're absolutely perfect as you are."

"Then, do you like me?" Jordan asked hopefully, and Taylor pulled his hand back.

"Um, well, I mean, I have Gabriel," he said awkwardly. He wanted to reassure Jordan, because the man was making himself so vulnerable right now, but he couldn't give false assurances of affection when there was none. Jordan was a friend, nothing more. And actually, Taylor had never really even seen him as a friend. He was a good roommate who was sometimes friendly. Maybe it was because Jordan pushed him away. He thought back to all those times when that unknown expression would cross his roommate's face right before an insult or something else to drive them apart. Had Jordan been fighting his feelings? Was that unknown expression desire that he then shoved away at the same time he pushed Taylor?

He couldn't imagine how hard that would be. Taylor hid the fact that he was gay but in all honesty, he wondered if he really were gay or if he were something else. He fantasized about men but the only person who had ever sparked his desire outside of his fantasies was Gabriel. Was it possible to be attracted to a single person and no one else?

Jordan snorted softly at the mention of Gabriel.

"He's a demon," Jordan said. "Don't you want someone who can return your affection?"

The words stung and he thought back to his accidental confession of love last night. Demons couldn't love. They couldn't form real, intimate relationships. Everyone knew it. So why was Taylor having such a hard time coming to terms with it? It seemed like Gabriel should be able to love him; everything else was there. Gabriel seemed to want to love him and felt guilt that he couldn't. But why couldn't he?

"I'm sure Callan's good for you," Taylor said, trying to edge away from the pain he felt at Gabriel's inability to love. "Don't you like her?"

"Of course I like her, but she's a demon. Don't you want a real relationship?"

Taylor was silent, the words stinging his heart. He wanted his relationship with Gabriel to be real. He wanted it to be reciprocated. He wanted to believe that the feelings he had for Gabriel were returned. And Gabriel did care for him, deeply. He knew it. What if Gabriel did love him, but just didn't understand that it was love? Maybe demons didn't understand love, or thought it was something different, and that was why they thought they couldn't love. Or maybe Gabriel was just an exception. Because he had to love Taylor, didn't he? What else could his feelings be called?

"I'm happy with Gabriel," Taylor said. "I guess it's not what you consider a real relationship, but it's real enough for me."

Jordan ducked his head as his cheeks flushed nearly as crimson as a demon's eyes. Anger or embarrassment? There was reason for both. He had just made himself very vulnerable by expressing his interest and Taylor turned him down. Taylor sighed. He didn't want his roommate upset. Jordan deserved better, and Taylor took his hand and squeezed it.

"But you're a great guy, Jordan," he said. "You're really fun to be around. You'll find someone who loves you."

"Does that mean," Jordan started, then he lowered his head again. "I suppose you don't ever want to see me again, do you?"

"Of course I want to see you," Taylor said, startled. "You're my roommate. You're a friend. I'm not going to abandon you or anything. To be honest, I was worried you would abandon me when you found out about Gabriel and it... well, it really meant a lot that you were still there for me. I guess you had other reasons for that, but I still appreciate it."

Jordan smiled, some of the fearful sorrow leaving his face. "I do like being your friend," he said. "I miss having you as a roommate. You always picked up after me and I didn't even realize it. Callan's been doing some of it, but I don't want her to be my maid or something."

"But you were fine with me being your maid?" Taylor asked dryly, and Jordan laughed.

"I guess I sort of took you for granted," he said. "I'm sorry for that."

"No problem," Taylor said, and gestured to the path. "Want to keep walking?"

Chapter 18

Sunday Revelations

"What was that about?" Gabriel asked rather jealously as Taylor returned and sank into the couch. He lifted an arm over his head.

"Don't tell anyone," he said, wondering if he was allowed to tell Gabriel. He had to be able to tell his demon, right? After all, Gabriel could read his mind if he really wanted. "Jordan came out to me. I don't think I handled it very well. I probably should have been more supportive, but I was just so surprised."

Gabriel was silent, then came and sat next to him. He wrapped an arm around his shoulders.

"That was bold of him," Gabriel said. He sounded completely unsurprised. "I'm sure you did great, Taylor."

"Did you... already know?"

"I knew he was interested in you," Gabriel said. "It's obvious to me, but I knew you were unaware. That's why I was troubled when Callan bonded with him."

"What does she have to do with anything? He said he liked women, too."

Gabriel was silent for a moment, stroking his arm.

"If you turned to Jordan, she was probably expecting me to turn to her," he said slowly. "That may be why she tried to get between us."

"Well, that's not happening," Taylor said, snuggling into his demon. Gabriel smiled and kissed his head. He was disturbed that Callan had potentially bonded with Jordan for that reason. How strong was their bond? Clearly, she could feed on him well, or else she wouldn't have taken form so quickly. But succubi almost always took form quickly. They fed on pleasure and if Jordan was attracted to women, it wouldn't be hard for him to feel pleasure with her. But he was also attracted to men, and to Taylor. He had never considered such a thing but the more he thought about it, the more comfortable he was with the idea. He felt bad for instinctively rejecting the idea, because he knew many people felt that way about his preferences and choices. He should have been more sympathetic.

"Want to watch something?" Gabriel asked rather hopefully.

Taylor laughed and agreed. He had work to do, but he could put it off. They had all day. He let Gabriel pick a show to binge and he got popcorn, and soon they cuddled together as they watched episode after episode. Finally, Taylor glanced at his phone and sighed. It was time to do homework, and he wasn't ready to stop yet. But Gabriel was sensitive to him, as usual.

"You need to work?"

"Yeah," he said regretfully. "But you can keep watching."

"I'd rather be with you," Gabriel said, and they moved to the table. As Taylor got out his homework, Gabriel took one of his textbooks and started reading. He didn't ever help Taylor with his homework but he was curious about everything and enjoyed reading Taylor's books. He wasn't entirely sure why, since Gabriel could just peek into his mind. Maybe there were limits to the knowledge Gabriel could take from him. Or maybe Gabriel just liked to give Taylor privacy. Either way, as Taylor got to work on his homework for Mr. Hill's class, Gabriel sunk into one of his psychology textbooks.

Taylor was able to complete the homework easily and as he worked through the problems with the equation Gabriel had given him, he paused. He had promised Mr. Hill to ask about this. He had several questions for Gabriel. With a start, he realized that even though he had brought up some of his questions, Gabriel had dodged the answers. He hadn't been willing to talk about what he was, or what exactly he fed on. He avoided the questions exactly as Mr. Hill had predicted he would. Was there a reason he didn't want to answer, or had the conversation just shifted on its own? There hadn't been anything suspicious about it when they were talking, but now, looking back, he realized how skillfully Gabriel had diverted the conversation. Why didn't he want to talk about it?

"Hey, Gabriel," he said, and realized that Gabriel was already watching him. Had Gabriel realized his sudden suspicion? Probably. Even if he wasn't scanning Taylor's mind, he was good at reading body language.

"This equation you gave me," he said, deciding to start with what he had promised to ask. "Did you know it's supposed to be a secret? Can I tell other people about it?"

"Everyone knew it the last time I was in this world," he said as he lowered his eyes and winced. "I just assumed you hadn't learned it yet."

"But can I tell people? My teacher really wanted to know it."

"I would prefer if you didn't," Gabriel said. "Your friend can know. I've already told Ariel to prevent Natalie from telling anyone."

"You didn't get in trouble, did you?"

"No," Gabriel said with a smile. "Demons are not expected to know everything about the time they enter, and it will still be kept secret. Neither you nor Natalie will tell anyone, and it isn't the type of equation that can be determined by working out those problems you have. Even if your teacher tries to analyze how you're getting your answers, it won't help him."

"Why is it secret, if everyone used to know it?" Taylor asked, thinking of what Mr. Hill had told him about the equation being abused.

"It reveals too much about me. About us," he hastily amended.

"Not just me, but all demons. Humans shouldn't have learned it in the first place."

Taylor nodded, but he wondered if that were an honest slip of the tongue. Was the equation directed at Gabriel personally? Or had he just meant to indicate all demons and referred to himself first? He wasn't sure, because he still didn't fully understand the equation and how it could be used. It was for telling a demon's power, and how much energy they needed, according to Mr. Hill. How would that reveal information about Gabriel? Could it reveal what Gabriel actually was? If Gabriel didn't want anyone knowing what he was, and the equation revealed it, then of course he would want it kept secret. But why would the other demons also keep it secret? No, it was more likely that he meant all demons, not just himself. That would explain why no human knew it. Except for him and Natalie, and Gabriel was right: neither of them would share it.

He had more questions for Gabriel, more things he wanted to know, but he wasn't sure if this was the time to ask. He wanted to ask Gabriel straight out what he was and noticed that Gabriel was gripping the book tightly, his brow furrowed. Did he know what Taylor wanted to ask? If it put him this much on edge, then maybe he shouldn't ask. The answer couldn't be that important, could it? Maybe Gabriel didn't like what he really was. Maybe it would be stirring unpleasant memories or thoughts. He wouldn't do that to his demon. So he got back to work on his homework and could see Gabriel relaxing. As he worked, Gabriel started reading again and soon they were working peacefully together.

Taylor switched to writing his essay next, trying to get a decent draft for their peer review. Last paper he hadn't gotten a peer review, since he missed that class, and he suspected his grade was going to reflect it. Even though it was annoying sitting there the whole class giving feedback to his peers, he really appreciated getting the notes and comments. He tried to give good information in thanks to his peers for helping him, and he hoped they found his comments as useful as he found theirs.

Finally, it was time for bed. He wondered again if he should ask Gabriel, but he didn't. He just cuddled against his demon in the bed and fell asleep. As he slept, he was vaguely aware of Gabriel holding him and was comforted. After what seemed like an eternity, he opened his eyes. He was in his dream, with an ebony canopy above him and Gabriel standing nearby. His eyes widened. Gabriel was in his true form, his wings spread and his chiseled legs covered in thick fur. He was so beautiful, Taylor thought idly. Gabriel smiled, probably aware of that thought.

"No one has ever admired this form before," he said, and Taylor's lips spread in a smile.

"You're gorgeous," he said shyly. "In every form."

"You didn't want me to look like this the first time you saw me."

"I was surprised," Taylor said, remembering his emotions at seeing Gabriel like this the first time. "And I don't think you'd do well in my world if you looked like that. Everyone would stare."

Gabriel was silent for a moment, probably trying to sense if that was true. He thought it was. He couldn't remember his initial reaction exactly, but he had worried about Gabriel looking like that and people being shocked by it. It was true, too. In Taylor's dreams, Gabriel could look like anything he wanted. But in the real world, the human world at least, Gabriel needed to look mostly human to fit in. Humans wouldn't appreciate seeing a true demon, even though Taylor didn't mind.

Taylor stood up and approached him, thinking of how good it had felt when Gabriel had held him and wrapped his wings around them. Gabriel extended his arms without a word, sweeping Taylor into exactly the type of hug he wanted. As he relaxed in Gabriel's arms, feeling like he was melting into his demon's strength, he could feel Gabriel feeding on him. Not much, but there was a faint pull that he recognized. It wasn't enough to make him dizzy or weak, but it was there. What did he feed on? There was pleasure in this touch, but not much.

"You wanted to know what I am," Gabriel said softly. "I know you've been thinking of that quite a bit, ever since you talked to that teacher. This is what I am."

Taylor backed away and studied him. What did that mean, exactly? He thought of the succubi he had seen. They looked exactly like they did in the human world. Nearly human figures. None had appeared this demonic. But there was nothing about Gabriel's inhuman form that he hadn't seen before in illustrations of demons. Whenever there were images of demons in their own realm, they looked like this. Didn't they? Thinking back, he realized that the only depictions of demons like this were of the demon king himself. No other demons were portrayed this way. Was it because Gabriel was the demon king's only true child?

"Yes," Gabriel said in answer to his unspoken question. "He made me in his image, with all the same limitations and potential."

"Wait, does that mean that he can't-"

Taylor stopped, blushing. He didn't need to continue. Gabriel knew what he meant. Could the demon king really not feel pleasure?

"He freed himself," Gabriel said. "It's why he doesn't need humans anymore. He gave me that potential. That's why I look for a specific human. There will someday be a human who can free me from my dependence, as well. There are other things associated with it, many things that will happen when that day comes, but I have no control over it. I can only keep searching."

Taylor drew in a sharp breath. He knew, without question, that this was more forbidden knowledge. Gabriel had probably never told anyone this before and he was honored by the trust being shown. So there was a specific human who could break through Gabriel's limitations? Who could make Gabriel feel pleasure on his own, so he no longer needed humans? But if he didn't need humans, would that mean he would abandon his partner? Because as much as Taylor wanted to be the one who freed Gabriel, he didn't want his demon to leave him.

"When my limitations are broken, many things will happen," Gabriel repeated. "My human will be affected as well. If it is you," he added in a softer voice, "I would not leave you. I would have the choice to leave, but I wouldn't."

Taylor rushed towards Gabriel, flinging himself in his demon's arms. His heart felt like it would burst from love, and he could feel Gabriel feeding more strongly now. He didn't care, and didn't bother trying to understand what exactly he was feeding on. His demon wouldn't leave him, even if he had the option. That had to mean that Gabriel loved him. Why else would he stay? Even if Gabriel couldn't say it, even if he didn't recognize it as love, it could be nothing else. It was enough for Taylor. More than enough. He would be that person, he decided. He would figure out how to free Gabriel so that Gabriel was staying willingly, and not because he was bound by hunger.

"You understand that you can tell no one any of this," Gabriel warned, and Taylor nodded. He would never think of betraying Gabriel's confidence. "Your teacher will try to trick you," Gabriel continued. "Watch your words around him."

"He studies you, you know," Taylor said. "He wrote his thesis or something about you."

"I hadn't realized that," Gabriel said, sounding displeased. "No one has ever studied me before. I hadn't realized there were people who made it their business to learn about me."

"I'll protect you," Taylor said, leaning back to meet Gabriel's eyes. "I won't let anyone know anything about you unless you want them to know it. I'll be careful what I say, and I'll never betray you. You're my demon. No one else gets to have you."

"Thank you, Taylor," Gabriel said softly. "If I could choose who the person could be, it would be you. But I don't know. Can't know. Not yet."

Taylor kissed him, hoping Gabriel was feasting on his love and pleasure at the words. As they kissed, he could indeed feel his demon drawing out his energy until everything went black. When he opened his eyes, he was in his own bed with Gabriel beside him. He didn't say a word about what had happened and knew he never would. Not outside of his dreams. Gabriel's words were to be protected, and he would never risk breaking his demon's confidence.

Chapter 19

Potential War

Taylor dreaded seeing Mr. Hill on Monday, but the teacher didn't say anything to him during class. He looked at him meaningfully a few times, but otherwise he treated Taylor exactly as he always had. Natalie continued to take notes, though she didn't need to. He wondered if they were notes on the lecture or if she was working on something else. Probably for the class, he decided. Maybe she was trying to figure out how Mr. Hill was attempting to learn the equation, and why people had forgotten it.

Would Mr. Hill approach her as well, since her test results were bound to be as noticeable as his? Probably more, since his grade had been lower due to careless mistakes. He was still embarrassed by that. Hers would be flawless. But she hadn't mentioned talking to the teacher yet, nor had he seen Mr. Hill talking to her. He did notice Mr. Hill looking at her quite a few times as well, though. He had to know, and just hadn't asked yet.

After class, Mr. Hill didn't leave immediately, but he also didn't call Taylor to the front. Taylor packed up his books and considered. He had the answer Mr. Hill had asked for, and it would be best to give it to him as soon as possible.

"Natalie, can you tell Gabriel I'll be right out? It's not a big deal," he added, wanting to reassure his demon that he wasn't about to spill his secrets. Natalie agreed, mystified, and Taylor made his way to the front of the class. Mr. Hill smiled, but neither of them said anything until the room was empty.

"I take it you talked to Gabriel," Mr. Hill said. Taylor steeled himself.

"I'll tell you his answer if you tell me why his name is important," he said, hoping this worked. Now that he knew more about Gabriel, his curiosity about the name had grown. Mr. Hill considered the request, then nodded.

"Two thousand years ago, there was a war. You know about it. The Great War."

Taylor nodded. It was the last recorded time that the demon king appeared in this realm. The demons had turned against each other, and against the humans. It was one reason normal people feared the demonborn, because during the Great War, the demons had targeted everyone, demonborn and normal alike. But the demons seemed focused on destroying the demonborn, oddly. No one had ever figured out why, because without the demonborn, the demons would have no one to feed on. And no one knew why the demon king vanished after that war. He must have freed himself then, Taylor realized. Just as Gabriel would eventually free himself.

"I learned about it, like everyone else," Taylor said. "I guess I didn't pay attention. I don't remember anyone with that name."

"You wouldn't have learned it," Mr. Hill said. "The only people we remember from that war are the humans, and this was a demon's name. The demon king's. Gabriel was the last name he ever had before he vanished from our realm."

Taylor drew in a sharp breath. If the demon king were named Gabriel before he vanished, before he was freed, then didn't it stand to reason that this would be his demon's last name as well? Was he indeed the one Gabriel was waiting for? Was this a sign that Gabriel would also be freed soon?

"Can you tell me why that's important?" Mr. Hill asked.

"No," Taylor said sharply, surprised that he would ask so openly. But Mr. Hill looked surprised.

"I didn't realize you actually understood," Mr. Hill said slowly, shoulders raising as if in excitement. "I was simply asking, as a teacher, if you understood the implications. Has he told you what he is? Do you know why the name is significant?"

Taylor blushed. He had inadvertently given something away, even if it was just the fact that he knew something. He really would have to watch his words, because it was clear that Mr. Hill hadn't even been trying to manipulate him and still managed it.

"I just meant that I don't understand," Taylor said. "Um, why is that significant?"

He knew why he thought it was significant, but he didn't understand why Mr. Hill would think it was significant.

"The demon king's last appearance sparked a war," Mr. Hill said. "A civil war between demons that almost wiped out the demonborn. Demons gain power from their names, and it may be that there's something in the name itself that caused the war. By calling him Gabriel, you've unknowingly risked another war."

"A war?" Taylor asked, shocked. "How could a war be caused by a name? Why didn't anyone ever warn me about that name? Surely there are other demons named Gabriel."

"There are some, and no one would try to dictate what you name your demon, no matter the consequences. It's safe to assume Gabriel doesn't intend on starting a war, then," he mused. "That's good. Gabriel must not understand the significance of the name, either, though I suppose that makes sense. I don't know why demons would share their human names with each other since they change so often."

Taylor's mind reeled. Gabriel had said there were many things associated with freeing himself, that both him and his partner would be affected. Was a war one of those many things?

There was a knock at the door and to Taylor's surprise, Gabriel entered and came up to him, wrapping his arm around his waist and glaring at Mr. Hill.

"You're upsetting my human," he said coldly. "I'll tolerate you talking to him, but that's it."

Mr. Hill's lips widened into a smile that crinkled his eyes. "Is something about our conversation threatening to you?"

Gabriel hesitated and glanced at Taylor, who could tell that he hadn't been eavesdropping. He didn't know what their conversation was about or else he almost certainly wouldn't have come in when he did and risk exposing who he was, and what might happen. He must have just felt Taylor's distress and assumed that Mr. Hill was pressuring him.

"I'm sure I'll find out what you were saying to upset my human," Gabriel said, "But from now on, I don't want you talking to him outside of class."

"Even if it relates to schoolwork? Would you prefer me to call him up during class for personal matters?"

"If you hurt him in class, I will come in," Gabriel warned. "No matter the consequences. He can test out of this class if necessary."

Mr. Hill smiled again. "I apologize. I won't distress Taylor again. I hadn't realized that my words were upsetting him enough to cause you distress as well. Very interesting."

Gabriel's eyes narrowed but he said nothing, because he didn't know what they had talked about. He honestly didn't understand why Taylor was upset and now Taylor felt even worse, because his fears had caused Gabriel to reveal something about himself. He had promised not to do that, and already failed.

"Taylor, I believe you owe me an answer as well," Mr. Hill added.

"The answer is no," Taylor said shortly, angry at his teacher. He took some small pleasure in being able to deny his teacher the equation and was glad Gabriel had asked him not to tell. He had never felt so negatively about a teacher before, but everything that Mr. Hill did set his nerves on edge.

Without a word, Gabriel escorted him out of the class and Taylor followed, upset about the whole conversation. Gabriel kissed the top of his head and led him to his next class. He was probably going to be late. He had expected to spend a couple of minutes talking to Mr. Hill and rushing to Ms. Winde's class, but he had spent more time than he anticipated.

"Do you want to skip your next class?" Gabriel asked softly, to his surprise.

"I can't skip class," Taylor said, shocked at the very idea. He had skipped before, but never after missing so many classes. He was still catching up from bonding with Gabriel.

They reached the class a few minutes late but before Taylor could enter, Gabriel stopped him and yanked him into a kiss. Taylor shied away in embarrassment, but there was no one nearby so he relaxed into the kiss and tried to enjoy it so Gabriel could feed on him, since Gabriel must be doing this to feed. Had Taylor's fears drained him? Was that why he needed to feed right now? The kiss ended and Gabriel stroked his cheek.

"That was not for me," Gabriel said softly. "That was for you. I will never do anything to hurt you, and I will always protect you. We'll talk later."

Taylor nodded, and couldn't help a smile. Gabriel had kissed him... and hadn't fed? Feeding was the entire basis of their relationship. If Gabriel was able to give him pleasure without the ultimate goal of feeding, then didn't that imply that he was the one Gabriel was looking for? Gabriel chuckled. They were close enough that Gabriel could no doubt pick up on his thoughts.

"I have always wanted a partner like you, but I don't know yet," he said. "Now go to class."

Taylor obeyed, his step light and Mr. Hill's disturbing words of war fading from his mind. He snuck in the class and unfortunately, they were already in groups. Perfect groups, too – every group already had three people. Wherever he went, he was going to stand out. Ms. Winde sailed over to him, serene as always, and without a word about his late arrival, she directed him to the nearest group and gave him brief instructions. The rest of the group filled him in and he got out his draft and passed it to his peers, getting a paper for him to grade as he dove into figuring out how to help his classmates.

Class flew by as they kept passing papers and then talked with each other about each draft. Everyone liked what Taylor had, luckily, so he wouldn't have to make many revisions before turning it in. Maybe no revisions, though he did need to run spellcheck as the grammar-conscious guy in the group found quite a few typos that were causing errors in meaning. He gathered his things and Ms. Winde asked him to stay a minute. She rarely called him out like this and he blushed as he finished packing his things and went to the front of the class. Everyone else filed out. This was his day for talking to teachers, apparently.

"You're not late very often," she said.

"I'm sorry," he said. "I was talking to Mr. Hill after class and lost track of time."

She nodded. "Be careful around him," she said, to Taylor's surprise. "Demonborn society is not as unified as you may think, and he belongs to a group that has, well, different goals than I believe you have."

"What does that mean?"

"The quest for that equation is not pursued by all of the demonborn," she said. "Some of us think it's best forgotten. If the demons wanted us to know it, they would tell us. They don't, so why look for it? But the president agrees with Mr. Hill, and made the class required for all students. Be careful around him, too."

"I don't understand," Taylor said honestly, though he could see how there might be a schism between people who wanted to know the equation and those who didn't. The people who didn't care probably thought Mr. Hill's class was a waste of time. But was there something deeper? She seemed to be implying that there was. She sighed.

"Just be careful," she said. "Gabriel is very special, but having the prince of demons bonded to you will attract all kinds of attention. Some will be good, but not all of it. Demon hunters aren't your only enemies."

Taylor shivered. Was Mr. Hill a danger? He was rather threatening. And Taylor had been quite intimidated by the college president.

145

"That's it," Ms. Winde said with that calm smile she always had. She always was in such a good mood while teaching and he couldn't understand how she did it. Surely she had bad days, like everyone else. But if she did, she never showed it.

"What is your demon?" he asked curiously, realizing that on the first day, she hadn't explained her demon the way most teachers did. Mr. Hill's demon didn't have physical form, nor did his other two teachers. No one ever volunteered what their demons fed on, of course, but they usually mentioned who their demon was.

"A raven," she said with a pleased smile. "He's quite beautiful. You've probably seen him flying outside the classroom, though I've warned him against it. He can be so distracting to the students."

"I have seen him," Taylor said, eyes widening. He sometimes drifted off and stared out the window and there was almost always a lovely black raven either flying around or perched on the nearby tree. The raven wasn't close enough that Taylor could make out the red eyes, so he had assumed it was just a local raven who liked flying in the area.

"He's very pretty," Taylor added. "Thanks, Ms. Winde."

"Of course, Taylor," she said, and went to pack up her own things.

Taylor headed out but didn't say anything to Gabriel. Yet. He would, in private, but not here in the public. If there was some sort of split in demonborn society, then he probably shouldn't talk about it in public. And if Ms. Winde thought that part of that society was a danger to him and Gabriel, then he definitely shouldn't say anything. Once he was in private, though, he would tell his demon everything. Everything Mr. Hill had said about a potential war, and everything Ms. Winde had said about a potential threat. Ms. Winde was right: having Gabriel as his demon was bringing quite a few changes and not all were good. But as long as he had Gabriel, he didn't care.

Chapter 20

Frozen in Place

Gabriel caressed his cheek as they lay together and Taylor thought back to Mr. Hill's words, and Ms. Winde's warning. Gabriel hadn't pushed for an answer, able to tell that Taylor's thoughts were still jumbled. Finally, Taylor rolled into his arms.

"Mr. Hill told me why your name is important."

"My name?"

"Right when I named you, he mentioned that your name was special. Were you aware of that? You were still in my mind at the time."

"I was enjoying my new name," Gabriel said, a trace of guilt as he squeezed Taylor tight. "I wasn't paying attention to what he was saying."

How cute that Gabriel liked his new name enough that his attention wandered. Taylor gripped the arm curled around him, inserting his hand into Gabriel's as the demon cradled him. He didn't resist as they held hands.

"Well, he mentioned it then, and I asked him about it. And your name is special. It's the last name the demon king had before he vanished."

"What?"

Gabriel's hand flinched; Gabriel flinched. He pulled away but Taylor clung to him.

"I don't know exactly what that means, but I can guess," Taylor said. "I know you won't want to talk about it though."

"No, I don't." Gabriel's voice was strange and distant, as if he were in another realm projecting his voice. Maybe he was. Taylor didn't know how demons worked since they could still communicate with each other without speaking. Gabriel and Ariel spoke several times this past week and she was a cat. Maybe he could do more than communicate with nearby demons and that was what he was doing right now. Then he cuddled Taylor again.

"He must have said something else to upset you. That's not enough."

Taylor nodded, his head bobbing against Gabriel's with the gesture.

"Right when the demon king vanished, there was a war. A big one. You have to know about it."

"Of course."

Taylor twisted to look at his demon. "Where you in it?"

Gabriel chuckled. "I wasn't created yet. Surely you could guess that."

"I hadn't thought about it," Taylor admitted. "But that makes sense. Anyway, Mr. Hill said that the name Gabriel might be associated with the war, that having that name means you might start another war. And I thought back to what you said... I don't want a war."

Another silence from his demon, then a sigh.

"I don't know the future, Taylor. I can't predict what will or won't happen." That wasn't reassuring. Gabriel squeezed him. "But this isn't a good place to talk."

"I know."

Unfortunately, he already knew Gabriel wouldn't want to talk here. Was he worried people were listening in? Or was it just a precaution? Either way, his demon didn't seem comfortable sharing truths outside of Taylor's mind. He didn't like the restriction, but he would honor it.

He just hoped tonight Gabriel would pull him from his dreams and they could really talk, because the fact that Gabriel didn't immediately dismiss a war worried him.

"Your mind is so full of thoughts lately," Gabriel said, snuggling close. "And I know you can't sort them out with me around. Do you need another walk?"

"I dunno, last one didn't go well."

Gabriel let out a low laugh. "Jordan will not try anything. I'll make sure of it."

"How?"

"I'll speak to Callan. She'll be willing to keep him occupied while you have time to yourself. You haven't had a minute alone since I formed and I know you like privacy."

"I'd really like that," Taylor said wistfully. "But you know I love being around you, right? I like talking to you and doing things with you."

"What kind of things?"

Gabriel's hand slid down his chest and Taylor drew in a sharp breath. Was Gabriel going to seduce him right now? Was he even in the mood? He wasn't, and Gabriel stopped short of his pants with a laugh.

"I won't try anything," he said. "I'll save that for tonight."

"I do like it though." The words were still difficult to admit. He was so used to hiding his lust he found it hard to acknowledge, but the more time he spent gasping under Gabriel's touch, the easier it was. The public scrutiny was already there; they assumed he and his incubus were already engaged in the type of sex he backed away from. Nothing held him back but his fears. Yolette was no longer in his mind when they were together, but the hesitancy she had created was. Gabriel eased him into intimacy, but not fully, not yet.

Gabriel kissed his neck.

"Do you want to go now? There are still several hours before dinner."

"You don't mind?"

"It should be safe. You'll stay in the protected area?"

"Of course."

Gabriel kissed him again, and he reluctantly pulled from his demon's grasp and looked back at him. Gabriel stretched seductively, showing off his body in that thing white shirt that hinted at his skin underneath. So beautiful. But Gabriel was right about needing time alone. And if he didn't mind if Taylor took that time, he wasn't going to argue.

He headed out to the path, dodging students. They bothered him less and less. The last few times he tried to take a walk, they swarmed him. This time, he avoided their notice and wondered if Gabriel had anything to do with it. He strolled along the path that the president had ensured was safe, being careful to stay on the dirt walkway and not stray. The trail stretched several feet across, as it was one of the main paths making a loop in the forest surrounding the campus. He wondered how it was guarded, if there were people around him that he couldn't see or if there had been a fence of some sort built, or perhaps electronic surveillance. He didn't really care, as long as he was protected, but he was curious.

Last time he walked like this, Jordan had approached him and come out to him. Even though Gabriel assured him this time he wouldn't be interrupted, his roommate was still on his mind. He hadn't seen Jordan since then. Had he been sympathetic enough? He should have embraced Jordan immediately. He should have handled it better. As he walked, he wondered if Jordan would show up again despite Gabriel's order to Callan, looking for another chance to talk in private. And when he saw a figure in the distance, he stifled a laugh. So Jordan was out here. Apparently Callan wasn't a strong enough lure.

Mist shrouded the figure, but he turned and started rushing towards Taylor, who stopped, startled. The figure was taller than Jordan. Who was it? The figure came into focus a few feet away, a man in a bulky hoodie and sweatpants as if he were out jogging in the woods. He probably was, but why was he coming towards Taylor? If he were just running by, why was he stopping a few feet away, his eyes locked on Taylor? Who was this? His mind flew to Gabriel. Could

Gabriel tell he was in an odd situation? Because he was worried, and Gabriel made him feel safe.

"You're Taylor, right?" the man asked.

It wouldn't have been unusual for a student to be out jogging like this. Students were out here all the time, dressed the way this man was dressed. But this wasn't a student. This was an adult. Maybe from a distance he looked like a student, but not up close. And pretty much all of the students knew Taylor by now.

"Who are you?" he asked nervously.

"We have a mutual friend," the man said with a disarming smile. Taylor was not reassured.

"Who?"

"She wants to see you again."

Taylor stiffened in fear. Yolette. It had to be her. This had to be a demon hunter. He was in danger. He needed to get out of here. He turned, preparing to run, but there was another figure behind him on the path. What was going on? Wasn't this path protected? Where was his protection? He couldn't be misinterpreting this, could he? Did they mean someone else? How could two demon hunters get this close to campus, in an area specifically protected against them?

"I think you'd better leave," he said in as strong a voice as he could manage. "This area is heavily guarded."

But if it were electronic surveillance, would backup get here in time? He wished he had paid attention to the president's discussion of how he and Gabriel would be protected. Gabriel, he thought with a start. Gabriel could rescue him. But what if this were a ploy to get Gabriel out in the open so they could kill him? After all, demon hunters didn't kill the demonborn; they were after the demon. They had ways of permanently killing demons so the demon couldn't escape back into their own realm. Would it work with Gabriel? Gabriel had a shadow of himself in the demon realm. Could he be killed here?

"No one will bother us," the first man said with absolute confidence. A chill ran through Taylor as he thought of Ms. Winde's words. Had the president let these men in because of some split in demonborn society? Ms. Winde said the president was a potential threat. How big a threat? He had seemed delighted that Gabriel was at the college; was it a ploy to put them at ease? Was everything a trap?

"You have nothing to worry about," the man behind him added. The two men approached, their arms ready to snatch Taylor if he tried to bolt. There was no way he could escape. He wasn't strong enough to fight both of them, nor fast enough to get past them. He wanted Gabriel, but not if it put Gabriel at risk.

"Who are you?" Taylor repeated as he edged back in panic. What was he going to do?

The man behind him lunged and Taylor whirled, but the man knocked into him and they fell to the ground. Hard. Taylor coughed and tried to get up, but the other man was on top of him, keeping him pinned. He struggled, trying to bite the other man since nothing else was working, but the other man was quick to avoid him while still keeping him down. Then the temperature dropped abruptly and he shivered. The mist flaked into a light snow and the man over him looked up in shock, then grinned at the other man.

"Looks like he took the bait," he said in a smug voice. What did that mean?

The cold intensified and the snow plummeted to the ground and shattered as if gravity clung to it and yanked it down. Gravity dragged him down as well and the man on top of him became unbearably heavy. He moaned and struggled to knock the man off. His breathing grew shallow as the man's weight pressed on his chest. The man's smugness was gone now.

"I can't move," the man said, and the cold intensified further.

The aching cold in the ground under his back crept into his body. He heard a sizzling sound and the man over him cried out. Taylor managed to turn his head to look, though the growing cold was turning to frost and almost locking him in place. The man's hand was on the ground beside them and it was blue, freezing into the earth itself. Ice spiked through the hand suddenly and the man screamed. The other man cried out as well. Taylor couldn't look at him. Ice slithered along his head, along his neck, and the weight still forced air from his lungs. His nose and mouth stung from the cold and the air itself seemed like daggers of ice: sharp and unbreathable. He heard the sound of footsteps.

"You," the other man whispered, and Taylor heard a thudding sound. Then feet entered his line of sight. Whoever it was, they were moving easily as if the cold and gravity didn't affect them at all. The figure knelt, one elegant hand touching the ground. No ice covered the hand, nor did the person seem to notice the painful chill in the earth that crippled Taylor. The hand grasped the man over him and flung him off. Taylor still couldn't breathe, though the weight was gone. Blackness edged his vision, and then Gabriel's face filled his fading view. He relaxed. Gabriel. Gabriel was doing this. And Gabriel would never hurt him.

Two hands grabbed him and sparked warmth within him. Gabriel picked him up and the earth tried to keep him in place. Shattering as Gabriel yanked him up, and the rip of cloth. His clothing must have frozen into the earth. He was just glad his skin hadn't. He wondered about his hair. His lungs were unfreezing and he took a deeper breath gratefully. Gabriel held him tightly and every point of contact between them revived him. Then everything went still, just as it had the time Gabriel moved them faster than humans could travel. He saw the campus pass them by, and then they were in his apartment and sound returned, movement returned. Gabriel lay him in the bed but he was still frozen. He still couldn't move. He moaned softly when Gabriel left. The sound of running water. Then Gabriel was back at his side, picking him up again.

Gabriel carried him into the bathroom and lowered him into the bath. His body arched in shock at the burning hot water, but his body was loosening.

"I know this feels hot, but it's not," Gabriel murmured. "I'll warm you slowly. Just relax. Let your body heat up."

He didn't know what Gabriel was talking about because the water was practically boiling. He tried to relax as Gabriel commanded, but he shifted uncomfortably. Sensation returned with sparks of pain and he moaned softly. As the water reached an acceptable temperature, Gabriel added more and again it burned. He repeated that process several more times and finally, Taylor regained control over his limbs. He could move and breathe easily. His body no longer ached. He was still cold, but the water was now pleasantly warm, not burning. Gabriel kissed him.

"I'm sorry, Taylor," he whispered. "I'm so sorry. There was no other way to disable them. I didn't want to target you as well but I had no choice."

"It's all right," Taylor said weakly. "I know you'd never hurt me."

He sunk into the bath as Gabriel added a little more hot water. It didn't burn this time. It felt good. He was still in his clothes, he realized. They must have frozen to him, and Gabriel couldn't take them off. As his mind revived, the events played through his memory and his eyes opened wide. What had Gabriel done? How had he manipulated weather and gravity like that? And who were those men? Had Yolette really sent them?

"We'll get answers soon," Gabriel said. "The president is questioning them."

Was that really safe? Could they trust the president? Gabriel stroked his head.

"I understand, but it wasn't him," he said. "I questioned his demon. Thoroughly. He had nothing to do with this. The guards who were posted have been taken care of. They're to blame, and the president is furious that they betrayed him."

Taylor nodded, and relaxed again. The water felt so good.

"Gabriel," he managed. "Can I sleep?"

"I'll protect you," Gabriel said softly. "Just rest."

Chapter 21

Feeding

Something warm pressed against his chest when Taylor came back to awareness and he puzzled. It wasn't big enough to be Gabriel, and too oddly shaped to be a blanket. The pressure started alternating, kneading against him. He opened his eyes and saw two cat eyes staring into his as Ariel kneaded him with her large paws. No wonder. The demon nuzzled him, then hopped off his chest as Taylor sat up.

Natalie was nearby and Ariel wound around her legs as she smiled at him. Gabriel was there, but turned away. He was on the phone, Taylor could see, but he glanced at Taylor and grinned. Taylor was reassured.

"You okay, Taylor?" Natalie asked.

"Tell me it's Tuesday or Wednesday," he said, remembering the last time something like this had happened and he lost an entire weekend.

"It's Wednesday morning," Natalie said. "You slept through the night. As long as it's safe, you'll be able to go to class later today."

"Oh, good," Taylor said, relieved. He did not want to keep missing classes. Having a demon wasn't helping his grades. "I feel better," he added, mostly for Gabriel.

Gabriel was still on the phone, talking quietly, but met Taylor's eyes. He looked relieved as well. Taylor wondered who he was talking to.

"What happened?" Natalie asked. "The whole campus just dropped in temperature. I mean, it wasn't exactly a warm day to start with, but it was suddenly freezing and started snowing. The woods out past the academic buildings are still frozen. Some of the trees shattered in the cold. All we heard was that Gabriel did it to protect you."

"That's about all I know," Taylor admitted. "It just got really cold."

"Everyone said his body was powerful," Natalie said, glancing at Gabriel. "I guess I didn't realize what they meant."

"Don't get on his bad side," Taylor joked, and Natalie's eyes widened. He laughed and punched her lightly. "I'm kidding. You'd never get on his bad side. You're my best friend!"

"Thanks," she said. "But what caused it?"

"You can tell her," Gabriel said, slipping his phone in his pocket and sitting beside Taylor. He was quite good with technology now. Gabriel stroked his hair and Taylor could feel a slight tug of him feeding. He hoped his demon wasn't starving. Unleashing that freezing storm couldn't have been easy, and Taylor hadn't been able to feed him properly yet. But if he were really hungry, wouldn't he just ask Natalie to leave and feed?

"I'm fine," Gabriel said, kissing his cheek. Again, Taylor felt the slight tug, but he trusted Gabriel to know his limits. "I'd like to know what happened to you, too."

"Well, I was walking," Taylor said cautiously. "And this guy appeared, then someone else behind me. One of them tackled me, and then it got cold."

"I apologize," Gabriel said. "They had a trap set for me made of fire. Freezing the area was the only way to disable it and rescue you. I may have overreacted."

"It was demon hunters?" Natalie asked sharply. Taylor nodded. "But I thought you were protected."

"There was a mistake," Gabriel said, tightening his grip on Taylor. "You won't be going out on your own anymore. I hope you don't mind."

"That's fine," Taylor said. It made perfect sense and really, he didn't mind. He hadn't mentioned what the demon hunters had said about Yolette—or who he assumed was Yolette—because he didn't want Natalie about it. But he would tell Gabriel once they were alone.

"Well, I'm glad you're safe," Natalie said, and Ariel meowed in agreement.

Taylor agreed to walk to their next class together and Natalie warned that there would probably be a lot of people crowding to see him again. Monday hadn't been bad, but apparently everyone knew the sudden cold was caused by Gabriel and would try to find out more. There was nothing he could do and Taylor's stomach sunk at the thought of another press of students asking intrusive questions. He shouldn't have gone out on his own. Maybe he deserved this. Well, he would never do anything like it again. At least Mr. Hill wouldn't question him about it, not since Gabriel warned the teacher off.

Natalie and Ariel headed out and Gabriel twisted until he was straddling Taylor.

"Now tell me everything," he said, and Taylor did. Gabriel's eyes narrowed when he mentioned Yolette, but he didn't look surprised.

"I was hoping she wouldn't find you," Gabriel said. "I suppose that was foolish thinking. She clearly has contacts among the demonborn, and all of them know I'm here."

"I'm sorry I went out alone, Gabriel," Taylor said. "I didn't realize it was dangerous."

"It's my fault," Gabriel said, embracing him. "I told you to go out. You should have been perfectly protected. I was hoping this wouldn't happen yet, that we would be safe for longer."

"What do you mean?" Taylor asked, frightened. "Are we no longer safe?"

"If one demon hunter has found me, others will follow," he said. "The president is aware of the danger, but there's only so much he can do. I need to stay with you, or near you, and you need to stay near me. Both of us are in danger."

"If something happens to you, are you," Taylor started, then paused. "I mean, I know you're still connected to the demon realm. If something happens to you here, can you go back?"

"It depends," Gabriel said grimly. "Under some circumstances, yes. Under others, well, all demons can die."

"I thought the demon king couldn't die," Taylor said, remembering that bit of knowledge from some old class. It gave him hope, because Gabriel was made in the king's image.

"He can't, now," Gabriel said, and didn't need to continue. The demon king had been freed from humans somehow and was free from death as well. That meant that once Gabriel was freed, he would also be truly immortal. But not until then. For now, he was vulnerable. But Taylor would do everything in his power to protect him. A fierce longing to protect his demon rose up in him and he leaned forward into a kiss. Gabriel met him instantly and he could feel Gabriel drawing on him.

Gabriel pushed him flat on his back, still straddling him, still kissing him as he pulled Taylor's shirt off. Taylor tried to pull at Gabriel's clothes as well, with much less success. Taylor was soon naked and Gabriel still fully clothed. Taylor pulled away from their kissing to laugh.

"This isn't fair," he said. "I want to see you."

Gabriel grinned and lavished a final kiss before standing up and slowly pulling off his white dress shirt, the style he preferred. As he unbuttoned the shirt, Taylor's body responded. Gabriel was so beautiful. But for some reason, he found himself aching for more. Not just for this version of Gabriel, but his true form. He wanted to see Gabriel as he truly was, without any deceptions or illusions. He wanted to love Gabriel in his true form.

"Gabriel, can you feed as easily in my mind?" he asked, wondering if Gabriel would mind entering a dream to continue.

"You would prefer to be asleep?" Gabriel asked, sounding puzzled. "You're not still hurt, are you? You felt fine."

"I want you," Taylor said. "All of you."

Gabriel stared at him in surprise. "You want me... while I kiss you? While I pleasure you?"

"Yes," Taylor said with a blush. He still wasn't entirely comfortable with saying these things out loud, but that was exactly what he wanted. Gabriel seemed moved, then lunged on top of Taylor with a laugh of his own. He peppered Taylor with kisses until he was breathless.

"You won't fall asleep on your own," Gabriel said, which was true: Taylor was quite aroused by the feel of his demon against him. "Shall I help?"

"Anything you want," Taylor said. "I just want you."

Gabriel told him to shut his eyes and he obeyed. Then Gabriel instructed him to open them again and he did. They were in his dream. That was fast. And Gabriel still straddled him, only now he was in his true form. The fur on his legs tickled Taylor's and his wings were extended but curved around them, as if to shield them from the world.

"Is that better?" he asked in a husky voice. Taylor squirmed with pleasure. This was exactly what he wanted. He nodded, then Gabriel leaned down to kiss him, his wings arching over them and brushing the outside of Taylor's arms. He loved being embraced by the powerful wings like this. He wondered if Gabriel could fly with him. That was a thought for another time, though. Right now, he just wanted his demon here, in this bed.

Gabriel kissed him soundly, then began mouthing along his neck. Taylor moaned softly as Gabriel sucked hard, probably leaving a mark. But this was a dream. Nothing that happened here was real. Gabriel could leave as many marks as he wanted. As Gabriel nibbled along his collar bone, that did seem to be his intent.

Taylor's heart pounded rapidly as his breathing stuttered. He was beginning to harden with the constant touching and arousal, and then Gabriel lowered his hips against him and the prickling of fur enticed him as he lengthened fully.

"I want you, Gabriel," he whispered.

Gabriel shifted so that he was cradling Taylor, staring down at him.

"How do you want me?" he asked in that beautiful voice.

For an instant, Taylor wanted Gabriel deep inside of him as his back arched and Gabriel penetrated him. His mind shied away from the thought instantly. He wasn't ready yet, even though he wanted it. What did he want? He wanted to feel Gabriel, to rub against him, to feel his mouth around him.

Gabriel grinned and began kissing down his chest. Apparently words weren't necessary; Gabriel could easily see what he wanted. Taylor's breathing stuttered again as Gabriel hovered over his belly button, then his tongue plunged in and Taylor let out a surprised gasp. It tickled, but was extremely sensual. Then Gabriel began licking his way down Taylor's waist as he shimmied down the bed, his wings rising to brush against Taylor's chest. The feathers teased his nipples as he moaned.

Then Gabriel's tongue lapped against the tip of his cock and his moan grew louder. His tongue wrapped around him, then he was sliding down Gabriel's throat and the sensation was incredible. Gabriel felt so tight against him, and his throat vibrated against his sensitive member. Gabriel shifted against him as his hips bucked and he began thrusting against his willing demon. He was ready to come almost immediately but Gabriel pulled off him. He could feel the tug of Gabriel feeding deeply and wondered how he was feeding while holding off Taylor's pleasure. Then Gabriel took him in his mouth again and the pleasure spiked. When it was almost too much to bear, Gabriel backed off again.

Taylor sweated heavily and panted for breath from the teasing, and he grabbed Gabriel's head and pushed him onto his cock forcefully. Enough play. He wanted to feel his demon and not be stopped. He was ready to explode. Gabriel kept moving on him and then, finally, a spasm sparked through his body and he cried out as a wave of pleasure swept over him.

The pulsations lasted forever, and then he gasped for breath as if he was coming off an incredible high. Gabriel shifted next to him, kissing up his body until he was snuggled against him. The tickle of fur against his legs was arousing, but he was exhausted. He leaned to kiss Gabriel and realized too late that maybe he should kiss someone who had just given oral sex. But Gabriel didn't hesitate and there was no tangy taste, just his demon. This was a dream, after all. Then he sighed and relaxed against his beloved demon.

He felt completely safe here. Maybe this was the only safe place left now that the demon hunters had found them. He wondered what that meant, and how much danger they would be in. Would Yolette find him? Could Gabriel protect him? Gabriel kissed him again and he drowsed into sleep. It was a worry for another time.

Chapter 22

A Unique Demon

Class started after lunch and as soon as Taylor ate his cereal, Gabriel informed him that they needed to talk to the president. Gabriel led the way, his arm looped around Taylor's waist. Taylor appreciated the gesture; he was growing more and more nervous as they approached. Not only was he intimidated by Samson in general, now he had Ms. Winde's warning to think about as well. But Samson had protected Taylor after the attack, and there was no reason for the level of anxiety he felt. As they entered the building, Gabriel brushed a kiss on his cheek.

"I'll do the talking," he said softly, and Taylor nodded in relief.

Two men who looked like bodyguards from a movie opened the door to the president's office. Were they security for Samson or for him and Gabriel? He had noticed several burly men and women nearby on their walk here, and Gabriel warned him that there would be security around them from now on.

Samson stood as they entered. He was behind a desk and there were two chairs in front of the desk. He leaned across the desk with his hand extended. Gabriel shook his hand and then sat in one of the chairs, and Taylor awkwardly followed suit, knowing his handshake probably wasn't as firm and decisive as Gabriel's had been. He shifted nervously in the chair as no one spoke, glancing at Gabriel and wondering who was supposed to start this. But Gabriel seemed content to wait. Perhaps this a power thing that he didn't understand, some way of asserting dominance. But then wouldn't they both want to speak first? Samson finally cleared his throat.

"Security has been established around the areas of campus you'll be frequenting," Samson said, and turned his gaze to Taylor. "I apologize for the lapse that allowed an attack to happen. I take full responsibility."

"As you should," Gabriel said, and Samson's eyes narrowed as they returned to the demon. "But I trust that it will never happen again. I'll overlook this mistake, given the quality of security you've now provided us."

"The safety of the demon prince is a top concern for this university," the President said. "If you need anything, or feel that anything is lacking, just let me know."

"We will," Gabriel said, then glanced at Taylor. "There is a very specific threat targeting us and I believe knowing who was behind the attack will help prevent further attacks."

Samson stared at Taylor. "You know the two demon hunters who attacked you?"

"He knows who sent them," Gabriel said, and Taylor was grateful he didn't have to say anything. He could sense the power play around him and didn't understand it at all. "A demon hunter named Yolette."

Samson's eyes widened. "She's found you already?"

Gabriel nodded and Taylor wondered how Samson had heard of her. Actually, how did Gabriel know her? He hadn't been in the human world for over a century, and Yolette was a human, not a demon. She couldn't live that long.

"That family has always been a thorn in our side," Samson muttered. "Well, we'll cater our security to that threat. Unfortunately, your movement will have to be quite restricted for the time being. Aid is being sent from nearby resources, but it takes time."

"I appreciate everything you're doing," Gabriel said. "Keep me informed on everything."

Samson agreed. It seemed like the meeting was over because both men stood and shook hands again. Taylor belatedly got to his feet and shook Samson's hand again, then followed Gabriel out. He felt lost. There was quite a lot of tension between the two men. Samson was a potential threat, but the man was also the only thing keeping them safe on this campus. Gabriel couldn't alienate him completely. But he trusted that Gabriel knew what he was doing, and he noticed the burly men and women were closer to them on the way back to the apartments.

One bonus was that the other students kept their distance. Natalie had a morning class and he was glad he didn't have to worry about other students yet. But his class started in an hour, so he would have to face them eventually. They'd be curious about the attack, since the temperature had dropped campus-wide and everyone knew something had happened. He would be fine in Mr. Hill's class, since it was lecture, but Ms. Winde's class would be more difficult, as they almost always worked in groups.

As soon as they were back in the safety of the apartment, Gabriel sighed and took Taylor in his arms.

"Things have changed, Taylor, but don't be afraid."

"I'm not," Taylor said, but it was partially a lie and Gabriel could tell. "How did you know who Yolette was? How did he know?"

Gabriel was silent, then pulled Taylor to the comfy couch and took his hands, stroking them softly.

"She's not the same Yolette that I knew," he said. "It's a family name. They give the name to the firstborn daughter of their family line. It's done so demons, who live many human generations, will always know to fear the person bearing that name. That family hunts all demons, but they hunt me especially."

Gabriel lifted his wrist and turned it to show the small mark that matched Taylor's exactly. It was bright red now, since they were bonded, but the imperfections were still visible, especially the little hole that Taylor had always obsessed and fretted over. He had been sure that he wouldn't bond with a demon because of those imperfections; instead, he had found a demon who matched him exactly. He snuggled into Gabriel's embrace.

"I always have a mark that looks like this," he said. "That family knows it. When she heard that there was a child with a strange mark, and when she saw yours and knew it fit mine exactly, she must have known I would bond with you. So she hurt you, tried to make you incapable of bonding with me. Her family has hunted me for centuries, but what she did to you was far worse."

Taylor thought of the hours he spent with Yolette and how at first it had been so simple, with her trying to persuade him that he could live as a human and not be demonborn. Had that been her first plan to prevent him from bonding with Gabriel? And when she realized he still wanted to be demonborn, she tried to poison his idea of love and sex? It almost worked, and still affected his relationship with Gabriel. He hadn't had sex with Gabriel, not really, or at least not the kind of sex he dreamed about. He still had lingering hesitations about himself, and about their relationship.

"Why do they target you specifically? And why is Mr. Hill so interested in you?" Taylor asked, and Gabriel sighed and stroked his arm.

"You know I'm not like other demons," he said. Taylor nodded, but Gabriel didn't say any more. Taylor considered what Gabriel had told him in private, where no one could hear. Obviously that was the reason, and Gabriel wasn't going to repeat anything where anyone could potentially hear. Many things would happen when he found the right person. Mr. Hill implied that war would be one of them and Gabriel hadn't denied it. Was Mr. Hill trying to stop that war? But then why would Mr. Hill and Samson be trying to protect Gabriel rather than kill him? And why would a demon hunter care if there was a civil war among demons that killed the demonborn? Demon hunters didn't care about either group.

The equation must have something to do with it. The equation measured a demon's strength, and Gabriel implied that the equation targeted him specifically. Maybe they wanted to calculate Gabriel's strength so that they could limit him and prevent a war. There were so many confusing questions, but there was an answer to all of it some-where. Would Gabriel tell him in private? Did Gabriel even know? They would find out eventually, though, because Taylor was deter-mined to be the person Gabriel was looking for. And once he and Gabriel were truly together, the demon would be free and everything would change.

Gabriel glanced at his watch. Taylor hadn't noticed the watch before; it was quite fancy and looked like one that was practically a miniature computer. Taylor's was simple: it told the time and nothing else. He was tempted to get something fancier, but didn't want to spend the money. Gabriel didn't have the same qualms about spending and it was a good thing the president gave him a credit card.

"We should go to class," he said.

Taylor sighed and shyly kissed Gabriel before standing up. They headed to the academic buildings with several of the guards nearby. As they drew near, other students started to get closer to them, since there were too many students for the guards to keep away. Taylor didn't mind. The students weren't a threat.

Gabriel waited outside as Taylor met Natalie in the hallway and entered the classroom. His eyes went to Mr. Hill first, who smiled at him, then he and Natalie sat down. The intrusive student from last class asked how he was doing and he smiled and gave a canned answer. That seemed to be the invitation to the other students because suddenly all of them were asking what had happened. It seemed like ages before Mr. Hill called the class to order and began his lecture.

Taylor doodled as he half-listened to the lecture. He still didn't understand what Mr. Hill was talking about, even though he knew the equation. The other students had lost looks on their faces as well. All except for Natalie, who took notes and paid attention as always. She was such a good student. He hoped the grades she made on these last few tests could raise her overall grade in the course. His own grade was pretty much determined; hers might be able to change.

He remembered when he had first bonded with Gabriel, before Gabriel took on his form, and how Gabriel had seduced him in the middle of the class. While he didn't want to be seduced again in public, he did wish his demon were in the class with him, able to talk to him without disturbing anyone else. It was rather lonely thinking of Gabriel waiting by himself outside, though it was unlikely he was alone. There were always a swarm of people around him peppering him with questions. He attracted more attention than Taylor, and luckily he didn't seem to mind. He was fairly critical of most people that they met, but he didn't mind being the center of attention. He had probably been the center of attention his entire life as the demon king's only son. Did the other demons flock to him the way the people did, looking for some sort of favor?

Callan wanted him. He wasn't entirely sure why the succubus was interested in Gabriel, since they couldn't feed off each other. Did the other demons gain favor with the demon king by befriending his son? That was what Samson wanted, it seemed. Having Gabriel here and treating him well meant that the demon king—and by extension all demons—would look more favorably on the campus. And the campus was then able to boast about the higher rates of bonding for its students. Natalie told him that everyone in their class bonded with a demon in their first season, and almost all of the upperclassmen had as well. That wasn't usually the case. Normally it was about sixty percent for the first year, then about half of the remaining students each progressive year.

Natalie suspected it had to do with Gabriel. The other demons went to the same place he did. He remembered the numerous succubi dancing around him the first night of the demon season as if trying to lure him from Gabriel. They all bonded to people nearby the way Callan had, and who knew what other demons were attracted to the same location as the prince of demons. It was a boon for the university. Would the numbers be the same every year he attended, or would it be different because Gabriel actively searched this demon season and now he was bonded? Only time would tell. He suspected the streak would continue. Otherwise Samson wouldn't be quite so eager to please.

Finally, Mr. Hill's rambling lecture drew to a close and Taylor put his notebook away as the students slowly came back to life. Class was dismissed and he waited for Natalie to put away her book before they headed out and met with a chaotic scene.

Chapter 23

Confrontation

A ring of students stood just outside the classroom, all of whom looked terrified, and Taylor and Natalie pushed to the center to see Gabriel facing three demon wolves, growling and clearly aggressive towards Gabriel. Gabriel appeared calm, holding one hand out as if to soothe them. Taylor started to push to his side but he shook his head sharply. One of the wolves also glared at Taylor and hunkered down, his growl more pronounced. Taylor shivered and backed into the ring of students. Natalie took his hand as Mr. Hill rushed up behind them.

"I understand your concerns," Gabriel said to the wolves in a polite voice. "But you know that's out of my control."

The wolves snarled. Then a blur of red emerged from the students and Callan stood between Gabriel and the wolves. She looked at them scornfully.

"In front of the humans? Really?"

The wolves glanced at each other, then at the crowd that had gathered. The one in the center let out a huff of air and the three wolves slunk away. Callan turned to Gabriel with a smile, as if expecting praise, but he just looked away.

"There was no need to interfere," he said softly.

"Then maybe I won't next time," she said with a sniff. He put his hand on her shoulder.

"Thanks, Callan."

She seemed pleased, then returned the way she had come. Taylor wondered how she knew that Gabriel was in trouble. She arrived pretty quickly. Could she travel as fast as Gabriel, or was that something only he could do? He wasn't sure. Gabriel turned his gaze to Taylor and extended his hand, and Taylor went to his side eagerly. The other students seemed confused and several of the female students glared as Gabriel swept him in a hug. Gabriel was studying someone in the crowd and when Taylor turned back, he saw Mr. Hill with a thoughtful expression on his face. Then Mr. Hill returned to his class and Gabriel pulled him towards his next class.

"I'll explain later," he said softly as Taylor slipped into Ms. Winde's class. Taylor hesitated, unsure if it was safe to leave Gabriel outside, but the demon gently pushed him into the classroom. He sat down and tried to pay attention, but it was hard. When they got into groups, one of the students from a different group came up to them as they moved around the room. He puzzled, since she was supposed to be somewhere else, but she blushed and spoke quietly.

"I'm sorry about Terran," she said. "I don't know what got into him. I thought he was with the others in the woods, where he usually is during class."

Taylor realized in surprise that one of the wolves must be her demon. That meant she had no clue what was going on, either, and hadn't directed the odd confrontation.

"It's fine," Taylor said, uncertain if it actually was fine. "I'm sure it's nothing."

She smiled uneasily and returned to her group. He glanced towards the door where Gabriel waited. Gabriel could sense when Taylor was in trouble; Taylor wished he could sense the same about his demon.

His group finished early, as his groups usually did, because he was prepared with answers, unlike most of the students. One of the guys in the group smiled at him.

"Your demon is a lot of trouble, isn't he?"

Taylor smiled weakly, not knowing how to respond. The student was probably fishing for information on today, or on what happened earlier with the frost, but he wasn't going to volunteer anything. He didn't like the slight against Gabriel, but he wasn't sure how to defend his demon without giving anything away. Gabriel *was* a lot of trouble, it was true. But he was completely worth it.

"It must be hard having a demon with a physical form," another student said. Her mark was red, but her demon must not have taken form. Most didn't, after all. It was fairly rare for a demon to be able to feed deeply enough to take on a body. He was still glad Natalie managed it.

A moment of silence as if they were waiting to see if he would respond, then the first guy shrugged.

"My demon has a form, but she never causes any trouble."

"What is she?" the girl asked, and the guy grinned.

"A hawk," he said proudly. "She can fly all over and keeps an eye on the campus while I'm at class."

"Then did you see what happened when-"

She paused and looked at Taylor. He knew what they meant and was curious. Had other demons seen what really happened? And if they had, did they share it with their humans? They seemed to keep a lot of secrets from humans. Gabriel seemed to keep fewer secrets than most, but he wondered if the others even knew how much they weren't being told. The equation couldn't be the only thing they were hiding.

"She was too far north," the guy said after a moment. "What did happen?"

They were looking at him again and he realized he had to say something. He glanced at Ms. Winde, hoping she would swoop in and rescue him with her usual flawless timing, but she was talking to another group. He was on his own. The girl leaned forward, clearly curious, and he considered. He wished he could ask Gabriel what he was supposed to say. Natalie said that everyone knew Gabriel was protecting him, but no one knew anything else. He didn't want to reveal that there were demon hunters after him. That might cause a panic, since demon hunters were widely feared and the students would think they were in danger. If they thought Gabriel was attracting that kind of attention, they might even leave the college. He didn't want that.

"I just got in some trouble," he said awkwardly. "It wasn't much. Gabriel overreacted. That's it."

"What kind of trouble?"

"Just minor trouble," he said. "Gabriel didn't really need to do what he did. We didn't expect anyone else to notice."

"He's really strong," the girl said in awe. "Is he really the son of the demon king?"

Taylor nodded, and she let out a sigh. "And he's really an incubus?"

The guy smirked and Taylor nodded again with a blush. It wasn't entirely true, he now knew, but it was close enough and besides, that was what everyone thought.

"You're so lucky," she said. "He's really handsome."

Taylor blushed further and luckily—finally—Ms. Winde appeared and asked if they were finished. Their groups broke up and they returned to a discussion with the entire class but the heat lingered in his cheeks. At least she hadn't asked him what he had done to give his demon his form. No one asked that yet, but he knew the assumption. To be fair, he made the same assumption about all of the succubi. He was at least pretty sure what Jordan and Callan had done.

But he and Gabriel hadn't gotten that far yet. They had gotten close. They'd had sex, of a sort. But Taylor still wasn't ready for everything. He wondered how much more powerful Gabriel would be if Taylor weren't so scared of intimacy. Was he weakening his demon? He shivered. He hoped not, but there wasn't much he could do about it. Now that Gabriel had his form, there was no changing it.

Ms. Winde ended the class after an interminable discussion that he barely paid attention to. She called on him once, for a question he should have known, but he wasn't paying attention and flubbed the answer. She paused, looking sympathetic, and moved on after correcting his response. She didn't call on him again. And then, finally, class was over and he rushed out to the hall.

Gabriel lounged against the wall, as usual, and a group of girls giggled around him. He ignored them. Taylor still wasn't sure why he talked to some people and ignored others. As everyone poured out of the classrooms, Gabriel strode to his side and took his hand, kissing it as Taylor's blush returned in full force. They headed to meet Natalie for dinner and Taylor was aware of the guards surrounding them, becoming more and more obvious as the crowd of students thinned.

"Natalie's running a little late," Gabriel said as they entered the apartment building. Neither of them felt comfortable eating in the cafeteria with everyone else and if the college didn't mind paying for their meals, Taylor wasn't going to complain. Gabriel had quickly mastered the new technology of the kitchen and decided to cook something for dinner today. Taylor was looking forward to it.

He dumped his bookbag by the door and collapsed on the couch. Gabriel locked the door and sat beside him, taking his hand and kissing it again. Taylor could feel the slight tug of him feeding.

"What happened today?" he asked. "One of the girls in my class apologized for it. Her demon was one of the wolves."

Gabriel sighed. "I'd hoped to avoid a public confrontation like that. For once, I'm glad for Callan."

"But what happened? Why were they acting so aggressive towards you? You're the demon prince."

"Exactly," Gabriel said, kissing his hand again. "And not everyone approves of me."

"They don't approve? That the demon king had a son?"

"You know I'm not like other demons," Gabriel said, and Taylor nodded impatiently. At some point, Gabriel was going to have to explain this in more detail because it was frustrating getting thrown the same line over and over again. Maybe tonight. "Well, not all demons want a demon as unusual as me."

Taylor softened, thinking of all of the obstacles Gabriel faced. He was limited in so many ways, and now the other demons didn't like him for that reason. His heart went out to Gabriel and he leaned over and kissed him.

"I'm sorry," he said.

A knock at the door and they both stood. Taylor let Natalie in, with Ariel at her feet, and Gabriel headed to the kitchen. Ariel trotted into the kitchen and leapt on the counter, watching Gabriel as he gathered the ingredients for spaghetti. What did Ariel think about Gabriel? She had to like him. She was too friendly for anything else. Callan liked Gabriel. And both Natalie and Jordan were friends with Taylor.

With a start, Taylor considered the people he had seen Gabriel talking to outside of the class. He had never understood Gabriel's criteria but he noticed that his demon generally favored the same people that Taylor did. Was Gabriel only interacting with people whose demons approved of him? And was there some correlation between the relationships between demons and the relationships between humans? Were the people that Taylor liked more likely to have demons that Gabriel liked? An interesting idea. Maybe he would ask about it, but he wasn't sure if Gabriel would answer. He should probably just observe and try to confirm the theory on his own.

"So what's for dinner?" Natalie asked, plopping onto the couch and looking over at the demons in the kitchen. It didn't seem like she was going to comment on what had happened earlier and he was grateful. Or maybe Ariel already explained it to her.

"I'm making you spaghetti," Gabriel said, hefting a bag of the noodles with a flourish. "I found a recipe online."

"You got used to things fast," she said as if in surprise, and Gabriel grinned and began chopping tomatoes. Was he going to make it from scratch? It looked like it, and Taylor was impressed. He and Natalie talked about their classes as Gabriel cooked and Ariel observed, and Taylor couldn't help but wonder if the two demons were having their own silent conversation while he and Natalie chatted. There were a lot of mysteries with demons, and it was becoming more and more apparent that they kept quite a few secrets from their humans. He just had to hope that Gabriel was honest with him, and that, perhaps, more would be explained in his dreams tonight.

Chapter 24

Lonely Day

Even though Taylor was looking forward to speaking to his demon in his dreams, he slept soundly and woke up about half an hour before his classes when he usually got up. Gabriel cradled him, his steady breathing brushing past his ear as he murmured and snuggled closer. If he wanted intimacy, he should have come to his dream, Taylor thought in annoyance. Or was Gabriel truly asleep and cuddling closer unconsciously? Did that mean Gabriel cared about him?

Gabriel opened his red eyes slowly, blinking away sleep, and Taylor's annoyance was replaced by a deep love. He felt a slight tug as Gabriel fed from him, probably from the intimacy of their embrace. He wasn't entirely sure what Gabriel fed on, but it wasn't necessarily when they were having sex or doing anything sexual. It was when they were close, intimate, and always seemed to be the times Taylor's feelings towards him were the warmest. But he knew Gabriel wouldn't tell him what he fed on. He would change the subject, as he had the one time Taylor asked and as Mr. Hill warned he would. For some reason, that knowledge was off-limits.

"Good morning," Gabriel said, making it almost a question as if he knew Taylor wasn't in the best of moods.

"I thought we'd talk last night," Taylor said. "Or do you think there's nothing to talk about?"

Gabriel kissed his cheek. "You needed rest. You were exhausted. You're not fully asleep when I control your dreams."

"You've never said anything about that before," Taylor said, still grumpy. But at least Gabriel wasn't trying to hide things; he was just trying to help him sleep better. Or that was what he said. What if this were just an excuse and Gabriel were keeping the real reason a secret, as demons seemed to keep so many secrets? Gabriel kissed him again.

"Is there anything I can do to improve your mood?"

"Not here," Taylor said, since Gabriel wouldn't talk openly outside of his dreams.

"I apologize," Gabriel said, and kissed him a third time. Taylor sighed. His kisses were sincere, at least. He would forgive the demon, and hopefully they could talk tonight. He did want to talk, and try to figure out what had happened with the demon wolves so that the situation didn't repeat itself. Why wouldn't other demons approve of Gabriel? And why had that one wolf growled at Taylor specifically when he had tried to go to Gabriel's side? Was he in danger because of whatever was happening between Gabriel and the other demons?

"You're safe," Gabriel said, and Taylor tried to believe it. At least Gabriel was reading his concerns and reassuring him. "What happened will not happen again, at least not where humans can see."

"But it will happen again?"

"Outside of your view? Probably," Gabriel acknowledged. "There's nothing I can do to stop it. This happens every time I take on a form. They're just making their displeasure known. It won't escalate into violence."

"It won't turn into a war?" Taylor asked, thinking of what Mr. Hill told him and what he remembered about the ancient war. Demon turned against demon, and demonborn were killed as a result.

"I don't want it to reach that point, and I'll try to prevent it."

177

Taylor turned to look at him. Gabriel's face was impassive, his red eyes glittering in the light coming in from the window. He didn't want a war, he would try to prevent it, but he wasn't ruling it out. Why couldn't he just say that there wouldn't be a war? Taylor shivered. Was a war coming? Would the other demons turn on Gabriel? What would happen then?

Gabriel kissed him yet again. "Please, don't worry about it," he said. "Anything that happens won't take place for a very long time. And don't tell anyone your worries and concerns. I shouldn't have said anything."

"You should have reassured me."

"You're not in a good mood, are you?" Gabriel said with a laugh. "I'm sorry. We'll talk tonight. No matter how much you need sleep. I promise."

Taylor grumped a little, but got up and started getting ready. He eyed Gabriel's gorgeous form as the demon dressed. They had showered together last night and the sight of that beautiful body was enticing, even though he had class soon and was still in a sour mood. He was getting more and more comfortable with his lustful impulses, but he couldn't satiate them right now. Too close to class time. He sighed as he dressed and brushed his teeth. Gabriel ran a hand through his hair playfully as Taylor shooed him off. He kept his hair like that, though. It did look good mussed. His mood was increasing rapidly, especially when Gabriel quickly whipped up some scrambled eggs with mushrooms, tomatoes, and jalapeños, his favorite. After breakfast, they headed out and were quickly surrounded by guards.

"Taylor, I need to talk to Samson today," Gabriel said. "I don't know how long it'll take. I probably can't be with you between your classes."

"That's fine," Taylor said, though he would miss seeing his demon during his lunch. He had an hour and a half between his classes today and he and Gabriel usually retreated to have lunch with Natalie. They would be on their own today. Still, he would rather be safe than have

Gabriel at his side every minute of every day. "The girls will be disappointed. They like seeing you."

Gabriel laughed. "Some of them are tolerable," he said, and Taylor wondered at his criteria once again. Maybe he would try to notice which girls looked the most upset that Gabriel wasn't there, and try to figure out who the demon was actually interacting with and who he was ignoring.

They reached the classroom and the bustle of students in the hall, and Gabriel took his hand and kissed it. Taylor wasn't comfortable with more public displays of affection and his demon knew it, but something this small brought only a flash of embarrassment.

"I'll see you soon," he promised, and Taylor nodded and entered the class.

Mr. Fischer was erasing the board and muttering about inconsiderate people. The teachers were supposed to erase the boards after each class, as his teachers were always careful to do, but not every teacher did it. Whoever taught immediately before this class almost never did, and Mr. Fischer was stuck erasing two boards full of tiny writing explaining the intricacies of biology. Taylor was glad he wasn't in that class. Not only was biology his least favorite subject, he would never be able to take notes from a teacher who wrote like that.

Taylor sat at the front of the room, as always, and could feel the eyes of the other students on him. They never worked in groups in this class and he was grateful, as he wouldn't have to deal with their questions. He got out his notebook and tried to ignore the creeping sensation on the back of his neck from their gazes. Two students entered and walked passed him, and one of them paused. She turned to face Taylor and he reluctantly looked up. It was the student from yesterday, the one whose wolf who had confronted Gabriel.

"Did your demon tell you anything else about what happened?" she asked.

"No," Taylor said, wishing he were lying. But it was true. Gabriel had told him almost nothing. "Did yours?"

"No," she said. "Sorry about that."

"It's not your fault," he assured her, and she and her friend went to their seats. Taylor could tell that the entire class had been listening to that conversation, limited though it was. Being the center of attention like this was exhausting. No wonder Gabriel had let him sleep.

Mr. Fischer got started and soon Taylor was busy taking notes on a tragic play he had read the night before. As Taylor took notes, his mind wandered. He should be paying attention, but his writing turned to doodles of geometric shapes and lines. Why couldn't Gabriel rule out a war? Was that a real possibility? Why was Gabriel so controversial to other demons?

Gabriel was going to find the right person and be free from a dependency on humans. He would find a person who could give him pleasure, a human who Taylor assumed he was capable of loving. A strong longing to be that person filled Taylor. He knew he was that person already. He loved Gabriel completely, so how could those feelings not be returned? But demons were incapable of love. The play they were studying today was about that very subject. It was a tragedy of a human who fell in love with her demon, and ended with her killing herself in an effort to prove her love and the demon turning away from her coldly. There were all sorts of plays like this, and poetry on this topic. Humans always wanted their love returned, and it never was. Why would Taylor's love be any different?

Because Gabriel was different, he thought wistfully. His love was different because his demon wasn't like the others. The other demons treated him differently, and some even seemed to hate or resent him. Maybe they resented the fact that he might someday be free of humans. Maybe what he was interpreting as aggression was actually jealousy. Taylor rested his chin on his hand and stared at the circles and stripes he had started drawing on the edge of his page. He heard movement around him and looked up in surprise. Everyone was leaving.

Taylor realized class was over. He slowly got his things together. He could take his time, since Gabriel wouldn't be waiting for him. Mr. Fischer was also packing up his bags and when everyone else had left, he smiled at Taylor.

"Were you paying attention at all?"

Taylor flushed. "I did the reading," he said, though he knew it was disrespectful not to listen even if he had prepared in advance.

"Did you learn anything from it?"

Taylor was puzzled, and Mr. Fischer sighed.

"People bonded to succubi and incubi tend to fall in love with their demons more than any other group," he said. "We were talking about the dangers of mistaking need for love. Watch out for that, Taylor. Your demon can never love you, no matter what you want. He's only doing what it takes to make it easier to feed."

Taylor's cheeks burned as he ducked his head and slung his bag over his shoulder.

"I know," he said, though a deep part of him disagreed deeply with that statement. Gabriel was different. Someday, if Taylor were the right person, Gabriel would be able to love him. He wouldn't end up like the woman in the play. He wouldn't kill himself to try to earn his demon's love. He would earn Gabriel's love without dying, because someday, he knew that Gabriel would love him.

Chapter 25

Unhelpful

"You're so quiet," Natalie said, spinning her fork in the spaghetti skillfully. Gabriel overdid his cooking and they would have leftovers for days. Luckily, it was spectacularly delicious so he didn't mind, and Natalie was happy to help.

"There's just a lot going on," Taylor said, and Natalie smiled sympathetically.

"Anything you want to talk about?"

Taylor glanced at Ariel, sitting on the couch cleaning her claws. Ariel wasn't looking at them, but her ears were angled towards them. She was paying attention, and he didn't really want to talk to Natalie with another demon nearby. Natalie followed his gaze and her brow creased.

"Should I ask Ariel to leave?"

"No, it's not important," Taylor said, though he did want to talk to Natalie alone. Ariel was far less intrusive than Gabriel, but he missed being alone with his best friend. He hadn't seen Natalie without a demon nearby a single time since they had bonded to their demons. Well, there was class, but that was different. He missed the privacy of their friendship.

Ariel stopped licking her paw abruptly and hopped off the couch. She trotted into the bedroom and batted the door shut behind her. She might still be able to hear them, since she was a cat and cats had good hearing, but at least there was an illusion of privacy.

"Is that better?" Natalie asked. "She's so much a part of me now, I almost don't notice that she's always around. I didn't know it bothered you."

"It doesn't," Taylor said, unsure how to explain. "It's just, I feel like I never get you alone anymore."

"You're always with Gabriel," she pointed out with a laugh. "I'm not the only one who spends all their time with their demon."

"I know," Taylor said. "He's part of the problem, too."

Her laugh faded. "He's a problem?"

"I just mean I can't be alone anymore," Taylor said quickly. "He's not a problem."

"So what's going on?"

She propped her chin on her hands and turned all of her attention to him. He sighed. This was what he had wanted—a chance to talk to Natalie privately—but now he didn't know what to say. There was so much he wanted to say, but he felt almost out of practice sharing with people. He shared a lot with Gabriel, but much of that was unintentional. Gabriel could read his mind; it wasn't like Taylor told him things. But he wasn't sure what to share, especially since there was a chance Ariel could hear and might relay it back to Gabriel.

"It's just different than I thought it would be," Taylor said. "Having a demon, I mean. I don't know what I was expecting, but not this."

"You did end up in an unusual situation," Natalie said. "I never thought you'd end up with an incubus. Or a succubus. You're the last person I would ever pick for that."

Taylor blushed. "Yeah. That's been... weird. We haven't really, well, I know everyone assumes... but we haven't."

Natalie's eyes widened. "How did he take form?"

Taylor sighed. So Natalie thought he and Gabriel already had sex too? He felt almost betrayed. She should have known him well enough

183

to know that he wasn't the type to jump in bed with anyone, let alone another man. Even if he were an incubus.

"I did think it was odd," she continued. "But he's an incubus. I guess I just assumed. I'm sorry."

"Everyone assumes."

"He's not pressuring you or anything, is he?" Natalie asked, still looking puzzled. "I don't know why a demon would go against his human's wishes, but he's kind to you, isn't he?"

"He's wonderful," Taylor said, thinking of when Gabriel held him after learning about Yolette. Gabriel had started the long, difficult process of healing from those wounds and only he could have done it. Without Gabriel, Taylor would still be trapped in his past.

"I guess that's a problem, too," he admitted. "I'm in love with him."

Natalie drew in a sharp breath.

"Taylor, you know demons can't feel love," she said. "You can't fall in love with one. I know he's the first person you've been in a relationship like this with, but he's not human. Your relationship isn't like a human relationship."

"I know that," Taylor said, his heart sinking. "But what if it's different? What if we're different?"

"You're not," Natalie said firmly. "Don't you know how dangerous this is? That's rule number one of being demonborn: you don't fall in love with your demon."

"It's not like I'm going to do anything," Taylor said. "And I can't help the way I feel."

"A boyfriend," Natalie said, perking up. "You need a boyfriend. You need a real relationship with a human so you can see how it's different."

"I don't want a boyfriend," Taylor said. The sense of betrayal grew. "I have Gabriel."

"Men with succubi have relationships all the time," Natalie pointed out. "And you've never been in a relationship before. You really need to know what it's like, so you can-"

"No," Taylor said, cutting her off as he set his fork down forcefully. Natalie froze, startled. "I don't want a boyfriend. I can barely handle Gabriel. You think adding another relationship is going to help?"

"I guess that might backfire," Natalie said slowly. "But you have to do something. You can't love a demon."

Taylor sighed and scooped up some noodles and sauce. He'd hoped to get some comfort out of this conversation, maybe some sympathy, maybe some good advice, but Natalie went straight to the typical demonborn solutions. In love with your demon? Find a human to take their place. But he didn't want that. He wanted Gabriel, not some human. And Gabriel would be able to love him eventually; he knew it. But he couldn't tell Natalie about it without revealing Gabriel's secrets, and he would never do that.

There was a whirring sound from his bookbag and Taylor blinked. His phone. Who would be calling him? He went to his bag and dug out the phone. It was Gabriel. He could probably sense Taylor's distress. Taylor sighed, but picked up.

"Hey," he said.

"Do you need me?"

It was such a simple question but implied so much concern.

"No," Taylor said. "Just having lunch with Natalie."

There was a pause, as if he were trying to figure out how having lunch with his best friend would put him in a bad mood. Well, Taylor had been in a bad mood since waking up. Nothing was going well today. He kept looking for something, some comfort, some truth, and everyone else kept coming up short. Including Gabriel.

"Call me anytime," Gabriel said slowly.

"I will," Taylor promised. "Bye."

He hung up and returned to the table. Natalie's cheeks tinted pink and her eyes cast down.

"I'm sorry, Taylor," she said. "I just don't know how to talk about this. I guess I don't even understand how it can happen, but I suppose if Ariel were an incubus, if I had a type of relationship like that, maybe I could see why I might love her."

"It's fine," Taylor said, returning to his spaghetti as she slowly did the same. "I know it's wrong. I know what I'm supposed to do."

"Probably doesn't help, though, does it?"

"No," he said softly. Because even though he knew Gabriel didn't love him, there was that note of genuine care when he had asked if Taylor needed him. Even over the phone, the emotion was clear. How was that any different than love?

"Plus, now there're guards everywhere we go," Taylor said, deciding to completely shift the conversation. "Gabriel's talking to the president right now. I'm hoping we don't have to be followed for long, but I also don't want to get attacked again. I don't know what I want."

"Yeah, your life really has changed," Natalie said. "But that's not necessarily bad. It's just different. You'll work something out that you're happy about, and you'll get used to your new life. I know it. You'll be happy again soon."

"Again?" he asked sarcastically, and she laughed.

"Well, not as moody as you are right now," she said, because they both knew Taylor had never been a cheerful, happy-go-lucky person in his entire life. He was good at pretending to be fine, but Natalie knew him well enough to know that he suffered from bouts of depression and had self-esteem issues. She did, too, though he noticed her mood and esteem had improved considerably after bonding with Ariel. He hadn't changed the same way, and he couldn't help but be jealous. But he would get there. He munched on the spaghetti and nodded to himself. He would adapt to this new life. And eventually, Gabriel would love him.

"We should probably head to class," Natalie said after they finished. She went to the bedroom door and let Ariel back in, and Taylor blushed. He forgot that they kicked Ariel out. But the demon didn't seem to mind, trotting to the door and looking back as if impatient to leave.

"We're going," Natalie murmured as she pulled her shoes back on and slung her bag over her shoulder. Taylor followed suit and they headed back out to campus.

Rain drizzled down as they left, with a thick fog rolling in. The guards stayed closer than usual and Taylor was extremely aware of the men and women flanking him. He smiled at the closest woman cautiously, wondering if he were allowed to talk to them, but she just stared at him impassively. Apparently not. It was weird being surrounded by people and not even knowing who they were. Did most people know the people protecting them? That was the impression he had always gotten from books and movies, which always featured relationships forming between bodyguard and protectee. No chance of that happening here.

They reached campus and there was a buzz in the hall. Natalie's class didn't start yet, so she walked Taylor to his. There were several students gathered around his door, looking delighted. Taylor approached and saw the sign on the door. Class was canceled. He got out his phone and checked, and yes, Ms. Salazar had canceled class and sent out an online assignment instead. He sighed.

"Now what?" He didn't always like being in class, but he liked the structure. And he was already here, ready to go.

"I'm headed to the library," Natalie offered. "Gabriel's still busy?"

"I think," Taylor said. "Let's go to the library. It shouldn't be too bad, right?"

Natalie's brow creased, then she looked around. While many of the students were looking at the note on the door, most were looking at Taylor and clearly curious about what he was going to do next. He'd been avoiding public places like the cafeteria and the library, but maybe he would risk it.

"We can get a private study room," Natalie said. "Come on."

"Sure," Taylor said cautiously. "It's worth a try. I just hope we get something done."

"We will," Natalie said optimistically, and while he didn't share her optimism, at least heading to the library would give him a place to finish the online assignment so he could focus on his demon when Gabriel returned. They headed down the road to the library, flanked by bodyguards in the drizzling rain.

Chapter 26

Heavy Rain

The rain fell hard as they walked to the library huddled under their umbrellas. It was difficult to see; the sky was washed white with rain and there was a mist as the raindrops bounced off the ground. Taylor could hardly see where they were going and was grateful for the guards guiding them. He glanced over at Natalie.

"This is a mess," he said. "Should we just go home?"

"I think we're almost there," she said. "Easier to just keep going. The rain can't last, right?"

So Taylor lowered his head and tugged his jacket tighter. His shoes and the bottoms of his jeans were soaked, but she was right. Rain like this never lasted long and they were probably past the midpoint. Unfortunately, the library wasn't near any of the other buildings and there weren't any other places they could duck inside. The only good part of the rain was that the other students probably hadn't followed them. Of course, there were probably also a ton of students waiting in the library for the storm to pass, so they would still get stuck in a crowd. Taylor sighed. There was no way to win.

They kept walking through the blinding rain, Taylor's eyes fixed on the ground. He was vaguely aware of the guards around them, but he was really only paying attention to Natalie in front of him. Minutes passed, and finally he looked up with a frown. How far was the library? He didn't go there often, but surely they had arrived by now. He took a few steps forward to match Natalie and glanced over at her. Her eyes were fixed on the ground, as his had been.

"How far is it, do you think?" he asked.

Natalie jolted.

"Oh," she said. "I guess the rain is really slowing us down. I haven't been paying attention to where we're going, to be honest. I figured those guys knew where they were going."

She gestured to the vague shapes around them. They were the ones leading the way, after all, since they had them surrounded. And the guards knew they were headed to the library, didn't they? Where else would they go in the middle of nowhere? The library was pretty far from the rest of campus, after all, and bordered on the forest. The forest was dangerous; that was where Taylor had been attacked. But maybe the guards weren't leading them in the right place. Safest to check.

Taylor sped up until he could tug the jacket of the bodyguard leading them. He turned back and Taylor's brow creased. He could have sworn it was a woman leading them. But maybe they shifted positions in the rain.

"Are we near the library?" he asked. The rain dripped down the umbrella so thick it was hard to make out the man's face, but it looked like he smiled.

"Almost there," he said, and Taylor retreated to walk with Natalie and shared the news. The rain really had slowed them down, because in good weather they could have gotten to the library and back in this time.

They kept walking, and after a few more minutes, Taylor turned to examine the area. This didn't look familiar, but the guard said they were almost there. What was going on? He glanced at Natalie. Her eyes were down, as they had been before, and she looked lost in thought. He elbowed her and she jolted again.

"You okay?"

"Yeah," she said. "Sorry. I was just talking to Ariel. She's curled up at the dorm all nice and cozy, trying to make me feel better about being out here in the rain."

"This is weird rain, isn't it?"

"Yeah, it's never lasted this long before. I heard some demons can affect the weather," she added. "Maybe that's happening."

Taylor fell silent. He'd heard that, too, and it was one reason the campus tended to be sunny, but why would a demon want it raining so hard it was impossible to see straight? It still didn't look familiar. There were looming shapes all around them but it looked more like trees than the library. Had they gotten turned around and ended up in the forest? He stepped forward and tugged the man's sleeve again.

The man turned and grabbed his hand, startling him. He noticed another guard taking Natalie's arm, and then the man stabbed something into her arm. Taylor was too shocked to react as the guard slammed a needle into his shoulder and stinging pain throbbed at the injection site. He yanked away and looked to Natalie, who was also wrestling off the guard.

"Keep them moving," said one of the other guards, and two men grabbed Taylor and started moving forward at a jog. Natalie was right behind.

"What's going on?" Taylor managed to ask. He felt fine. The needle stung, but why had they done it? It didn't hurt anymore, and it didn't seem like they'd done anything. Was this supposed to protect him somehow? The guards were there for protection, weren't they? What else would be happening? His thoughts were slowing, somehow. It was hard to think about what was going on and why he was now being almost dragged into what had to be the forest, because they were nowhere near the library.

He remembered the men attacking him in the forest. They had somehow gotten past the bodyguards, hadn't they? Or was it that they had been bribed? A shiver ran down his spine. If the bodyguards weren't helping him, and were taking him into the forest where he had been attacked, then were they working for Yolette?

"Natalie," he said, trying to shout but his voice felt weak. Had they drugged him somehow? Had they drugged Natalie? Where were they taking them? Terror swept through him and he tried to reach out to Gabriel, to let Gabriel know he was in danger and needed help. Gabriel could get here quickly. Maybe not instantly, but he would be here soon.

The rain stopped abruptly and the sudden sunlight briefly blinded him as they stumbled out of the storm into bright light. It was definitely demon-made rain, then. The guards pulled him to a stop and he struggled to stay on his feet. There was a figure in front of him in a heavy rain jacket and it turned as they approached. The figure pulled the hood down and Taylor's heart turned to ice. It was Yolette.

She smirked as he stared at her in absolute terror and disbelief. Where was Gabriel? Why wasn't he here yet? Gabriel was supposed to protect him from her, where was he?

"Hello again, Taylor," she said in that voice that had crept through his nightmares for years. "Who is your friend?"

"Who the hell are you?" Natalie demanded, shoving off the guards holding her and taking an aggressive step forward.

Yolette smiled. "An old friend of Taylor's. You remember me, don't you, Taylor?"

He wished she would stop saying his name. He remembered her saying his name as a child when she coaxed him, instructed him, taught him to do things he didn't want to do. He couldn't move, couldn't speak. But Gabriel would be here soon. Gabriel would protect him.

"I knew you were trouble the moment I laid eyes on your mark," she said. "You may not have known your destiny, but I did. I'm surprised the incubus still wanted you after what I did."

Taylor shivered. So she *had* abused him as a child to try to make him unable to bond with Gabriel. Gabriel suggested it and Taylor considered it, but didn't want to acknowledge that it might be true. Because it almost had turned Taylor away. Oh, Taylor still would have bonded with Gabriel. But he might not have strengthened their bond enough to let Gabriel take form. If Taylor hadn't been willing to confess what Yolette had done to him, Gabriel wouldn't have been able to start the healing process and without that, he wouldn't have been able to get close enough to give his demon form. They still would have ended up bonded, but Gabriel had almost lost his form because of this woman, and she had done it deliberately.

It also stung to know that the abuse he had suffered as a child wasn't even directed at him. He suffered and felt shame and humiliation at her hands, and she hadn't even cared about him. He wasn't the one she was even thinking of when she hurt him. He wasn't sure why that stung so much, but he could feel a heavy, scratchy feeling in his eyes that usually preceded tears. He wanted to hide somewhere and cry, but he was in the open and exposed.

"Your demon has haunted this world for a thousand years," Yolette continued. "My family has hurt him before, but it's never been enough to kill him. This time, though, I know his weakness. This time, I will kill him."

She reached into the pocket of her heavy jacket and pulled out a gun. The blood drained from his face, from his body. He went stock still as she hefted the weapon.

"My family has been working on this for quite a while," she said. "The bullets are designed to poison and kill demons. Now I just need a way to keep him in place."

She pointed the gun at Taylor and smiled.

"Can you think of anything? Any way to keep him in place long enough for me to shoot him?"

"No," Taylor whispered. It was an answer and a plea. This could not be happening. Where was Gabriel? Did he even want Gabriel here right now, when Gabriel might be killed? Where was he, and would he know to stay away?

"I know what will keep him there, but he has to be close first," she said. "Unfortunately, we had to give you something to hide your location to get you here."

She gestured to one of the guards, who grabbed Taylor's arm.

Taylor flinched. He thought of the needle. Was that what it had done? It had blocked Gabriel's ability to find him? That was dangerous.

"Don't worry," she said with a smirk. "He'll know where you are soon enough. It should take him two minutes to get here, and I'll have a gift waiting for him when he arrives."

"No," Taylor repeated weakly.

"What the hell?" Natalie asked, and he saw that a guard had grabbed her as well and she was fighting him off. That was what he needed to be doing, Taylor realized. Not just standing here passively, he needed to be fighting.

Abruptly, he yanked away from the guard and ran towards Natalie. Or tried to. Three guards moved to block him and he punched one, struggling to get past and get out of here. They grabbed him easily and hauled him back in front of Yolette, who laughed cruelly. She gestured to one of the guards, who pulled out another needle and before Taylor could react, plunged it into his shoulder again. He winced and pulled away. The guards released him and he was dizzy for a moment.

"Two minutes," Yolette said, glancing at her wrist. "Are you going to try to run? That might make it more interesting."

"Run, Taylor," Natalie called.

Taylor turned to run, but he was surrounded by guards. He dashed forward, hoping to dart between them, but they moved to block him instantly and he ran into them hard. They shoved him back and he turned and tried to run the other way, but again he was blocked. Tears filled his eyes. He was helpless. Just like when he was a child. His weakness was on display as she watched coldly, the same way she had watched him struggle to obey her. And he was obeying her even now. He was running away at her command. He straightened and turned to face her. He would not be her pawn anymore.

The guards backed away and Yolette raised her gun. He glared at her. She wasn't going to shoot him, just threaten him, and he was done being threatened.

"Ten," she said. "Nine."

She continued counting down and he glanced around in confusion.

Was she counting down to when Gabriel arrived, and then she would shoot the demon? But how would she know where he would arrive? Did she think he would show up between Taylor and the gun? Surely Gabriel would know Taylor wasn't the target and not make himself such an easy target.

"One."

There was a crack and Taylor's eyes widened. The gun was pointed straight at him. He barely had time to think before something blasted through his side, burying into his belly. He dropped to his knees and heard Natalie screaming. Yolette... shot him? But why? And where was Gabriel?

He fell onto his back, stunned. He must be in shock because while his side hurt, he knew it would get a lot worse as soon as his body figured out what had just happened. He took a gasping breath and flinched as his side convulsed. A blur in front of him, and suddenly Gabriel was crouching over him, panic filling those beloved crimson eyes. A way to keep Gabriel in place. He gasped as he realized what Yolette meant. Gabriel was focused on him, on the bullet wound, and not on Yolette. He was completely vulnerable and didn't even realize it. But as he tried to speak, to warn his demon, to do anything, his mouth filled with blood and he found he couldn't even move. He was too weak. He had always been too weak. Tears filled his eyes and the shame of failure rose over him.

Chapter 27

In Flames

"Taylor," Gabriel cried, grabbing him as he fell. Yolette smirked.

"I've got you now," she hissed.

The pain was crippling as Taylor gasped for breath. The bullet had passed through his belly and Gabriel was pressing his hand against the wound, but it was too late. Natalie took a step forward as if to help him, but Yolette pointed her gun at her and she paled. Tears streamed down Gabriel's cheeks and Taylor reached up to cradle his face with wavering hands. He never thought that his demon would be so distraught. Did Gabriel love him, or would he react this way to losing any partner? No, he thought. No, this was different. Gabriel loved him, and he loved Gabriel. He would do anything for Gabriel.

A click and Taylor's eyes widened. Yolette had the gun pointed at Gabriel and the demon seemed too upset by Taylor to even notice. He heard the blast of gunfire and grabbed Gabriel, trying to drag him down and out of the way, but it was too late. He shut his eyes, unwilling to see the bullet piece his beloved demon's body, and suddenly everything went still. The sobs of Natalie stopped abruptly and there was only silence. Was Gabriel moving them out of the way faster than sound?

He peeked his eyes open and saw darkness around him. There was no pain, he realized with a start. He opened his eyes.

Gabriel knelt beside him in his true form and he clutched his demon. But Gabriel felt wrong, unfamiliar, and he backed away in fear. The demon smiled.

"Do not be afraid, human," he said, and his voice was similar to Gabriel's but definitely not his.

"Who are you?" Taylor whispered. "Why are you pretending to be Gabriel?"

The demon laughed. "He does look like me, doesn't he?"

Taylor drew in a sharp breath. Gabriel looked like this demon, not the other way around? There was only one demon Gabriel looked like. The demon king. He stared at the demon, now noticing that the horns were longer and more elaborately curled, and a long tail escaped from beneath his glorious wings. But why was the demon king here? Where was Gabriel?

"Gabriel?" he asked. "Where is he?"

"He's about to die," the demon king said.

"No," Taylor cried, reaching out to grab the demon king's arm. The king drew back and Taylor snatched his hand away, frightened that he had grabbed the demon king but unwilling to believe the words.

"No," he repeated. "I'll take the bullet for him. Let me die for him. Please. He can't die."

"You would give your life for him?" the demon king asked softly, with an undercurrent of longing. "Would you sacrifice everything for him? Not just your body, but your soul as well? Would you become his, in every way, to save his life?"

"Yes," Taylor said. Maybe he should think about this, but he didn't need to. All of that was already true. He was Gabriel's, body and soul, and he would sacrifice whatever he needed to sacrifice to save his life. "I don't care," he added. "Let me save him."

"If you give your soul to him, he will survive," the demon king said, and Taylor grabbed his arm again, not caring about who this was. The king didn't pull away this time.

"Yes," he said. "What do I have to do?"

"It will hurt," the king warned.

"I don't care."

The king nodded, a pleased smile lingering on his lips. Did he perhaps feed on pain? No one knew anything about the demon king except that he was free of humans. Gabriel would still be reliant, he thought with a pang. He knew in his heart that he was the one Gabriel was looking for, the one who could unlock his love, but Gabriel had never seen it. Gabriel would still be tied to humans and would move on from him. He would find another partner and continue his endless search. But it didn't matter. He would be alive. Taylor would do anything to keep his demon alive. He might die, and he might lose his soul, but he couldn't let Gabriel die.

The king helped him to his feet and Taylor shivered. What was involved in losing his soul? He was afraid of the pain, but he would do it. The demon king held out his hand and Taylor hesitated before taking it.

"You promise that Gabriel will survive?"

"If you sacrifice your soul, he will survive," the king affirmed, and Taylor took a deep breath and put his hand in the demon's.

The king yanked him forward into an embrace, wrapping his arms around Taylor to trap him and then wrapping his wings around them. When Gabriel did this, Taylor felt cocooned and safe. He loved it. But here, in the grip of an unknown demon knowing his soul was about to be painfully ripped away, it terrified him. As the wings brushed against his back, stirrings of fire sparked. Everywhere the wings touched, pain lanced through him and he screamed in surprise. It seemed as though his entire body filled with agony and he writhed against the king but the demon's grip was too tight.

But he didn't want to escape. This would save Gabriel. He bit his lip and tasted copper blood as a wave of pain cascaded through him, crashing against every nerve and setting it aflame. He wanted to faint, to lose consciousness, anything to get away from the fire scraping against his mind and chipping away at his control, but he couldn't. The pain was too much for his mind to fade. He was trapped. The pain. All he could think about was the pain.

Gabriel, he desperately reminded himself. He wanted to beg for mercy, to beg for it to stop, but he had to do this to save Gabriel. There was no other way for his demon to survive.

The pain somehow intensified and he screamed again, his body rebelling against his control to shove against the king and try to escape the wings that crashed against his skin, but his mind held firm. He wouldn't survive this. He was going to die. Maybe he would be like this for all eternity. Maybe this was his hell and he would have to suffer this forever in order for his demon to live. He would do it. His body shuddered helplessly and his throat felt like it was being ripped out from the screaming, but he accepted it.

Acceptance didn't help, didn't ease the pain or make it more manageable, and his tears evaporated as they hit his enflamed skin. How long before he went insane from the pain? How much time had passed? Was he even aware of time passing? Had minutes passed? Years? Would he ever lose his ability to feel every flicker of the wings this intensely?

And then other arms were holding him, other wings stroking him, and they held no fire. He still screamed, his body still burning, and something essential ripped out of him and entered the figure holding him. A shadow tore itself from his mind, severing the link between him and his soul, and then the pain overwhelmed him again and he screamed.

But the pain wasn't increasing, he realized with shock. Now that the shadow had torn away, it was fading. The wings were cool against his skin, and he realized the figure was kissing his face. The lips brought desperately need relief from the fire. He tried to open his eyes and after struggling with the pain, he managed it.

Gabriel. It was Gabriel holding him. He was changed, though. The demon's eyes were black, like the demon king's eyes. Black. They weren't bonded anymore. Terror wracked his body as he realized that there was nothing connecting him to his beloved demon anymore, but he tried to calm himself. Gabriel was alive. That was all that mattered. It didn't matter that their bond was shattered, that nothing lay between them.

They were still in the darkness, not the real world, he realized. His screams stilled to whimpers and Gabriel was saying something, but the rushing in his ears was too loud. He saw other shapes out of the corner of his eye and realized there were other demons nearby, in mostly human form. Many had wings, some had horns, and all had black eyes. Was this really a dream of his? Why would he imagine this? But it had to be a dream, because it wasn't the real world and Gabriel was holding him. Had the pain addled his mind and he was imagining his beloved demon holding him?

Taylor took a shuddering breath as the pain continued to lessen. His body ached and felt like cooling embers, and there was an emptiness in his heart. Gabriel wasn't his anymore.

"Taylor," he heard, and realized that Gabriel was repeating his name.

"Gabriel," he whispered, voice hoarse from screaming.

Gabriel beamed and kissed him, and the pressure of those lips on his eased the ache in his heart. Gabriel wasn't his, but there had to be some affection between them.

"Taylor," he whispered. "You did it. You're the one I've been waiting for."

Taylor blinked in surprise. This had to be a hallucination from the pain. Gabriel stroked his cheek.

"I love you, Taylor."

Chapter 28

A Different Realm

Taylor's heart sang at the pronouncement of love from Gabriel, and the words washed through him and soothed even the memory of pain from his body and mind. Gabriel loved him. He wrapped his arms around Gabriel's neck.

"I love you, Gabriel," he whispered.

Gabriel slowly lowered his wings and folded them behind his back. There were many other demons around them. Where were they?

"You're alive, right?" he asked, remembering the demon king's words and suddenly fearing that Gabriel had been killed and this was some sort of strange afterlife.

"Not yet, but I will be," Gabriel said. "You will be, too."

"I was shot," Taylor pointed out. "So were you."

"No," Gabriel said firmly. "You were shot, but you'll recover. I wasn't shot. Not yet. And now, I have the strength to avoid it and take out the one who threatens us."

"But where are we? Why aren't you doing that?"

Gabriel pushed him back and gestured around them.

"This is the realm of demons," he said. "Only one human has been here before, and he was too weak to survive. You were wounded, but still have strength. Thank you," he added softly. "Thank you for being true to me. I will always be true to you."

Taylor's mind whirled and he looked at the demons around him. That did explain why their eyes were black. If they were in the realm of demons, then these were all the demons who weren't bonded with anyone. He had only seen bonded demons before. But why were Gabriel's eyes black? If he was the one Gabriel had been looking for, why weren't they still bonded?

The answer dawned on him slowly. Gabriel had said that once he found that person, he wouldn't be dependent on humans anymore. They wouldn't be bonded, but Gabriel would choose to stay with him. Many things would happen, Gabriel warned, that would impact Taylor as well as Gabriel. Obviously their bond was gone and Gabriel still wanted him, but what was going on? How was he possibly in the realm of demons? Humans couldn't survive there. No one besides a demon could exist in that realm. This had to be a dream. This had to be some hallucination from the pain. If it was, he was grateful. This was everything he had ever wanted.

"I'm sorry, Taylor," Gabriel said softly, and Taylor tensed, knowing he was about to be plunged back into the pain and this mercy taken away from him. "You're no longer human."

Taylor frowned.

"What do you mean?"

"You sacrificed your soul for me," Gabriel said. "Humans can't exist without a soul."

Taylor touched his chest, looking down at himself. He looked exactly the same. But he was in the realm of demons. Perhaps he was trapped here now. Gabriel would live, and so would he, but he would be eternally trapped in this realm. He would never see the real world again, never see his mother or Natalie or all of the people he cared about. He would never even see the people he hated.

"I can't read your mind anymore," Gabriel said, stroking his cheek. "But you're safe. We won't be here long."

"I'm really confused," Taylor admitted. "What happened?"

Gabriel took his hand and squeezed it. The other demons were drawing closer and he tensed.

"You gave your soul to me," Gabriel said. "Now I'm complete. I told you what I was looking for, and you gave it to me. I wanted it to be you so badly, but I couldn't demand your soul. You had to give it freely, and prove your devotion by surviving the transition to this realm."

Taylor shivered at the memory of the pain of that transition.

"There are so many things we need to do, but we can't stay here long," Gabriel said. "We need to return to the human world. I need to dodge that bullet and save your life. I would never be able to live with myself if I let you die now. I don't know how my father lives."

"Your father?" Taylor asked, puzzled. "I saw him. He's the one who-"

"Yes," Gabriel said sadly. "He held his own human the same way and his human survived into this realm, but his body was so badly damaged that when they returned, the human died. He was unable to fully join with his human, and all of demonkind lost our hope until I was created. With you, we have another chance."

"Another chance for what?"

Gabriel placed his finger on Taylor's lips.

"You will learn in time, after we return. For now, you must hold on to hope. Your body is weak in the human world, but you will survive. Hold on to that. Believe that. Can you do it?"

"I would do anything for you," Taylor whispered.

"I know," Gabriel said with a hint of regret, and Taylor wondered if perhaps he didn't want Taylor's love. No, that couldn't be it. Gabriel shut his eyes. "I wish it could have been easier for you. And things won't be the same for you when you return. You aren't human anymore."

"What does that mean? Am I a demon now?"

Gabriel's lips curled upward. "Perhaps. It's never happened before. I guess we'll have to see. But first, you must survive. Are you ready?"

Taylor took a deep breath. The demons around him looked oddly hopeful, and almost desperate. They wanted him to survive. He wondered about the demon king. This had happened to him, too, then. His human must have given his soul to the king and that was how he could survive without humans, but his human died. Taylor would not let that happen to Gabriel. He could tell that Gabriel was free now—his black eyes said as much—and he wouldn't doom Gabriel to live alone forever. What good was immortality if your love died? He was afraid of what would happen to him, but he would stay at Gabriel's side and as long as he had his demon, he could face anything.

"I'm ready," he said with as much confidence as he could muster, and Gabriel enfolded him in his wings once again.

Taylor nearly screamed as he felt the bullet tearing through his belly and the pain returned abruptly. Something rushed past him too quick to see and he heard a thud as a bullet smashed into the wall behind him.

"Damn it," Yolette muttered.

Taylor opened his eyes to see Gabriel's back as the demon blocked him from Yolette's gaze. Gabriel was unharmed but Yolette was smirking.

"You can't dodge forever," she said. "Should I shoot him again to keep you in place?"

"You won't be shooting anyone," Gabriel said.

He heard Natalie gasp, and then Yolette's eyes widened.

"Your eyes," she said in shock. She looked at Taylor. "But he's still alive. How are you here?"

"How do you think?" he asked in a low voice. "Everything that you and your kind fear is coming. The end of the regular order. The end of the demon hunters. The end of you."

Yolette laughed, but she sounded scared. "My family has always been here to fight you, and we always will. Even if you kill me, there will be others. There will always be others, and we will always destroy you and your kind."

Gabriel raised his hand to point at her. It was difficult to see from Taylor's position on the floor, but he thought Gabriel grinned. The pain was making it hard to think and unlike with the demonic pain earlier, this time he could feel blackness edging his consciousness. But he could tell that if he let himself sink into that darkness now, he would never wake up. He had to survive for Gabriel.

"This is for what you did to Taylor," Gabriel said. "Goodbye, Yolette."

Taylor stiffened as a beam of light sparked from Gabriel's hand. He shut his eyes quickly but the afterimage burned his retinas. It was fire, exactly like the fire he felt in the demon king's arms. He heard a scream, an agonized, terrified scream, and knew that Yolette was feeling the fire he had felt for what seemed like an eternity while the demon king's wings scorched his skin. The scream cut off abruptly and there was a thump. Taylor tried to open his eyes but he was still blinded. He heard Gabriel curse.

"Natalie, give me your phone," he said.

Taylor heard agreement and then a shuffle. He heard Gabriel's voice asking for emergency first aid to their location, as soon as possible. Then arms were around him, a hand pressing at his belly again, Gabriel whispering for him to hold on. He could feel Gabriel's love pouring into him and it soothed him and gave him strength. It drove the darkness away just enough for him to hold on. Minutes passed as Gabriel's love formed a chain between them. He clung to that love as he struggled to keep from the inky blackness lurking beneath him. He knew without question that he would die if he slipped and fell, and he felt as if he were dangling over a cliff with only a thin rope holding him up. He could tell Gabriel was trying to make that rope stronger, thicker, but as time passed, the rope grew thinner and thinner. Soon it would snap under his weight, and he found he wasn't as afraid of death as he had been.

He was hardly even aware of when that thin rope vanished. All he felt was the sensation of falling, endlessly falling, as his fears faded into the darkness around him. A swooping sound interrupted his drifting thoughts and a figure with ebony wings spread wide dove towards him. He stretched out his arms to the figure. It wasn't Gabriel, he could tell, but it was rescuing him and he could vaguely feel that he wanted to be rescued. There was some reason he couldn't die but now that he was so close, he could hardly remember. Then the figure caught him and suddenly those ebony wings were on his back and he was supporting the other figure.

The figure was too heavy and to his surprise, the figure kicked him and he let go instinctively. He floated in the air, staring as the other figure fell into the darkness of death. He could feel that darkness rising towards him. His wings flexed as he stared up and saw a faint speck of light. Gabriel was there. He flapped his wings and felt them carry him up, towards light and life and love.

As he flew, more of his awareness returned and he began flying faster, remembering what Gabriel had said about how he couldn't die, remembering that Gabriel would spend an eternity alone if he died now. He gained in strength, gained in speed, and suddenly the light was all around him and a shadow passed over him. His wings were gone. His body formed around him, awareness spreading outward. He felt different. This wasn't the body of a moment before. But it was definitely his body.

Taylor opened his eyes and saw Gabriel's tear-streaked face above him, those black eyes wet with worry. Taylor lifted a hand to stroke along Gabriel's cheek as his demon let out a relieved sob and clutched him in a hug.

"Taylor," he whispered. "You're alive."

Chapter 29

Demon Eyes

T aylor couldn't speak for a moment. His body felt so strange. He could still feel his wings in his mind, but they were gone. And his legs, they were different. His eyes burned, but that sensation faded. Gabriel blocked most of his view but he could see a hospital room around him, filled with people.

Natalie was standing nearby holding Ariel, and her eyes and nose glistened red as she shed nearly as many tears as Gabriel. Jordan and Callan were there too, exchanging looks of relief. Jordan must have been crying because his cheeks were wet. Ms. Winde was talking to several nurses and they were coming to his side now. He was hooked up to several machines and there was a dull ache in his belly. He was dizzy; he must be on some sort of drugs. He had been shot and lost a lot of blood and even though he wasn't going to die anymore, he would probably be in agony without something to dull the pain. Just out the door, he made out the shapes of Samson and Mr. Hill. Everyone was here, it seemed, but the only one he cared about was Gabriel. He could feel Gabriel's love pouring into him and it filled a deep need within him. He grew stronger as the love sunk into his soul.

A nurse set her hand on Gabriel's shoulder and gently pulled him off. She blinked in shock when she saw Taylor and he wondered why. She reached out and put a hand on his forehead, staring into his eyes.

"Can you hear me?" she asked.

"Yeah," he managed.

"Can you sit up?"

Gabriel moved back to give him room and he pushed himself up carefully, making sure not to tangle the IV in the crook of his elbow. There were several wires attached to his chest as well, and he was in a hospital gown. He wondered how much time had passed as he looked for a clock. He heard gasps from Natalie and Jordan. Ms. Winde appeared shocked, but Callan didn't, so it couldn't be something too wrong. Maybe he just appeared weak, or his color was off after losing so much blood.

"Taylor, your eyes," Natalie said.

He lifted a hand to his face, shutting his eyes and feeling the lids. He felt normal.

Gabriel placed his hand over Taylor's and pulled it down as Taylor opened his eyes again and felt like he was drowning in his demon's love. Nothing had ever felt so good.

"What happened, Taylor?" Gabriel asked softly.

"Someone saved me," Taylor said, thinking of the figure giving him his wings.

Gabriel sighed and Taylor could feel a sharp grief from him.

"Father," he whispered, and Taylor drew in a breath, the scene suddenly making sense.

He was falling to his death and a figure that was but wasn't Gabriel saved him. It had to be the demon king. How had he missed that? Of course it was the demon king. And the demon king had given Taylor his wings and fallen into death. But the king was immortal, wasn't he? Or had he sacrificed his immortality and his life in order to save Taylor and give his only son a chance at love? Was he that selfless? Did he love his son that much? Feeling the sorrow welling up in Gabriel, he knew that was what had happened. The demon king was dead, but Taylor lived.

But in addition to the sorrow, he felt acceptance from Gabriel, and gratitude.

"I'm sorry, Gabriel," he said, taking his demon's hand in his. "I didn't know who it was."

"What did he give you?" Gabriel asked as if afraid.

"His wings," Taylor said in a low voice, not really wanting anyone else to know about it. He didn't think anyone else heard. Gabriel shut his eyes and nodded, then smiled faintly.

"The greatest gift he could have given you," he whispered. "Though it will change everything in your world."

"What do you mean?"

Gabriel backed up from him and gestured for the nurse to bring him something. Although he didn't say anything to indicate what he wanted, she must have known. She handed him a mirror and he handed it to Taylor without a word. Taylor stared in it and two bright red eyes stared back. What was this? It was his face, but the eyes were crimson like a demon's. He looked at Gabriel. The demon's eyes were now black, but Taylor's eyes were red? What was going on?

He thought back to the demon king giving him his wings. His body felt different after that, and he could still feel the shadow of those wings in his mind. He remembered what Gabriel had said in the demon realm about him no longer being human. Had the demon king given him his form? Exchanged Taylor's weak, dying body for the demon king's strong one? The greatest gift he could give, Gabriel said. Was he now the demon king? Surely that couldn't be true.

He glanced at Callan and she bowed her head slightly as if in acknowledgement of that fact. Ariel blinked slowly, dipping her head as well. He couldn't have inherited the demon king's body. That meant he was a demon. But the demon king didn't need humans. Why were Taylor's eyes red, which indicated a bond with someone? He gave a start and stared at Gabriel. He could feel Gabriel's love and it gave him strength, and he could read Gabriel's emotions. Was he bonded to Gabriel?

"Say as little as you can," Gabriel murmured. "No one must know the truth."

Taylor nodded, still stunned and struggling to figure out what was going on. Then Samson and Mr. Hill turned as if to check on him. Both went stock still, staring at his eyes, and then they looked at Gabriel in unison. Gabriel was fearful of them. They wouldn't kill Gabriel or Taylor, he didn't think, but they would try to manipulate them. They were a danger, as Ms. Winde had once warned. And Yolette...

"Yolette?" he asked Gabriel, and satisfaction flooded through his bond.

"Dead," he said. "You're safe."

"So are you," Taylor said, wrapping his arms around Gabriel's neck and kissing him. He didn't care that people were looking; he wanted to feel his demon. His belly felt fine, surprisingly. He wasn't even hooked up to any machines, he realized. It was just him and his demon and when he opened his eyes, they were in darkness. Gabriel chuckled. He was in his true form.

"You learned that quickly," he said. "But I suppose my imagination isn't as rich as yours. I'm not used to creating my own realities, just using my humans'."

Taylor looked around at the darkness. "We're in your dreams? What's happening in our world?"

"Time is moving so slowly we could stay here for hours and still return right where we left off," Gabriel said. "Normally we would have fallen into a faint if you did this, but you've already mastered slowing time."

"Am I really a demon? Bonded to you?"

"It seems that way."

"Did the demon king really give me his form?"

"Look at yourself," Gabriel said, and Taylor looked at his body.

It was the demon king's. He had wings and when he felt his forehead, he felt horns. But they weren't as long or as elaborate as the demon king's or even as Gabriel's. His legs were different, he realized. They were like Gabriel's, more like the legs of a horse than a man, and fur covered them. He flexed his wings, surprised at how *right* his body felt. No wonder Gabriel wanted to wear his true form as much as possible and felt betrayed when his partners were frightened by it.

Gabriel was in his true form as well, and Taylor wondered again at the differences.

"He gave you his form, but you're young," Gabriel said gently, as if in explanation. "He could give you the outline, but your body, your face, is still your own."

"That means I have the potential to find someone, right?" Taylor asked, puzzled. "But I've found you. I love you."

"The two of us have one human soul to share," Gabriel said with a chuckle. "We're both demons now, and we're not demons. You're bound to me, but because I'm now immortal, so are you."

Taylor smiled. "An eternity with you?"

Gabriel pulled him into an embrace and kissed his head. Taylor shut his eyes and held his demon close. This was everything he had ever dreamed of: him and Gabriel, able to love each other and stay with each other forever. He remembered the pain he always felt when thinking of Gabriel and wondering if the demon thought of him as anything beyond a meal. Of course Gabriel loved him. He just hadn't been able to recognize it or admit it, because that meant that Taylor would have to give up his soul.

He understood now why Gabriel always hedged on when he would know that his human was the right one. And he remembered Gabriel asking him once if Taylor wanted to belong to him completely. At the time, Taylor backed away, still uncertain of his own feelings. But when the demon king asked the same thing, there was no hesitation in his mind. He did belong to Gabriel, body and soul, and now that belonging had become a bond. He wondered what other abilities he would have as a demon, and whether or not Gabriel kept his demon abilities. He thought of how Gabriel killed Yolette. Clearly, he wasn't human and maintained his demonic power. Would Taylor be able to do the same? Possibilities flashed through his mind as he thought of all the things he had heard about demons, all the myths and rumors, and all the things he knew for a fact Gabriel could do.

"Thank you, Taylor," Gabriel murmured. "Thank you for your patience, for your sacrifice, for your love."

Taylor sighed and relaxed into him. Then he opened his eyes with a grin.

"So if you're free now, if I'm the one, then that means all of the restrictions on you are gone now, right?"

"Yes," Gabriel said, clearly not following. Taylor's grin widened.

"I want you," he said in a husky voice. "And you're not allowed to pull away this time."

Gabriel's eyes went wide as he must have realized that he was now capable of pleasure, of orgasm, and then his lips split in a matching smile.

"I couldn't ask for anything more," he said, and kissed Taylor hungrily. "Do you think you can hold us in my mind that long or should we wait to do it tonight?"

"Now," Taylor said. "I've waited long enough."

Chapter 30

Finally Together

Taylor blinked in surprise. Without warning, there was a room around him and Gabriel, lushly furnished with a bed that appeared to be the exact bed that Taylor always fantasized about. Only the sheets, instead of black silk, were now a deep purple that gleamed in the light of a cozy fire. Gabriel's fantasy was detailed and complete. Taylor had only ever imagined the bed, but Gabriel set the entire mood and as Gabriel led Taylor to the bed and pressed him against the cool silk, a fuzzy warmth entered his mind. He was feeding. Feeding on love. That was what Gabriel had been feeding on all this time. Lust would do, but he needed love to survive and now that they had each other, he would never starve.

Taylor shut his eyes and adjusted his wings, then sighed as Gabriel kissed his neck and sucked hard enough to leave a mark. Only there were no marks here, and there would be no evidence when they returned to the real world. He clutched Gabriel tight to him and knew that he was ready for this. He always drew back before, never quite sure that he was ready, but now it was right. Yolette was gone and Gabriel loved him. He could finally give in to his lust and do all of the things he fantasized about.

Gabriel grinned at him.

"Look into my mind, darling," he murmured.

Taylor almost responded that he didn't know how, but when he focused on Gabriel's thoughts, he was suddenly enveloped in an image, complete with sensation and emotion. It was the image Taylor envisioned the first time he heard that the demon prince was looking for a partner: a handsome incubus lying him back into the bed and pressing down on him with a kiss. That fantasy had come true. The scene shifted and he saw one of his first fantasies about sucking Gabriel off, the first time he had allowed himself to fantasize about what he might possibly do with the demon. He blushed as he realized that fantasy had come true, too. Then the scene shifted to a blur of other images that Taylor had pictured these past few weeks, of Gabriel above him, kissing him and entering him, of him kneeling as Gabriel entered him from behind, of them together in every possible way. Those fantasies hadn't come true yet, but he was ready for it.

"Yes," he whispered, and Gabriel grinned.

Then they kissed and all of the fantasies were blown away by the reality of Gabriel's lips against his, their tongues dancing together, their bodies writhing in time with each other, every touch sparking new sensations in his new body. He could feel Gabriel's pleasure welling, and his love, and he drew deeply from it. A flicker of weakness from Gabriel, along with surprise, and he pulled back. He remembered how, at first, a simple kiss from Gabriel was enough to weaken him. He built up his tolerance, but Gabriel hadn't learned to do that yet. He needed to start slow or else Gabriel would be spent long before he was ready.

"Sorry," he said softly, then kissed Gabriel again.

Gabriel pressed him into the bed just as he had once imagined and he adjusted his wings until they were comfortable. Gabriel's wings shielded them and brushed against his arms as they embraced. While usually he was ready to go much faster than Gabriel, he was surprised that the opposite suddenly seemed to be true. Gabriel was already panting, he realized, and rubbing against him as if desperate for relief, but he was still warming up. Then Gabriel lowered his head and locked his lips on Taylor's nipple, and he arched his back at the unexpected pleasure. Gabriel continued to tease his body and he was beyond ready in moments, breathless and gasping.

He clutched Gabriel's head against his body and took a deep breath. He wanted this. He really did. There was some fear, but it was right.

"I want you, Gabriel," he said. "I want your first time to be with me."

It wasn't his first time, not really, but it would be his first time to orgasm and he wanted to feel that. Gabriel moaned against him and leveraged himself on his elbows so he was looking down at Taylor. A sly smile spread across his lips.

"You've imagined it so many times," he said. "How do you want it?"

Taylor considered, then reached cautiously into Gabriel's mind. He had never felt when Gabriel was doing this to him and suspected it would be the same and Gabriel wouldn't know he was doing this. But he wanted to match Gabriel's fantasies, not his own. And it was true; he imagined so many variations he would be hard-pressed to choose. Gabriel's mind overflowed with sexual need and joy and relief and pleasure and Taylor carefully fed, not wanting to drain him. But one image dominated: making love like this, facing each other, with Taylor crying out and losing control as... there was a blankness in Gabriel's fantasy because Gabriel honestly didn't know what pleasure felt like, so he couldn't even imagine it in his fantasies. Well, that would change. Taylor licked his lips at the thought.

He bent his knees and crooked one leg around Gabriel's.

"Like this," he said breathlessly, feeling extremely vulnerable as he spread his legs apart and Gabriel's eyes hooded with lust. Gabriel kissed him again and as their tongues threaded together, the demon's hand traced down his belly. He stroked Taylor briefly, then let his hand slide between his legs to his opening. He hesitated.

"I'm so used to being in charge," he said with a soft laugh. "Imagine yourself slick, darling. Ready for me. I don't want to hurt you."

Heat flooded his cheeks but he did as commanded. He knew

people used lube for sex and imagined that for himself, and then Gabriel slicked his fingers along his opening. He gasped at the sudden pleasure and tensed as Gabriel gently entered him with his finger. He murmured at the unexpected pressure, but it felt incredibly arousing. He wanted more.

He could sense that Gabriel wanted to go slow and ease him into it to avoid hurting him, but he didn't want to wait. He wanted Gabriel, all of Gabriel, right now. He grabbed the demon's hips.

"Now," he moaned.

"Darling," Gabriel started, but Taylor lunged forward into a furious kiss. He controlled this, didn't he? He focused on diverting Gabriel's attention from wanting to protect him to wanting to be with him and could feel Gabriel's reluctance to enter him quickly fading. He knew how badly Taylor wanted this. He wouldn't wait.

Gabriel gripped him tightly and positioned him at a slightly different angle, then something pressed against him. A flicker of panic sparked through him, but he pushed it aside angrily. He was so ready for this. There was no reason to hold back, not anymore. He wanted this, wanted Gabriel, wanted the experience of feeling the demon he loved, the demon who loved him, inside of him.

He gasped as Gabriel entered him and began a long slide that tingled through his entire body. It was pressure and pleasure combined, and as Gabriel slid into him, he arched his back and longed for more. He wanted this so badly. As soon as Gabriel was inside him, he moaned and shifted, needing more. Gabriel gave him what he needed; the demon began thrusting into him and as he did, something sparked to life inside him, some place deep inside that Gabriel rubbed against that flamed when it was stimulated. It was almost like the fire that had ripped his soul away, except instead of pain, this flame brought only pleasure. But it was just as all-encompassing, and he gasped and shuddered in the pleasure as Gabriel quickened against him.

Usually Gabriel extended their lovemaking, getting him to the brink and then pulling away, but this time his demon was eager. Normally Gabriel was at least somewhat removed because he couldn't fully participate, but now anticipation flooded through Gabriel's mind and he fed on it. Gabriel was aroused not just from the sex, but from the promise of what was to come, and his pleasure fed Taylor's own.

"Now, Gabe," he said, using the nickname he had carefully selected. This was exactly why he had wanted the name, he realized with a shiver. For when it was too intimate for his full name. For when his demon was deep inside him and his world was about to burst from pleasure. Gabriel nipped his ear and then dove inside, and Taylor threw his head back and nearly screamed as something shuddered through him, a wave of pleasure that dwarfed anything he had felt before. Only it wasn't coming from him. It was Gabriel's orgasm flooding his senses. It didn't take much for his own body to explode but Gabriel's pleasure continued to swamp his senses and combined with his own orgasm to overwhelm his senses.

His entire body was limp as Gabriel collapsed on top of him, panting. He could feel pleasured disbelief in his demon's mind and could easily read what he was thinking. Gabriel had given this pleasure to numerous humans, had seen their reactions and felt their pleasure through their bond, but he never imagined it could possibly feel so good to experience himself. He was grateful for Taylor, loved Taylor, would do anything for Taylor. Taylor blushed and pulled out of his mind, wondering how often Gabriel had snooped on his thoughts that closely.

They lay together for a long time as Taylor slurped up the remnants of Gabriel's pleasure and love. But eventually, Gabriel lifted himself to look down at him.

"We need to go back," he said, still breathless. "You can't hold us here for much longer and we need to be in control when we return. No one can know what just happened."

"We'll go back to exactly how we were?" Taylor asked. What had they been doing before he took them here? He didn't even remember. Were they sitting next to each other or had he embraced Gabriel?

"They'll probably be able to tell that you brought me here," Gabriel said. "It's hard to spend any time here outside of sleep without giving away that something has happened. But they mustn't know what happened."

"All right," Taylor said. Gabriel took a deep breath and shut his eyes. He took another breath, then grinned at Taylor.

"I think I'm ready. I think I can pretend that didn't happen."

"You only have to pretend until we're in private again," Taylor pointed out with a grin of his own.

Gabriel laughed. "Let's return, darling, and as soon as we're alone again, I'll make sure that wasn't just a fluke."

"How do I return us?"

"Right now, you're holding us in my head," Gabriel said. "It should feel like a web that you're holding. Just release the web, and we'll return. But Taylor..."

Sudden vulnerability appeared on his demon's face and he wondered at the sudden wave of insecurity he felt from him. He reached up to stroke Gabriel's face and the demon blushed in an uncharacteristic way.

"Thank you," he whispered. "Thank you for everything."

Taylor smiled and ran his finger over Gabriel's soft lips.

"We're still linked," he said. "There will be plenty of chances to thank me."

"You know what I mean," Gabriel said with a glint of humor in his eyes. And Taylor did know.

This was not a simple thanks. Gabriel had searched for a human who would be willing to sacrifice their soul for him for centuries, possibly longer, and he never found one. Until Taylor. And Taylor hadn't just freed him from his physical constraints, he wanted to remain with Gabriel. Gabriel was willing to stay with him after being freed, but he could see that Gabriel had been terrified that Taylor would no longer want him at that point. He was afraid that Taylor would reject him because Gabriel had demanded his soul in exchange, but instead Taylor had bonded with him. They were linked together now, irrevocably bound.

Gabriel hadn't expected that, and neither had Taylor, to be honest.

He could feel Gabriel's love and relief and continued to feed, but he himself felt the same love. This was everything he could have asked for. Well, maybe he wouldn't have asked to be a demon. But if he had to lose his soul, if Gabriel had to be free from humans, at least this way they were still tied together. Nothing would tear them apart now, and he could finally bask in his demon's love without any fears of what society would think or what Yolette would do. They were safe, and they were together.

He reached out and felt the web holding them in Gabriel's mind. He didn't remember what they had been doing and knew that when they returned, they would both be confused for a moment at the sudden return to reality. It was inevitable that the others would suspect something. But no one would know how life-changing this brief dip into Gabriel's mind was. Once they returned, everything would be different. He was a demon now, and nothing would ever be the same for him or for Gabriel. They were safe, but new challenges would arise. Mr. Hill and Samson were still a threat, as were the other demons who didn't approve of their prince. There were still other demon hunters. Together, though, they would overcome all of that. With a deep breath, he prepared himself for a return to reality, and then he released the web and felt his human body tighten around him. They were back.

Epilogue

D ays passed in a blur as Taylor healed. His doctor and the nurses were impressed at how quickly he healed, but it felt like forever. Natalie visited everyday with Ariel at her side. Ariel often jumped on his bed and curled beside him, and he discovered that he could communicate with her when he tried. It was almost like telepathy, just like when Gabriel used to speak in his head, and he wondered if that was what Natalie felt with her. Jordan stopped by a few times, but Callan stayed away. When he asked about her, Jordan explained with a blush that Gabriel didn't want her too close. Apparently the conflict between the two of them was ongoing.

And Gabriel was almost always at his side. He did leave sometimes, mostly to talk to Samson and arrange everything happening outside the hospital room, but he was a constant companion as Taylor fed on his love. Even when Gabriel was away, Taylor could sense him. A few times he could sense that Gabriel was troubled, but he was never in danger, so Taylor tried not to worry. Of course Gabriel would be troubled. Yolette was dead, but there were other demon hunters to worry about, and news of what happened was spreading across the demon-born world no matter how Gabriel tried to stop it.

People knew that Gabriel, the demon king's son, had unlocked his dependency on humans the same way the demon king had. But while the demon king retreated into the demon realm and never emerged, Gabriel was still here and people wanted to know why. So far, only a few people knew about Taylor and he was glad. Once people found out that a human had become a demon... well, he had no idea what would happen. There might be panic, or people might decide to try it themselves, he had no clue. And so far no one knew that Gabriel had been capable of loving him as a demon, or that it was that love that had unlocked his abilities. Samson and Mr. Hill assumed that Gabriel had first freed himself from humans—and in doing so, become more human—and then became able to love Taylor. They assumed that Taylor was capable of loving Gabriel because he wasn't truly a demon. The fact that they loved each other was impossible to hide.

For some reason, Gabriel wanted to hide the truth of their love and Taylor was willing to let him. He could sense that something was happening in the demon realm, something related to that love, but hadn't been a demon long enough to understand what. Gabriel knew. Gabriel had already returned to the demon realm several times even though Taylor remained here. It was safer, Gabriel said, though he didn't know why he would be in danger among other demons now that he himself was a demon. He didn't question it, though. He would do anything Gabriel wanted.

Finally, the doctor announced that Taylor was ready to go home. Taylor let out a cheer and immediately began gathering the things people had brought him to pass the time. Gabriel let out a laugh and placed his hand over Taylor's.

"Let other people get those, Taylor," he said. "I want you home as soon as possible."

Thought Gabriel didn't say why, it was obvious to Taylor. They had been together in Gabriel's dreams, but never in this reality. Never in these bodies. As much as he loved his other form, he wanted to know what it was like to make love to Gabriel as a human. If Gabriel wanted to hurry him home, he wouldn't complain.

He stood up and stretched. He felt great. Gabriel took his hand and they finally left the room where Taylor had been trapped for so long. Mr. Hill waited in the lobby of the hospital, to his surprise. Gabriel's mood darkened. Clearly, Gabriel didn't want to see the professor. All of Taylor's professors had stopped by to give him short lessons so he wouldn't get too behind. He wasn't entirely sure why Mr. Hill did, since Taylor knew more about the subject than him, plus the man always put both Taylor and Gabriel on edge. Still, it was thoughtful for him to stop by. Now, though, he was unwelcome.

"I'm glad to see you strong again," Mr. Hill said, his eyes lingering on Taylor's. No one really talked about the fact that Taylor was now a demon. Everyone skirted around that issue. Even Natalie seemed uncomfortable in bringing it up.

"Thanks for your help," Taylor said politely.

"I'm sure you and Gabriel are eager to begin your lives now," he continued, looking at Gabriel. "Is there anything I can do to assist you?"

"Be careful choosing sides," Gabriel said softly, and Mr. Hill blinked as if in surprise.

"Choosing sides in what?"

Gabriel grinned, his grip tightening about Taylor. Taylor could feel that Gabriel had been keeping a secret and didn't want to keep it anymore, that it was finally time to acknowledge something Gabriel had known about this whole time but, like his love for Taylor, hadn't wanted to admit.

"The revolution," he said.

Mr. Hill went white and Taylor remembered fearfully what his teacher said about the name Gabriel, and how war broke out when the demon king had that name. Was Gabriel really going to start a war?

"Let's go, Taylor," he continued, and Taylor snuggled against him and pushed past the stunned Mr. Hill. If there was going to be a revolution, at least he had Gabriel at his side.

About the Author

Elizabeth James hails from Portland, Oregon and spent many hours of her childhood tucked away in the Gold Room of Powell's Books, reading science fiction and fantasy masterpieces and hidden treasures. She writes romance with strong elements of science fiction and fantasy as a result, focusing on LGBT characters.

Thrall of Darkness

Thrall of Darkness was founded because there is a shortage of good, quality literature featuring gay protagonists that does not reduce gay characters to stereotypes or dismiss them as secondary characters. Every story seeks to challenge the status quo by focusing on gay characters and combining drama, action, and sex into an addicting blend of fun-filled narrative.

thrallofdarkness.com

You can find more information on Thrall of Darkness novels and short stories at thrallofdarkness.com, including free interactive stories featuring LGBT dating simulators in realistic and fantasy settings.

Also by Elizabeth James

A Vampire's Desire

Kairos takes a job in an ancient vampire house knowing nothing about them and their society, and immediately falls in love with his boss, a powerful but cold vampire. As he tries to get closer, threats from a rival house threaten to tear them apart as threats to his life mirror threats from the other vampires and he finds himself running up against an entire society turned against his love.

Tarragon Academy

Tarragon Academy is a college at the foot of a smoldering volcano surrounded in mist and mystery. First-year student Jamie is having a hard time adapting until he meets an upperclassman named Scott. Will Scott help him thrive in his new school, or does Scott have his own reasons for helping the beautiful young freshman?

Dragon Tamer

Luke has heard dragons all his life and when a dragon summons him to raise her dragonlings, he runs away to help her. But the world he enters is fraught with danger and he knows little of the outside world. As the dragons begin dying off and dragon tamers like him become scarce, a rival tribe kidnaps him and everything he knows is thrown into question.

Sagent

Gabriel is a sagent, a sex agent, at the start of his career, but he is already scarred by his previous agency. When he is sent on a dangerous mission to the underbelly of Destiny, everything starts to fall apart. Isolated from his agency and not knowing where to go, Gabriel must choose between returning to safety and Destiny, or staying and forging his own path.

First Prince

Wren is the beautiful yet rebellious first prince of Fontain, forced to move to the Imperial Palace as part of a treaty. Upon arriving, he receives a frigid welcome and realizes his stay will be fraught with danger. When he finds romance in an unexpected place, he realizes that his life may not be as dire as he imagined and pleasure can be found where it is least expected.

Prisoner of Love

When Prince Tristan is captured in battle, he fully expects to be tortured and killed. But the torture turns to erotic pleasure as he learns that his enemy, Prince Ryan, is in love with him and has been planning his capture with meticulous care for years. Will Tristan hold firm to his principles, or will Ryan's forceful seduction overpower his senses?

Dark Offering

Nightmares are a nightly occurrence on the planet of Ylse, and they're strong enough to lure humans to be fed on by the creatures who haunt the night. Jarl is charged with risking the night to feed the colony. He comes across one of the creatures offering peace. Is the creature sincere or is this just a new way to lure the humans to their deaths on this inhospitable planet?

Bride of Albis

Sam and his small crew of space-faring traders have their usual routine permanently shattered when they are kidnapped by pirates. Sam makes a deal with the head of the pirates: he will be sold as a slave in exchange for the freedom of his crew. But when he discovers that the pirate lied and sold his crew as well, he vows vengeance.

Seeking More

Seeking More is a collection of eight contemporary gay romance stories that range from the deeply emotional to action-packed, from hapless MFA students to couples on the brink of a new relationship. Each story is focused not only on steamy romance, of which there is plenty, but also on character development and an emotional connection between reader and character.

Eve of Eternity

Sabine is a young woman searching for her identity while fleeing the powerful man trying to steal her heart and mind. She's almost under his control when she is kidnapped by a man with conflicting loyalties and a mysterious past who claims to kidnap her in order to rescue her. Will she break free from the men around her?

Treacherous a Dragon's Love

In the middle of the final battle against the great dragon Arostrath, a woman appears bound in golden chains. The King claims her as his reward but the youngest son has an unusual fondness for her that could cast the kingdom into ruin. Will his love for the beautiful and strange woman destroy the kingdom, or does her mystery hide the answer to all of their prayers?